The Secrets of the Morrow

Stephanie Le Roy

Dedication

To my husband, for showing me that my value doesn't come from my willingness to sacrifice—and for loving me even when I have nothing left to give.

Acknowledgments

Thank you to all those who shaped my worldview, each encounter contributing a piece to the lens through which I write.

They say,

The deepest pit in the blackest part of hell is where a soul—destined to endure the raw torment of loss in the mortal realm—is forged.

Those who commit unforgivable sins are not simply punished; they are dissolved into the fluid of fate itself, melted and reformed in the hammering grip of the Old Gods. From that crucible, new souls are born. Broken. Fragmented. Cursed to roam the surface world in search of pieces of themselves that may never come to be.

Contents

Prologue

Oliver slogged through the thick mud outside the communion center, drenched and shivering. He prayed for either the rain to cease or the endless ceremonial prayers inside to conclude—but judging by the way the clouds hung, it seemed the stars might fall before either granted him mercy.

He pressed himself against the warmest wall he could find—one of the crude baked-hut alleyways facing the center—and tried to steal what shelter he could. Across the street, the massive mahogany doors of the communion center loomed, dark and closed. He exhaled into his cupped hands, the warmth doing little to stave off the gnawing cold that made his fingers feel like splintering glass.

The chill had become so vicious it caused his entire body to tremble. Still, he waited, eyes scanning for any sign of his master—the Head Dragon Priest of the enclave. If he could just get a moment with the man, perhaps plead for clemency, then maybe—just maybe—he could be released from this humiliating punishment.

During the last counsel, accusations had flown. Breaking his vow to Enlil had been called the gravest sin a priest could commit. Not only had he betrayed his sacred bond with the god, but he'd sullied the trust of the brotherhood bound to it.

Oliver didn't see it that way. Yes, he felt guilt, mostly for what happened afterward, when his temper had exploded. But he'd vowed to double his efforts in the fields to atone. It was penance enough. Let the lesser priests work the fields. His presence would likely intimidate them anyway. And if he was being honest, he found some satisfaction in the idea of sending Victor back out into the sweltering sun for that smug little speech he'd given the night before.

A gust of wind sliced through the alley, sending a fresh wave of tremors down Oliver's spine. His teeth chattered loudly. A man could die in this kind of cold.

How the hell was he supposed to know he'd almost killed the girl?

She'd danced her way into his bed, smiling, playful—willing—and then turned around and insulted him like some conniving brat. Maiden or not, she should've known better.

Cursing beneath his breath, he shifted from foot to foot, trying to generate some warmth. "Damn that old priest. Hurry the hell up," he muttered.

He didn't hear the approaching footsteps until a hand the size of a bear's paw slammed down on his shoulder, spinning him around like a rag doll. His eyes went wide with panic.

Standing before him was a towering figure cloaked in shadow, the face completely hidden beneath a deep hood. But what struck Oliver most were the eyes—icy blue, glowing faintly through the impenetrable blackness.

Then lightning cracked behind the figure, illuminating it—and Oliver realized the blackness wasn't from the hood. It *was* the face. A void of pure, unrelenting darkness.

"What the—?" Oliver stammered. But this time his trembling wasn't from the cold.

A sudden warmth spread down his leg as the creature's massive hand tightened, pressing directly into the nerve beneath his collarbone. Pain surged.

"AH!" he screamed, thrashing. He struck the stranger's chest, but it was like hitting stone.

The grip shifted. His right arm was twisted behind his back, painfully wrenched until he slammed face-first into the wall, breath knocked out of him, pain blooming across his ribs.

"I'll give you whatever you want! Just don't kill me!" he gasped, his voice cracking in terror.

"Oh, that's rich," the figure growled, a low, guttural chuckle rumbling in Oliver's ear.

"Considering you're the reason I'm not getting what I want, I'd advise you to shut up, you stupid fuck."

The voice was deep, otherworldly, vibrating with restrained fury.

"All you had to do was get laid and hold up your end of the deal. But no—you had to grow a damn attitude."

Before Oliver could respond, the figure's arm swung. A thunderous right hook struck his cheek, sending him sprawling to the ground, dazed and blinking through stars.

He spat blood. "What? This is about *her*?" he asked, half-incredulous, half-terrified.

Across from him, the cloaked man paced, fists clenched, shoulders rising and falling with fury.

"No, dumbass," the figure snapped, spinning on his heel. "This is about you screwing up *my* plans!"

Those glowing eyes flared brighter, searing inches from Oliver's face. He flinched, retreating into himself, expecting another blow—but instead, the light dimmed.

"I—I'm sorry," Oliver whimpered. "I didn't know…"

The figure ignored him, pacing again, muttering under his breath, one hand gesturing as if conversing with invisible councilors. Oliver dared not interrupt.

The silence turned heavy. Then, suddenly, the figure stopped. Looked up.

"Fuck it," he muttered—and with one motion, slammed a blast of power into Oliver's chest.

***

Ashur discarded his soaked cloak upon entering the temple—a towering monument erected in his honor during his era of godhood, when he ruled the Earth under the name Enlil. The cloak slapped wetly against the silver-plated floor. A slave girl appeared instantly, retrieving it without a word and wiping away the trail behind him.

In the ancient days, mortals had given blood and body in offerings to the Initials—primordial deities born from the chaos before form. In time, these deities took mortal lovers, elevated themselves to gods in the eyes of man, and demanded worship.

Now, only three of the divine remained on Earth: two gods and one Initial. Roman—and his venomous wife, Noctis.

Ashur would see them bleed.

They would pay for what they'd done to Lux—his radiant Lux, the luminous essence of the universe. She had once been the very embodiment of light and sound. The first Initial. The cosmic source from which beauty and balance flowed.

He still remembered how she'd told him their origin. She and Noctis were born of Earth's first expansion—twin forces of opposition, light and darkness locked in eternal push and pull.

Lux had descended to Earth in human form, gifting fire, art, and culture to man. Noctis, ever her rival, ushered in the dark ages. Each chose a consort among mortals. And Lux had chosen *him*, pulling him from a festival crowd and shaping him into a god.

For ages, they had danced in delicate opposition. But Noctis, selfish and sanctimonious, had ruined everything. She'd grown a conscience.

Ashur longed for the old days. The smell of burnt offerings. The chants that echoed his name. The throne beside Lux that glowed with celestial flame.

Those days would return. Soon.

Oliver remembered nothing now—Ashur had seen to that. The priest's mind had been wiped clean, save for a violent compulsion to fulfill his end of their agreement.

And Layla—poor, naïve Layla—was now writhing in agony behind the walls of Ashur's chambers. If she survived, she might yet have a chance at redemption. If not... well, there was always the other sister.

For now, he would wait.

Roman paced the length of the bedchamber he and his wife had shared for the past twenty thousand years, unease twisting deep in his gut. The disappearance of their daughter, coupled with the brutal murder of the High Priest just the night before, weighed heavily on his mind. After centuries of military service, Roman had come to rely on his instincts—and right now, they were screaming. None of this sat right with him. The timing was too precise, too orchestrated to be mere coincidence.

His embroidered crimson robe whispered against the grain of the polished hardwood floor, each bare step landing with a muted thud that kept his spiraling thoughts at bay. He had never been able to think clearly with shoes on.

Noctis had already scolded him once that morning and twice again in the afternoon for his brooding, but he couldn't shake the heavy dread clinging to him. Layla was still a child by their standards—fifteen, wide-eyed, and full of tender need. She still sought comfort the way she had as a babe, curling into arms that promised safety. The world beyond the palace walls—or even the village—was a cruel unknown to her, and Roman knew it was his failure not to have prepared her better. He had miscalculated, but there was still time to correct it. He would not lose her to his own oversight.

Layla was a princess—valuable, but only alive. That cruel truth offered some measure of hope. Her worth was her shield. Noctis, however, seemed utterly unbothered by her absence, her attention caught up in other matters. Roman could almost hear her dismissive scoff at the idea of a ransom.

"She's the daughter of an Initial," Noctis would say. "She should be able to handle herself. This is good magic practice for her." A harsh reminder, always, that Layla struggled with her powers—another worry Roman didn't need right now.

Running a hand through his thick, raven-black hair, he made a mental note to get it cut. Noctis liked him scruffy, with that wild soldier's edge, but old habits were hard to shake. He had been a warrior far longer than he had been a husband. He exhaled sharply, pressing his fingers to his eyes, trying—and failing—to ease the frustration that came from being shackled by the throne. The duties of kingship kept him confined while his daughter was out there, somewhere, alone.

He knew he wasn't being fair to Noctis. Over the past two days, fear had warped his thoughts into something bitter and unjust. She wasn't a terrible mother. In truth, Noctis was a remarkably devoted one—an unexpected contrast, given her role as the creator and commander of many of the world's darkest forces. Over the last century, she had grown increasingly affectionate toward him, but when it came to their daughters, her devotion had always been fierce.

Though often impatient with Roman as a husband, she transformed entirely when training the twins in magic. Patient, encouraging, and oddly joyful, she coaxed power from them with a gentleness he could never emulate. Every small success was a cause for celebration in her eyes. Roman had canceled the first parade she organized when Layla sneezed and accidentally sparked a gust of wind.

"A sneeze," he had argued, "is not an intentional spell. If we start celebrating that, we'll need to throw a party for every cold in the kingdom."

He'd later been forced to decommission a whimsical parade float shaped like a giant nose, which Noctis had dubbed *The Centerpiece of the Snot Parade*. Unsurprisingly, he hadn't seen that going well.

The door creaked open, pulling Roman out of his thoughts. A slight figure peeked around it—nervous, hesitant.

"Joel," Roman called, his voice softening. "Come in."

The young man in black robes stepped fully into the room, closing the door quietly behind him.

"You wanted to see me, Your Majesty?"

"I did," Roman said with a small smile. "Wanted to see how the initiation went. It's not every day I lose my best servant to the Brotherhood of Dragon Priests."

Joel flushed with pride, eyes dropping to the floor, eliciting a quiet chuckle from the king.

"You've never been great at taking compliments. Too much humility. That's one of the things I admire about you, Joel."

"Thank you, sir." The boy hesitated, shifting from foot to foot. "Since I'm here... there's something I'd like to ask you, my lord."

Roman tilted his head, eyeing him curiously. "Oh? And what might that be?"

Joel cleared his throat, nervousness prickling at his voice. "The new High Priest has asked whether it might be possible for Her Majesty to personally ward his chambers. After what happened last night... he's concerned, sire. He thinks the attack might've come from within, and he doesn't trust a low-ranking mage to protect him."

Roman's expression darkened slightly, but he nodded, understanding the young man's concern. "I can't blame him. It's still hard to believe it happened at all. I spoke with Jasper just last night."

At the mention of the murdered priest, Joel looked down again, clearly shaken.

"Tell your new master I'll speak with Noctis. He'll have her answer by the end of the day." Roman's tone was firm but kind.

Joel bowed low. "Thank you, Your Majesty." He backed out of the room, closing the door behind him with a gentle click.

Chapter One

10,000 Years Later

It was shaping up to be a beautiful day in the Moro. The rising sun melted the dew clinging to the leaves, and birds stirred from their nests, their morning chorus slowly filling the air. The cry of an early songbird echoed through the forest, piercing the fragile silence as a soft veil of golden light crept between the towering trees beyond the glen. All around, elemental creatures began emerging from their dens—silent, graceful figures drawn toward a quiet gathering at the heart of the clearing.

There, beneath a cascading curtain of wildflowers blooming in shades of pink and purple, sat a small woman—still as stone, her presence striking in its solitude. Her pale yellow dress moved gently in the breeze, brushing against the warm, honeyed tone of her skin. The contrast was softened only by the raven-black curls swept neatly atop her head. Her deep blue eyes—piercing and unyielding—drank in the beauty around her, though they did not reflect it. She saw none of the serenity. Only loss.

This was the place that haunted her: the site of her sister's betrayal, a shrine to centuries of enslavement. The landscape, breathtaking in its untouched splendor, mocked her grief. It was a place of reverence for some—but for Layla, it was a wound that refused to close.

And yet, she remained.

There was a strength in her stillness, in the rigid set of her shoulders and the steel behind her gaze. A single tear slipped free, betraying her composure. The air behind her shifted—gathering force—and the strands of loose hair at her temples lifted in the charged wind. He was near.

She didn't turn. She had been waiting for over an hour, but she was not surprised that the bastard was late. Ashur was never punctual.

Once, his very presence had made her stomach turn, his arrogance enough to leave her breathless with rage. But now… now she craved him.

That craving disturbed her.

There was a raw magnetism in him—an ancient, practiced dominance that drew her in like a drug. It radiated from him in waves, intoxicating. It was power. Unforgiving. Unrelenting. Unnatural. And in some part of her still bound by need, she welcomed it, hoping it might numb her anguish, even for a moment.

He approached silently, his presence announced only by the shift in the wind and the quiet hush of disturbed leaves. He crouched beside her without a word, brushed the tear from her cheek with a heavy sigh, and brought it to his lips.

For a breath, it was tender.

Then came the blow.

The backhand cracked against her face with enough force to nearly send her sprawling. Layla caught herself just short of the earth, her hands sinking into the soft moss and blades of grass. Her lip split open, the warmth of blood mingling with the sweet scent of crushed greenery.

She gritted her teeth.

Ashur usually removed his wedding band before striking her— today, he hadn't. Half-convinced she'd provoked it, she steadied herself with a bitter exhale, rising slowly.

He hated hitting her. That's what she told herself. If he didn't, he would've done it more often. And gods knew, she had given him reason enough over the years.

Meeting his icy gaze, Layla masked her pain behind stoicism. Her eyes—glassy from the sting—nonetheless drifted over his face, drinking in every detail as shame twisted inside her, braided tightly with a dark, lingering desire.

The tousled fall of dusty blond hair framed eyes the color of frost. A small scar cut through his left brow—the mark she'd given him the night he claimed her as his. That scar, he'd once joked, was merely an "unfortunate side effect" of his mortal days. But she knew the truth—it had been her last act of defiance.

Even now, with centuries between that moment and this, he looked no less regal.

Ashur stood with the poise of an aristocrat, arms folded over the loose white tunic that clung to his broad chest and pulled at the shoulders. His stature wasn't towering, but the way he carried himself made him seem larger. The black leather leggings wrapped tight around his lean waist, emphasizing his hardened frame.

By every measure, he was beautiful. A god among men. And damn him, he knew it.

Layla remembered her desperation, her voice trembling as she begged, *"Save my family from this injustice, my lord, please."*

He'd laughed.

In return for his help, he'd proposed she become his concubine. She had responded by smashing a candlestick over his head. But desperation has teeth, and in the end, she had agreed to his contract of eternal servitude.

The condition? Vengeance.

A promise still unmet.

Her eyes lingered on the rough stubble along his jawline, the trace of disorder in his otherwise composed appearance. She found a sliver of satisfaction in it—proof that even gods could unravel. And in their private moments, she had come to appreciate those cracks.

"Why am I here?" he asked, his tone edged with irritation.

Her open appraisal of him had not gone unnoticed. He raised a brow—just slightly—but it was enough. A warning. His patience was thinning.

"I found him, my lord," she said softly. "And he's more powerful than we ever imagined."

Ashur didn't respond immediately. His eyes narrowed, calculating. It was in these moments of reflection that she found him most compelling—silent, thoughtful, unknowable.

She resisted the urge to remind him that *he* had summoned her here.

Finally, he spoke.

"Well," he said, the corners of his mouth curling into something between a smirk and a smile. "I suppose you get to have your vengeance, then."

The words hit her like a thunderclap.

For a heartbeat, all rationality abandoned her, and an unrestrained smile broke across her face. Joy—pure and unguarded—lit her features.

Ashur answered with a smile of his own, but it didn't reach his eyes.

"Try not to enjoy him too much," he muttered, voice slipping back into displeasure.

He stepped closer, tilting her chin with the faintest brush of his fingers. His gaze passed over the damage he'd done to her mouth.

"I'd hate to ruin this pretty face any more than absolutely necessary," he whispered.

And then he kissed her—softly, cruelly—before vanishing into the wind, leaving her alone with the promise of blood and long-awaited justice.

Chapter Two

Leah stood at the center of a circle of children who had suddenly appeared, now seated cross-legged on the mossy forest floor.

"Now, remember to hold the circle. Do not let it break or…" she warned, her voice trailing off just as the entire group blinked out of sight—vanishing into thin air.

Their immediate disappearance startled a small fox whose curiosity had drawn him within sniffing distance. The swift reappearance of the children just moments later had a similar effect on the rest of the woodland creatures, scattering them with alarm. Only the dragons, perched high in the branches of the Great Oak, remained undisturbed—watching with what could only be described as amused fascination.

"Ryanne, this is your last chance," Leah scolded, turning to face a girl whose wide eyes now brimmed with panic. "If you can't follow instructions, there'll be no more magic trips for you. I mean it."

Ryanne's eyes widened in horror at the thought of being left behind. After all her persistence to join, the idea of being excluded now was unbearable. She gave a reluctant but obedient nod, her head dipping in submission.

"Maja Leah? Why did we come to the Great Oak?" asked one of the smaller boys, looking around with genuine confusion. His voice was soft, his uncertainty plain. Their prior adventures had taken them across distant parts of the kingdom—why stop here?

Leah took a moment to consider her answer. The Great Oak towered just above the village, a colossal marvel said to have stood for thousands of years. A cascading curtain of pink and purple blossoms draped its thick, gnarled trunk, which stretched an astounding twenty feet in diameter. Many believed it to be the very first tree planted by Ashur, the great God of the Skies, on the day Earth was formed. The presence of the ancient dragons—still nesting in its blossoming canopy—was said to be proof of this origin. Their shimmering scales, flashing reds, greens, blues, and silvers, adorned the thick branches in familial clusters, bringing the tree to life with every shift and flick of movement.

Each child's gaze of awe was met with hundreds more. In the distance, the Twin Mountains marked the far edge of the valley, where an enormous waterfall poured from their midpoint, a silver ribbon cascading down in endless motion. The waterfall created a striking backdrop for the ancient palace nestled below—a place Leah had once known intimately in her youth. Though long unused, today it teemed with villagers who scurried through every corridor and corner, preparing it for the evening's grand feast.

The lake beneath the mountains wrapped like a protective arm around the palace's outer gate, its glistening waters feeding the lush forest that ringed the village. A wide stone bridge arched gracefully over the lake, allowing for a quicker route to the palace gates. Floating lanterns, suspended above the water's surface, would be ignited by dragon fire once the sun disappeared beyond the hills—a breathtaking feature prepared in honor of a long-awaited event: the prophesied return of their princess.

Leah had been haunted by visions of destruction in recent nights. The images had driven her to seek clarity and solace among the ancient branches of the Great Oak. Perhaps that was why they had come. But as she looked down at the boy who had asked the question, she softened and offered a different truth.

"Well, this trip marks a rare and exciting time of celebration for the people of Moro, Adam," she replied warmly, smiling at him with a maternal tenderness. Though she had no children of her own, Leah had once cared for the boy, raising him until his adoptive mother came to claim him.

"Now," she said, clapping her hands and bouncing slightly where she stood, "can any of my brilliant secret magicians tell me what we're celebrating today?"

Laughter bubbled up around the circle at her playful tone.

"The Day of the Black Sun!" came an enthusiastic squeal from behind her.

Leah spun around dramatically—only to lose her balance and land flat on her rump.

Laughter erupted. Children shrieked with amusement, and Leah, cheeks flushed with embarrassment, joined them. She flopped back onto the ground, arms splayed, giving in to the hilarity of the moment. When the giggles finally began to subside, she sat up, brushing leaves from her long, raven-black hair and adjusting the rumpled skirts of her robes. She waited patiently as the last of the chuckles faded before continuing the lesson.

"For generations, the arrival of the Black Sun has been anticipated. It brings peace and prosperity, a time of birth, fertile harvests—and the renewal of magical gifts…"

A small hand shot up before the girl tightly grabbed the hand of her neighbor to avoid breaking the circle.

"Yes, Ryanne?" Leah said with a chuckle, already anticipating her question.

"Will the princess be coming to the feast today?" Ryanne asked, her voice breathless with excitement. Her brilliant magenta eyes sparkled as the words left her mouth.

That intensity, paired with her striking features, gave away her lineage in an instant—she was Dark Fae. Her Elven mother had fallen in love with a Dark Fae warrior while serving as a healer during the war that erupted following the princess's disappearance. Without Ryanne's existence, many villagers would have believed such a union to be impossible.

Like most of the children in the circle, Ryanne had been born during or shortly after the Thousand-Year War. This celebration marked the first Day of the Black Sun that any of them could remember. Even the youngest, Adam, was already six hundred years old.

Adam was Leah's most gifted student. He possessed a remarkable magical instinct—though his talents sometimes caused unexpected trouble. Small explosions occasionally erupted in the market after a scolding, or objects of desire would drift into his hands as he walked by, much to the exasperation of his mother.

Leah recalled the day she had found him—swaddled in blankets, alone in the woods near town. No one had any idea where he had come from, and Leah herself had no memory of how she'd stumbled upon him. Though she believed she had only been gone for minutes, the villagers told her she had been missing for several months. The memory was a blank void in her mind, a black cloud she had never been able to lift. The villagers searched the forest for weeks, seeking his parents or even a body—finding nothing.

Each child in her circle had unique gifts, and Leah cherished them as if they were her own. She often cared for them when their parents were away, sharing stories and tutoring them in the use of their abilities. Through her guidance, they had learned to respect each other's differences and found strength in their shared identity—just as Leah's parents had once taught her.

Ryanne, though gifted, had a habit of challenging authority. She possessed an uncanny ability to read the movements and intentions of others—a trait inherited from her father—and a natural tendency to lead. Even at eight hundred years old, she had earned the admiration of her peers and often took the helm in classroom disagreements.

Then there was Catria, the eldest in the circle, just shy of her thousandth year. Her rare heritage granted her perfect memory; she remembered each day of her life as clearly as if it had happened moments ago—a gift that set her apart in a community where most younglings struggled to remember anything before their five-hundredth birthday.

Leah's class was well-prepared for anything that might happen in her absence. She had trained them for years, knowing that one day, they would lead their people—especially if the village was ever forced to stand united again.

"I certainly hope so," Leah answered softly, her tone turning wistful. "There was a time, long ago, when the princess didn't need the Black Sun to return. She walked freely among us—laughing, dancing, playing in the meadows with the children of the village. She brought joy wherever she went."

A weight settled in Leah's chest as she spoke.

"But one day, the Goddess of Anarchy grew jealous of the love and praise the princess received. Taking on a human form, she slipped into the palace under cover of night and cast a cruel spell—trapping the princess in the moon. Since then, she's been forced to watch her people retreat to their homes in slumber, unseen and unheard."

Leah paused, her voice thick with memory. She could still see the princess as a child—her tiny hands tugging at Leah's, laughter ringing through the palace as they twirled together in the Great Hall on feast days. The face had faded with time, but the feeling remained, imprinted on her heart.

A faint smile touched Leah's lips.

"Luckily, our princess is a clever girl," Leah stated with quiet pride.

"She discovered powerful magic on the moon that allowed her to escape after a thousand years of war between kingdoms."

Unwelcome memories surged within her—visions of the final battle she'd fought through, and the moment she'd learned the princess had returned.

"She couldn't celebrate with us before she was called back to her prison that year," Leah continued, her voice gentling, "but she ensured the release of countless men and women. She ordered that all soldiers of our kingdom, myself included, return home before her departure."

Leah looked around the circle of wide-eyed students. Each face reflected wonder and awe.

"Maja Leah?" a tentative voice asked.

"Yes?"

"You were in the Thousand Year War?" Catria's astonishment lit up her spectacled face, giving Leah the humorous image of a startled owl. Leah chuckled warmly.

"Yes, actually. Ryanne's father and I fought side by side in many battles over the years. And her mother—well, she saved my life more than once."

A ripple of whispers swept through the circle as every child turned to stare at Ryanne, who sat frozen in astonishment, her mouth slightly agape. Another hand flew up eagerly.

"Maja Leah?"

"Yes, Adam?" she replied patiently.

"How old are you?" he asked with disarming honesty, triggering a wave of laughter that rippled around the group.

Leah laughed along, the sound chasing away the sting of her earlier embarrassment.

"Old enough, I think... That's quite enough storytelling for today. The moon will soon cover the sun, and your parents will want you cleaned up. Let's get ready for the feast, shall we?"

A chorus of cheers erupted. Leah rose from the ground, brushing leaves and specks of dirt from her golden-brown dress. She straightened the dark leather belt that cinched her waist and adjusted the heavy metal ring securing a long strip of leather cascading down her skirts. With a small shake of her head and a broad smile, she cast the enchantment that would carry them all home.

***

As the moon's shadow crept closer to the sun, the Priests of Ashur assembled in the village center to prepare for the feast. Each wore flowing black silk robes tied with a cotton cord at the waist—the shade of red indicating their rank. At the heart of the gathering stood the High

Priest, his cord a vibrant crimson, as tradition demanded. The seven senior priests stood beside him, their deeper red sashes arranged in order of seniority. All bore the exhausted expressions of men who had not slept for days.

Below the platform, the remaining seventy-plus priests flanked the gathering in two lines. Their younger faces made a stark contrast to the aged leaders above.

Leah observed the transformed village with quiet, almost wistful attention. As a child, this place had been a far cry from its current splendor. The streets were once choked with filth and desperation—garbage tossed carelessly into gutters while the destitute fought over scraps of rotting fruit. The stench had been unbearable.

It was the Dragon Priests who had changed everything. They gathered the poor and the starving from the streets, offering them food and shelter in exchange for service to the brotherhood. Soon, they began raising swine in the back of their communal hut to sustain the growing number of acolytes.

The community's excitement swelled when the newest priests were divided into task groups. One such group was charged with collecting refuse and food waste to feed the pigs—a simple yet transformative act that lifted the village from squalor to cleanliness.

Now, the feast had become a symbol of that renewal. Color flooded the streets in every direction—bold ribbons of red, pink, and yellow wound around buildings that had sprouted vibrant blues, purples, and greens. The village seemed to bloom with life, a stark contrast to the earthy browns of the huts. The decorations curled and danced in the breeze, stirring a sense of anticipation and wonder.

At the raised center of the square, the village elders gathered— first in line to receive the sacred blessing that would bind them to the Father God Enlil. Only then would the pilgrimage to the sapphire-blue lake begin.

By late afternoon, the sky shimmered with the crowd's elation. Dragons circled overhead, gliding and spiraling in rhythm with the music filling the square. Sunlight fractured through their wings like stained glass, sending dazzling bursts of color across the gathering. They waited for the signal, the same one they had learned for the very first celebration—held exactly one thousand years ago.

Leah noted a new ritual element since the previous day's rehearsal: a large wooden bowl of elixir now sat in the center. With each added ingredient, its aroma grew more enticing. One by one, the elders drank deeply, connecting themselves to Enlil through the sacred brew.

As the feasting ceremony began in earnest, villagers formed a line, moving in groups of families and close friends toward the palace. Each paused to drink from the elixir before continuing on.

At the back of the line walked Leah alongside Ryanne's parents, Alec and Lydia. They kept a modest distance from the crowd—habits formed from years of managing war-scarred memories.

Large gatherings often triggered vivid flashbacks. After Alec's outburst during the last Dragon Fire Celebration—when he tore through six young priests and hurled a seventh from a second-story window—the Dragon Council nearly exiled him.

Eventually, the healers confirmed similar symptoms in many war veterans. The following year, fifteen more experienced intense reactions during the festivities, causing chaos when young disciples released fireworks too close to the crowd. The Council finally acknowledged the need for caution, though they remained firm in their requirement that Alec be supervised—given his formidable battle instincts.

Only Lydia seemed capable of that task. Leah had always admired their bond. It was rare to witness a love so steady and enduring.

She watched the pair walk arm-in-arm, Lydia's red hair cascading over Alec's back as they leaned into each other, trading quiet smiles and occasional kisses like lovestruck teens.

Ryanne darted up from the stone bridge, hurling herself into Alec's arms. He caught her with ease, spinning her in the air as Lydia clapped with mock amazement, her laughter ringing like a bell.

Ryanne was a lucky little girl.

Leah stood in silence, a warm smile flickering on her lips. But deep within, an ache stirred.

For the first time in centuries, she felt completely—and painfully—alone.

Chapter Three

Joel entered the outer chambers of the High Priest, pulling back the hood of his robe and freeing the tangle of light brown curls that crowned his head. The soft fall of curls framed his face, setting off a pair of nearly violet eyes that gleamed with quiet unease.

From within the hall, unmistakable sounds of pleasure echoed faintly—moans that sharpened Joel's frown as he approached. He moved with cautious distaste, unwilling to hear what his ears could not unhear. The guards flanking the great doors stood stiff and silent, their weary expressions betraying the fact that this had been going on for some time.

Joel's upper lip curled just beneath the pale scar that curved across his cheek. It was more than discomfort—it was disgust. The ancient customs of the Dragon Fold forbade any sexual acts while under the Oath of Ashur, the Sky God. This oath had bound the brotherhood for over a thousand years and had remained unbroken until the current High Priest's reign.

Like the rest of the priesthood, Joel had been deeply disturbed by this degradation of sacred law. Yet he understood the consequences of interrupting now would be far more severe than his discomfort. This wasn't the first time.

In all his years, Joel had never seen anyone but the High Priest enter or exit the inner sanctum. He'd questioned the guards, who were posted day and night. Their answers were always the same—no one had passed through. That room was sealed tight, warded against all intrusion, particularly from powerful mages capable of teleportation within the village. Only a select few even had that strength.

The High Priest had grown paranoid after his predecessor was murdered. That tragedy had shattered the peace and triggered the first breach of the Oath. Many attributed the High Priest's moral fall to grief and the weight of sudden power.

The killer had been discovered—Roman Titus, a mage whose power was unrivaled across the Moro. His wife, Noctis, had aided him and was said to have created the wards that now protected the chamber. Ironically, they were designed to prevent the very tragedy that they had allegedly caused. The murder weapon, still wet with blood, had been found in Roman's chambers. The sentence was swift. The High Priest had ordered both Roman and Noctis executed for religious treason.

Joel had been stunned when he learned of their fate. Noctis had always shown him kindness. Roman had never struck him as capable of such treachery. The memory still unsettled him, and now, he found himself wondering about their children—daughters, he believed. Their names were gone to time, but the phantom of that memory stirred faintly.

He pushed the thought aside. The past was a distraction, and there was work to do.

"Who is with him?" he asked curtly.

"We've seen no one enter through this door but the High Priest, my lord," one guard replied.

Exactly as expected. The woman's identity remained a mystery—heard but never seen.

"You're excused," Joel said.

The guards nodded in relief and withdrew.

The cries from within had faded, leaving a tense stillness in their wake. Joel seized the opportunity and knocked.

To his surprise, the heavy doors flung open with an almost theatrical flourish, revealing a breathtaking woman who stood entirely nude. Raven-haired and glowing-eyed, she met his stunned expression with a knowing smile. Her eyes shimmered with unnatural blue light, and her bare form was unabashed, bold in its allure.

"Do come in, Joel. We've been expecting you," she purred, stepping aside with a fluid grace that sent a jolt down his spine.

High Priest Oliver stood at the far corner, pulling on his robes with a smug grin twisting his lips. The doors slammed shut behind Joel, and he jumped. A soft laugh escaped the woman's full, crimson lips.

Joel tried to look away—tried, and failed. His gaze trailed helplessly over her flawless skin, from the elegance of her collarbone down to the delicate curve of her hips. A tiny freckle just to the right of her navel caught his attention, and it was as if time stopped.

"Who are you?" he asked, voice low and reverent, almost a plea.

The woman moved around him with the grace of something untamed. Every motion was precise, smooth, predatory. He felt like prey drawn to her without resistance.

"That's not important, dear," she said, her fingers brushing lightly against the one part of him betraying his thoughts. His arousal was undeniable. It had been far too long since he'd touched a woman.

"What is important," she whispered, "is that you're here now."

She pressed herself against his back, her warmth radiating through his robes. Her hands roamed over his chest, across his shoulders. Her hips shifted in rhythm, and Joel was lost.

Usually, he found comfort in the beauty of the High Priest's chambers—the elaborate murals of dragons carved into the stone walls, the black marble floors inlaid with golden sigils, the centuries-old furnishings crafted by the ancient high elves. But in this moment, his senses registered only her.

"Where is the boy, Joel?" she whispered, lips brushing his ear before leaving a kiss behind it.

Joel turned, gripping her wrist with firm but gentle intent, drawing her close. His body pressed against hers, breath catching in his throat.

"What boy?" he asked, voice rough with desire.

She gave a sultry chuckle, slipping from his grasp like mist. He blinked in frustration. Seconds ago, he'd reminded himself to be gentle—now, he felt foolish for even thinking he could control this moment.

"There will be time enough for that later, love," she teased. "Now, where's the boy?"

Her question was edged with impatience, but her tone was still playfully seductive.

"You'll have to forgive his single-mindedness," the High Priest interjected. "I'm sure it's been quite some time since Joel's known… release. Or seen a naked goddess like yourself."

The woman frowned.

"You may have to persuade him, as you once persuaded me."

Her eyes narrowed.

"So it would seem," she said with an exhale that was part sigh, part warning. "You've outgrown your purpose anyway, murderous swine."

The High Priest stiffened. Confusion clouded his eyes as he studied her face. But her expression had changed—now bloodlust flickered in her gaze, mingling with old hate.

"Joel," she said softly. No command, no force. But he moved instinctively.

She touched him again. His body trembled at her touch, as if all his instincts had awakened. Her hands wrapped around him, her lips kissed him lightly, and Joel kissed her back—hungrily, mindlessly.

When she pulled away, he gasped.

"There's only one way for us to be together," she whispered. "Kill him, and I'll be yours forever."

The promise in her voice ignited something primal within him.

"Consider it done, my lady."

The High Priest sputtered. "What…?"

Joel stepped forward, shoulders squared.

"You think you can destroy me?" the High Priest scoffed, half-laughing. "I am power incarnate! You, Joel, are nothing beside me."

Under ordinary circumstances, Joel might have agreed. The High Priest had demonstrated incredible strength time and again. But now, something inside Joel surged—an ancient energy buried deep in his chest, flaring to life. He drank it in like the breath of the divine.

She smiled as though she had been waiting for this moment for centuries.

"Very well," Oliver snapped. "Let's end this charade."

With a flick of his wrist, he launched a bolt of fire into Joel's chest. The impact sent him flying across the marble floor, sliding with a crack and a grunt. The force left him winded, pain blooming like wildfire.

The High Priest looked to the woman, a sneer on his lips. But she merely watched, calm, as though this was all part of a much larger plan.

"You would rather have this pup of a man than me?" he spat at her.

A sweet smile and a flick of her wrist were the only responses she offered.

Joel stood, chest heaving, pain rippling through him like a second heartbeat. His legs trembled beneath him, but he managed to find his footing. Then, something shifted—strength surged through his limbs, unrelenting and raw. Still, it took all his focus to harness it as he launched himself at the High Priest. Blow after blow, strike after strike, each attack more furious than the last.

At first, the High Priest parried with ease. His expression betrayed no concern, only mild amusement. But that composure didn't last. Joel's newfound strength was climbing by the second, and the Priest, once so invincible, began to falter. The edge in his movements dulled. His breathing grew more ragged.

The High Priest retaliated with volley after volley of fire magic, a singular flame flaring from his palms—but Joel stood unfazed. Each wave of magic collided with his defenses, and Joel swatted them away with growing ease. The surge inside him was overwhelming, a force that seemed to burn brighter with every step he took. He felt untouchable. Invincible.

Glancing across the battlefield, Joel caught her watching. His heart stuttered at the sight. Her smile, dazzling and laced with a pride he'd never known, locked with his eyes for a fleeting moment—and it was enough. Intoxicated by her gaze, Joel pressed his attack harder, striking with unrelenting fury.

Years of pain flooded his memory.

He remembered the humiliations—the way the High Priest had tormented the younger acolytes. The cracked bones. The broken spirits. Joel could feel the sting of the beatings again, could almost trace the scars along his own flesh. His fury deepened.

And then, the memory of *her*—bloodied, broken, discarded like garbage in the alley—seared through him. Her swollen eyes. Her shaking hands. The flinch when he had reached for her. He had known then. Only one man was cruel enough to destroy something so beautiful over a perceived slight.

Joel's rage became focused, surgical. He struck with precision, no longer a barrage of emotion but a calculated assault.

The High Priest stumbled backward, crashing into a table in a desperate bid to retreat. He was wheezing, hunched over, his once-proud robes now scorched and tattered. The years caught up to him in a blink—he looked ancient, as if he had aged a millennium in moments.

Joel knew it was over.

He stepped forward, calm and deliberate, drawing power into his palms. No shield was needed now. A ball of lightning formed between his hands, its glow so intense it burned his vision. When the power threatened to spill from his control, he released it.

A violent explosion cracked through the air, shaking the walls. The High Priest's scream was brief and guttural before he dissolved into a pile of ash.

Joel stepped forward and kicked at the remains.

"Go to hell, you arrogant prick."

The silence that followed was broken by slow, deliberate applause.

"My, my. Very impressive, darling."

Joel turned, sheepish, a grin spreading across his face. She lay sprawled across the single bed that now belonged to him.

"Come closer," she purred. "Bask in my presence."

She giggled, and Joel obeyed, driven by a hunger that had nothing to do with food or power. The need in him was feral, untamed. With each step toward her, it grew harder to control.

She wasn't helping.

She crawled across the bed, her movements deliberate, every sway of her hips and bounce of her breasts stoking the fire in him. She sat back on her heels as he reached the edge of the bed, close enough to touch.

"Tell me how much you want me," she commanded, her voice a melody laced with challenge.

"There's no need," he growled, "I'm about to show you."

In a flash, he grabbed her and kissed her, hard and desperate. His grip was fierce on her wrists, pinning her as centuries of restrained desire exploded into motion. His tongue demanded entry, seeking something only she could give. She moaned, arching into him, surrendering.

Joel's lips left her mouth to explore the softness of her neck. Her breath caught as he traced the sensitive skin above her jugular. He released her wrists, needing to touch more of her, but forced himself to slow, to savor.

He stepped back briefly, untying his trousers, letting them fall in silence. He took her in—the curve of her lips, the blush on her cheeks, the faint red mark his scruff had left on her pale skin. A deep, animalistic sound rumbled from his chest.

If he had any self-control left, now was the time to turn back.

But he didn't.

That control had vanished with her first moan.

As her eyes widened at the sight of him, Joel smirked.

"Oh my god," she whispered, eyes devouring him. A teasing smile crept across her lips, cheeks glowing with heat.

"Why would you keep that to yourself?" she teased. "That's just rude."

He grinned at her approval and pounced.

In one swift motion, he had her beneath him, kissing her again with the same urgency, breaking only to whisper against her neck before trailing kisses lower. His tongue found her nipple, swirling, teasing. Her back arched, her moan vibrating through him, tightening the heat in his core.

She writhed under his mouth, pressing her body to his, pulling him closer, guiding him to where she ached for him most. Joel held her there, just shy of the edge, until her soft whimpers shattered his restraint.

With a groan, he thrust into her.

Her entire body arched beneath him, her eyes fluttering shut, lips parting in a silent cry as he filled her. Joel bent to tease her breasts again as he drove into her, harder, faster, their rhythm frantic and in perfect sync.

Her clipped cries echoed through the room.

Then, with a sharp twist, she rolled over, pressing herself against him from above, her caramel curves fitting perfectly into his hands. She lowered herself slowly, torturously, taking him in inch by inch.

Joel let out a frustrated growl and slapped her rear, eliciting a scream as she shattered around him, trembling and gasping, her body spasming in release.

The sight—her convulsing, clutching at him, utterly undone—pushed him over the edge. With one final thrust, he came with a shout, gripping her hips so tightly he feared he might leave bruises.

"Holy shit," he panted, collapsing on top of her.

He lay there, spent, riding the aftershocks of her pleasure as she twitched beneath him. The silence was thick with satisfaction.

"What's your name?" he asked suddenly.

She turned her head to face him, her eyes soft.

"It's Layla," she answered with a sad smile.

Joel returned a genuine one. "Did you enjoy that as much as I did, Layla?" he asked, rolling off her.

A shiver danced down her spine. "Oh yes."

He chuckled, clearly proud of himself.

But then, everything changed.

Her expression shifted. Though her head still rested on the pillow, and her tousled hair framed her like a goddess, the warmth in her eyes cooled. The Layla he had just been with vanished in a heartbeat.

"Where's the boy, Joel?"

He sighed. "He's being taken to the palace—for the final ritual."

"Unharmed?" she asked softly.

Joel nodded, sleep creeping into his voice. "Unharmed."

"Thank you, Joel."

"Uh-huh," he mumbled, eyelids growing heavy.

A breeze brushed against his skin, gentle and strange.

Joel's eyes shot open.

He sat up, searching the room.

She was gone.

Somehow, Layla had vanished without a sound.

***

Leah stepped forward, almost involuntarily, pushing deeper into the growing crowd at the palace gates. Something in the air tugged at her—familiar, intoxicating.

A scent.

It wrapped around her like a spell: a warm, heady mix of herbs and spices that stirred something deep inside her. She blinked rapidly, trying to focus.

Just then, Marcus, the baker's son, bumped into her from behind. Leah stumbled, nearly falling for the second time that day.

"Oh gods, I'm so sorry! I wasn't paying attention. My deepest apologies, my lady," Marcus stammered, flustered, his hand gripping her elbow to steady her.

"It's quite alright," Leah assured him with a laugh, brushing herself off. "I wasn't paying attention either."

She meant it. That scent—it had distracted her completely.

As she turned toward the source, she spotted a priest at the gates, passing goblets to the crowd. The drink shimmered in the light, and the scent was unmistakable.

"This drink smells amazing, doesn't it?" she asked, inhaling deeply.

"It's almost... sinful," Marcus replied, desire creeping into his voice.

Leah nodded slowly. "I'm glad the children are playing by the lake," she said, grinning.

Marcus blinked at her in confusion.

She laughed again—soft and knowing.

"It's just that with the thick crowd, I shudder to think what poor elder the children might trample to get hold of one of these goblets!"

Her words rang true to Marcus, who had often watched the children battle one another for the last fresh treats he and his father set out for the public each day. His laugh was hardy and earnest—a warm, rich sound that somehow felt like home.

The priests moved through the gathering, passing the gleaming goblets from one villager to the next. The crowd pressed closer, eager to receive the mysterious brew, each person drinking deeply in turn.

"It's true. I'm afraid none of us would stand a chance at tasting that intoxicating concoction before it ended up on the ground."

Their exchange drew the attention of several nearby townsfolk, who joined in the laughter sparked by the image. Still, not a single eye strayed from the vessel moving through the sea of eager hands.

"I wonder why they're handing out so many goblets…"

A flicker of unease crossed Leah's face as she caught up to Alec and Lydia, glancing down into the liquid-filled goblet now cradled in her hand.

A hush fell over the room as one of the priests stepped forward into the main hall. Leah paused to glance around and realized, with faint confusion, that she and Marcus had drifted at least twenty feet during their short conversation.

That's odd. I thought we had stopped.

Her thoughts were cut short by the sudden echo of the priest's voice.

"Two thousand years ago, our world fell into chaos. Our princess had disappeared…"

A low hum rose in Leah's ears, growing stronger with each passing second until it was nearly all she could hear—save for the lure of the brew.

"…war among brothers…"

The hum swelled into a roar.

"…the ceremony…"

Her mouth began to water as she watched villagers—those ahead of the newest arrivals—gulping down the brew like parched animals. *Greedy bastards.*

"Remedy our past actions…"

Without meaning to, Leah began pushing forward. Some invisible force compelled her, drawing her into the mass of bodies now buzzing like flies around spilled honey.

"Let the feast begin!" the priest bellowed.

Several villagers shoved the people behind them and clawed toward those in front, desperate for a better position. But the crowd, as if shaken from a collective trance, swiftly subdued the chaos. The offenders were ushered out, and order returned before the commotion could escalate.

Leah steadied her steps as she neared the bowl, eventually forcing herself to turn away and retreat to her seat at the great mahogany table in the adjacent dining hall. It stretched fifty feet in length and four in width, yet occupied only a quarter of The Great Hall's massive floor space.

The grand room hadn't changed in all the years she'd been away. Six towering white marble pillars still bore the intricately carved stag crests, accented by ivy garlands and small, strategically placed candles that flickered softly against the stone. The dust-free finish of the emblems shone in the dim light, as did the rich emerald banners dyed with silver thread. Silver-plated antlers—some curved, others jagged—served as ornate chandeliers suspended from above, freshly adorned with draping moss and arrangements of pale pink and yellow roses, woven among decorations in red, purple, and blue for the celebration.

Though the once-lustrous light brown wallpaper had faded with time, the dull gold undertones gave the hall a mellow warmth that softened its grandeur, lending it a rustic charm that felt both noble and lived-in.

At the far end of the room, a raised platform held four mahogany thrones. Two stood at the center, equal in size and elegance, while the two to the right were slightly smaller. Only the far-left throne bore a heavy crown carving along its high back, denoting the king's seat.

Leah's eyes lingered on the smallest throne at the far right. Something in her chest twisted—an emotion sharp and sudden, too close to longing to dismiss. The lightness she'd felt earlier dissolved into an unfamiliar grief that clutched her throat and stung her eyes.

A soft touch on her hand startled her. Leah blinked, her trance broken, and found herself staring into a pair of brilliant magenta eyes, wide with concern.

"Maja Leah, are you okay?" Ryanne's whisper barely reached her ears.

Leah forced a small smile, nodding gently.

"Yes, honey. I'm alright. It's just so pretty—I couldn't help myself."

The lie tasted false the moment it left her lips. Judging by the flicker of suspicion in Ryanne's gaze, it must have sounded worse than it felt.

"You don't look okay. I'll go get Mama!" the girl cried. Before Leah could stop her, Ryanne darted off into the crowd.

Well, now you've done it… That girl is too smart for her own good. Dammit. Just blame it on the wine.

Lydia appeared moments later, weaving through the gathering with Alec and Ryanne close behind. Two more children raced up behind them, tugging excitedly at Alec's tunic and halting his steps just shy of the table.

Leah watched him—really watched him—for perhaps the first time in ages. There was something about his eyes: a vivid glow she hadn't noticed before. He bent to whisper to his daughter, who squealed with delight and dashed away with the other children.

His black leather vest hugged a deep purple shirt and matched the sleek hide of his trousers. The ensemble rendered him nearly invisible in the fading light. A wicked-looking sword hung at his side, its obsidian blade marred with deep dents and ancient carvings. The edge, however, remained pristine and sharp.

Leah knew that weapon well. It had claimed countless lives.

She remembered the first time she saw it—during the Thousand Year War. She'd been little more than a girl at sixteen hundred, an orphan with no memory and a gift for magic so potent that the priests had called her the perfect warrior. Back then, she and Lydia had been close—closer than anyone else. Leah still recalled the terror on Lydia's face when she'd come to share the news that they were being sent to the front lines.

Together, they'd joined the troops for their first battle. Leah had been grievously wounded in the initial assault on Gravin Raw—Chaos Mountain, as it came to be known. She was fighting for her life when a stranger appeared, wielding a black sword like it was forged in the hands of Ashur himself.

He fought at her side without pause, cutting down the mindless enemy with inhuman resolve while she, bleeding and faltering, hurled fire and lightning with what strength she had left. Rain mixed with blood, her vision blurred, and still she cast protection spells, doing all she could to survive.

When the flames of the mountain finally ebbed and the battlefield lay quiet—charred bodies, scorched stone, and molten ash covering the earth—Leah collapsed in the mud.

Three days later, she awoke to Alec standing over her, and Lydia desperately trying to pull her back from the edge of death.

Alec had become a steadfast friend after that. And Lydia, well—Lydia had fallen hopelessly in love with the Dark Fae who had saved them both.

Alec took the seat next to his wife, who was clearly trying to get Leah's attention. Waving her hand in Leah's line of sight had done little to snap her out of the daze. Just as Leah opened her mouth to respond to Lydia's concern, a familiar cackle echoed softly in her ear.

She spun around, searching for the source, but no one nearby could have made the sound.

"Where are you, Leah?" a seductive voice whispered, curling around her like smoke.

"Did you hear that?" she asked, her voice low and uncertain, barely believing it herself.

"Hear what?" Alec replied, his eyes narrowing as he gave a wary glance at the ornate tapestries lining the walls.

"Leah, are you okay?" he asked again, his voice tight with concern. Lydia, now wringing her hands, looked just as worried.

Leah gave her head a quick shake to clear it.

"Yeah, I think this potion is getting to me," she muttered.

"You sure? We can step out for a moment if you need air," Lydia offered, her maternal instincts on high alert. Leah had never been great at hiding how she felt.

"I'm all right, I swear. Thank you, really, but I'm fine. It's just the wine talking," she insisted, forcing a reassuring smile.

Around them, Dragon Priests continued distributing more elixirs as the long line of villagers tapered off and the table approached full capacity.

Lydia gave the room a quick scan, then blanched.

"Alec, where's Ryanne?" she demanded, pushing up from her seat.

Alec caught her wrist and gently eased her back down.

"The younglings have a separate table by the lake," he explained calmly. "Ryanne was invited to join them—supervised, of course."

Lydia let out a breath and swatted him on the shoulder.

"Don't do that to me! I nearly died just now!" she scolded, turning back to her plate.

Alec glanced helplessly at Leah and mouthed, *What did I do?* over his wife's shoulder.

Leah giggled and shrugged, which earned both of them another swat from Lydia—though this time her glare was softened by a grin. The trio's laughter spread to others at the table, the unsettling moment quickly washed away by the levity.

A young priest made his way down the length of the table, refilling goblets and trying to keep the more impatient villagers in check by announcing the feast would be served in just a few more minutes.

To his credit, he had barely covered a third of the long table before a parade of servants burst through the kitchen doors, each carrying enormous platters.

Towering piles of meats and golden potatoes filled the air with the rich scent of spices and roasting fat. Bowls overflowed with vegetables— some roasted and caramelized, others steamed and buttered—until the entire table groaned beneath the growing bounty.

Rice, corn, cheeses, stews, and custards filled every space. Jokes about the table's structural integrity passed between guests as the feast commenced with a flurry of silverware, chatter, and clinking goblets.

Leah had eaten beyond fullness, stuffed to her very core. She leaned back in her seat, observing with mild amusement as a few highborn men discreetly unbuttoned their trousers to make room for another helping, their wives turning crimson and hiding giggles behind delicate hands.

Just as the food began to dwindle and platters emptied, the priests returned bearing desserts—sweet cakes glazed in honey, delicate pies paired with whipped puddings, and frozen delicacies that shimmered in the candlelight. It was a marvel that the table could still hold it all.

Leah and Marcus leaned in to hear Lydia share a memory.

"You remember the rations?" Leah asked.

Lydia nodded, then elaborated for Marcus's benefit, knowing he hadn't served in the war.

"Well, toward the end, our supply chain kept getting hit by the enemy, and we were put on strict rations. That is, until we discovered that weasel Aspen was behind it. I never liked him—even before he ran you through! Oh, I could never—" She paused, collecting herself, her cheeks flushed.

Leah teased, "That wine's getting to you."

Lydia gave her a playful slap on the arm.

"Oh hush. Anyway, we were rationed, right? And my charming husband decides we should have a picnic. In the middle of a war. So, we head out, and Alec checks the traps, thinking we'll have rabbit stew. But no rabbits."

Leah and Marcus were already grinning as Lydia continued, gesturing animatedly.

"So, Alec says, 'No problem. I'll teach you to use a bow real quick, and we'll catch something.' He gives me a crash course, then heads off one way, and I go another. Picture it—me in the woods, lugging this bow three times my size, barely knowing how to hold it, stalking through the trees for movement."

She mimed drawing a bowstring, her elbows pulling back dramatically.

"I finally spot something an hour later, and I swear it takes me five minutes just to draw the damn thing back. I shoot, and a second later,

Alec comes hopping into view, screaming about rabbit stew—with an arrow in his foot!"

The table erupted into laughter.

"He asked me to marry him three days later," Lydia added with a proud little grin.

Several hours passed in this cheerful way until, at last, the revelry dulled and the guests could eat no more. Drowsy from wine and overindulgence, they leaned back in their chairs as priests cleared the remnants of the feast.

One priest stepped forward and announced the princess's arrival was imminent.

***

Outside the palace doors, Layla stood, glaring at the over-the-top grandeur with nothing short of contempt.

She had allowed Joel his little delusion—for now. In her experience, men often turned hostile when a woman suggested their performance had been lackluster or worse, dared to say so aloud. Her first lesson in this had been with the former Head Dragon Priest, the same man who murdered his predecessor and framed the king.

Back then, just like now, Layla had seduced men not with magic, but with allure, keeping herself just out of reach until they proved themselves useful. After years of manipulating the priest—without a single spell— he had finally completed his first task: convincing the village elders that crowning a new king would be dangerous.

In return, he had demanded his reward.

Still a virgin when she entered into her pact with Ashur, Layla had no experience outside the god's bed—and had never once been left wanting. This mortal's fumbling attempt at pleasure was her rude awakening.

Ashur, ever indifferent to pity, had intervened only after she lay bruised and broken, gifting her a power siphon once he was sure she'd live. With it, she cast a memory spell strong enough to repair the bridge her wounded pride had burned.

In the end, it had all worked out. And now, having watched the High Priest die, knowing he'd meant nothing to her, Layla felt cleaner, freer.

She forced the sneer from her lips as she sensed Leah's presence inside the palace.

Let's see what she really remembers.

Drawing on her power, a gust of wind circled her, stirring dust at her feet. Her yellow dress whipped around her legs, cinched at the waist with a black cord. Raven-dark hair thrashed in the breeze, as if resisting her will.

Reaching out with her mind, she brushed against the edges of Leah's consciousness and waited.

Nothing.

No reaction. No defense. No recoil.

She doesn't remember anything, Layla realized with glee.

She let out a low, delighted chuckle.

"This is going to be way too easy," she whispered.

Leah's mind trembled faintly—recognition without clarity. Layla nudged her thoughts, searching, and found her: in the Great Hall. Fitting. It had been their favorite place as children. They'd run wild between the pillars, nipping at each other for attention like mischievous pups.

Leah had always been stronger, more grounded—but things had changed. Now, Layla held the upper hand.

Now, she had the ear of a god.

The smile on her lips never reached her eyes. The village, its people, its fools—she had them all right where she wanted them. A few more hours, and everything would fall into place.

Her vengeance was almost complete.

Only one last thing remained.

She reached out again, this time toward Joel. A soft brush across his cheek snapped him awake from his post-coital haze. To her surprise, he responded almost instantly.

His predecessor had required shaking, coaxing, and temptations of the flesh to wake. This one was different.

Less work. Less chatter. Less time wasted on mediocre sex.

Yes, she thought with smug satisfaction, she was definitely going to like this one much better.

Chapter Four

A struggle erupted around the sacred bowl. The elixir had become the object of uncontrollable greed—and Leah needed it. They all did.

She had never felt such ravenous desire.

A blast of magic tore through the crowd, followed by a strangled cry as a villager was hurled from the sweet, shimmering concoction. Steel flashed—daggers drawn by men pressed closest to the bowl. Leah felt an urgent panic rise in her throat. She wasn't going to make it. She wouldn't taste it.

She surged forward, kicking and clawing through bodies, her fingers tangled in fabric and hair, each breath hot with desperation.

Then a sudden wave of searing heat exploded outward, knocking her to the earth beneath a storm of trampling feet. Screams filled the air as people crashed around and over her, their bodies slamming into one another with primal abandon.

The blow jolted a memory—Adam's first day in class.

A boot smashed into her chin, snapping her back to the present. She was being crushed.

Panic clawed up her throat. She twisted her head, gasping, her limbs caught beneath the dead weight of others. The riot was on top of her. Teeth, elbows, knees—none spared her. Her lungs screamed, vision blurred, and still she fought, crawling through limbs and sweat and dirt.

She cried out, her voice muffled beneath bodies, her hands scrabbling for purchase. Slowly—agonizingly—the pressure began to lift. One person stumbled off her, then another. She sucked in a breath.

Another. Her chest seized with the relief of oxygen—and the hunger for the elixir surged back with terrifying force.

And then—fear. Cold, sudden, and absolute.

Clawing at her skirts, she tore a strip of cloth free and tied it around her face. She would not become an animal again.

The last weight lifted from her back. She pushed up to her knees, inhaling deep, greedy breaths as her body trembled.

Just moments ago, the crowd had been peaceful—smiling, laughing, telling stories as they slowly filtered toward the exit. Dragon Priests lined either side of the pathway, flanking the villagers, retrieving goblets of elixir with firm but polite insistence.

Then, a second bowl had been brought forth.

Everything changed.

A thunderous crack split the air, followed by arcs of lightning that lanced out from the form of a woman now standing at the threshold.

The riot stopped.

The princess was early.

Every eye shifted—first to the newcomer, then to Leah, then back again.

A breath, sharp and stunned, whispered behind her.

"They have the same face…"

Leah stepped forward, and the crowd parted instinctively. It felt… strangely right, as though the air itself recognized her.

She approached the woman—identical in every way but for the eyes. Cold. Calculating.

A crown of silver and diamonds rested among her dark curls, drawn back tightly from her face. Leah knew in her bones it didn't belong.

The Dragon Priests fawned over the woman, murmuring their devotion.

Leah knew the truth.

She was an imposter.

The proclaimed princess pushed through her worshippers and walked straight to Leah, stopping just short of touching her. She reached out, gently brushing a strand of hair from Leah's cheek, grinding out a smile as sharp as broken glass.

"It's good to see you again, sister."

A collective gasp rippled through the villagers. Murmurs rose, half of them now swearing they'd *always* suspected the resemblance, eager to gain favor.

Leah blinked, stunned.

"What?"

"Where is Adam?" the princess asked sweetly. Too sweet. Her smile remained fixed, her eyes void of warmth.

Something inside Leah recoiled. The air around the princess buzzed with danger, like a pit full of resting vipers waiting to strike.

"I don't know," Leah answered flatly, forcing her expression into stillness.

The princess stared deeper, probing. A silent challenge passed between them. Why? Leah wasn't the eldest. Was she?

Without warning, the woman flicked her fingers and smiled.

Leah flew across the room.

Her body slammed into the stone wall, and she crumpled to the floor. Chaos erupted. Villagers shrieked and surged toward the exit.

"Find the boy!" a booming male voice thundered over the riot.

The Dragon Priests sprang into motion.

Leah's head swam. Through her blurred vision, she caught sight of a red cord slithering through the crowd, disappearing beyond the exit.

Gas hissed through the air. It clouded the room and her thoughts.

The elixir—whatever was in it—it turned people into something else. They weren't themselves anymore.

A flash in her mind.

The secret mages.

The children!

Her mind snapped into focus. There was no more time.

Leaping forward, she grabbed the knees of three nearest villagers and clutched them together, shouting,

"Rigor Forum Transport Anta!"

The air twisted.

They hit the ground outside the village with a heavy thud. The three villagers rolled forward, tumbling into The Great Oak. Two more fell beside them with startled grunts.

Leah yanked the cloth from her face and collapsed on the cool grass, gasping for air. Her limbs ached with the unexpected strain of transporting more than she'd intended.

But she was alive.

As the villagers slowly regained their footing, Leah recognized them one by one:

Marcus, the baker's son.

Catherine, Adam's adoptive mother.

Katrina, the midwife mage.

Alec, Ryanne's father.

And Freya, the village matriarch.

They looked from each other to Leah, bewildered.

"What the hell happened?" Catherine demanded.

"I'm sorry," Leah panted. "There was no other way."

She started to explain, but a second explosion split the sky—sharper, louder.

Alec took off running, panic flashing across his face. Marcus hesitated only a second before following.

"Wait!" Leah cried.

She vanished, reappearing in front of them in a swirl of lavender magic. Her hands shot up, conjuring a barrier just as the men barreled into it. The force hurled them backward.

"Seriously, Alec? Your judgment is obviously still clouded."

"Get out of the way, Leah!" Alec roared, voice thick with rage and fear. Marcus groaned on the ground beside him, stunned.

"No, you idiot! The priests did this!" she shouted, fury searing her voice.

"Why would they?" he spat.

"The elixir caused the riot—don't you see? I know you're scared, Alec. I am too. But we're not helping anyone if we charge in blindly and die."

She locked eyes with him, forcing him to listen.

"We have to get in and out before the gas takes us too. You know what happens if we breathe it in…"

Finally, Alec gave a tight nod. Leah released the shield.

"We'll find them, Alec," she said more softly, laying a hand on his arm. She prayed it was true.

Katrina, Catherine, and Freya joined them, having descended the slope. Together, they began forming a plan.

"Is everybody ready?" Leah asked, wrapping the cloth around her mouth and nose once more. The others nodded.

The sun had nearly disappeared beyond the horizon. Twilight settled, and with it came the cover of darkness—just as the eclipse approached.

Gripping Marcus and Alec by their belts, Leah whispered again,

"Rigor Forum Transport Anta."

Back at the hilltop, Catherine watched them disappear. She turned to Freya and Katrina.

"Do you think this will really work?"

"By the love of Lux, I hope so," Freya murmured, worry etched deep in her features.

Moments later, Leah reappeared—this time with four more villagers.

The women startled, their fear snapping like a taut cord. They turned to strike, ready to defend.

Too late, Leah realized their mistake. She seized Marcus and Alec once more, vanishing in a blink.

The three women rushed to the newcomers, checking for injuries.

"What's happening down there?" Katrina asked, kneeling beside a dazed man.

"The priests—they're everywhere," he rasped. "They're searching for Adam…"

His voice shook with horror, guilt rising in his throat.

"Oh gods no… not Adam," Catherine whispered, tears spilling from her eyes.

"They ransacked the village. I don't know what they're planning, but they took him to the Palace," another man added grimly.

Leah's group reappeared with two more villagers in tow.

"Leah! They've taken Adam!" Catherine's voice cracked with urgency, halting Leah in her tracks.

"Where?" she demanded sharply.

"The Palace! Please—bring him back to me!" Catherine sobbed, clinging to her last sliver of hope.

Leah nodded grimly and vanished alongside Alec and Marcus.

When they landed in the village, the acrid smoke of burning wood filled Leah's lungs. She released Marcus with a firm instruction.

"Go find the children and tell them it's time for a magic trip. They'll take you to The Great Oak, but you'll need all of them. Go quickly!"

Marcus nodded without hesitation, already sprinting toward the lake, his silhouette vanishing into the swirling smoke that now billowed from the rooftops of several huts. He shielded his eyes from the heat and ash, driven by urgency.

"Gods," Alec murmured, horror etched into every word, "it's like we're back in the war."

Leah scanned the destruction around them—the fires, the cries, the air thick with fear—and knew he was right. But now wasn't the time to dwell on memories.

"Alec, we need to go," she said gently.

A shift passed over Alec's face, and in an instant, she recognized him. The soldier. The version of him hardened by centuries of conflict—merciless, focused, fearless. It was like watching someone don a familiar armor. And strangely, a part of her felt relieved. This was her Alec, the one she had fought beside, the one who had always stood steady in the chaos.

Lydia's love for him had always stood between them during the war. But now, a memory, uninvited and deeply unsettling, flickered through Leah's mind—an image of her and Alec walking arm in arm toward the palace, Ryanne skipping ahead, laughing, calling "Mommy! Mommy!" as Leah rested her head on Alec's shoulder, whispering sweet nothings into the crook of his neck.

Shame washed over her like cold water. She shook the vision from her mind, buried it deep, and whispered the incantation.

The world shifted.

Colors twisted and spun around them—violet, gold, silver—an opulent display of magic that never failed to momentarily distract Leah from the shadows in her heart. Stars swirled, then stretched into streaks of light as they traveled. The spell grew in intensity, then fell away, revealing the great hall as their feet touched solid ground once again.

"Dammit, Leah!" Alec barked as he stumbled, doubling over the heavy oak table she had teleported him into.

In her defense, the table took up most of the room.

A silver goblet clattered to the floor, the sound echoing across the high ceilings.

"Sorry. Still working on that," she muttered, giving him a sheepish grin.

The hall looked nothing like it had moments ago. Once lively and warm, it now felt abandoned. Dirty dishes and toppled goblets littered the dining area, remnants of chaos. The flowers and garlands that had adorned the chandelier and marble pillars just a quarter-hour ago had withered, blackened by some unnatural force.

Leah ducked behind a marble column, instinct kicking in. If the priests had heard their abrupt arrival, surprise would be their only advantage.

She reached out and touched one of the garlands. A brittle leaf crumbled and fell at her feet. Death had settled here like dust.

Alec took position behind a pillar opposite her, eyes trained down the adjacent hallway. Leah's focus snapped to the massive wooden doors across the room.

"Where do you think they may have taken him?" she whispered, barely audible above the pounding of her own heartbeat. Adrenaline coursed through her, her voice nearly lost even to herself. But Alec heard.

"If it were me?" he muttered dryly. "I'd hold him in the dungeon. But hey, I'm old-fashioned."

His flippant tone forced a small snort from Leah, one she tried to stifle—unsuccessfully. She choked on it, coughing awkwardly.

Alec turned sharply, eyes narrowing.

"You've obviously never done this before," he whispered, exasperated. "You're going to get us killed. Remember what happened in Gravin Raw?"

"That was not my fault! OK? If anything, it was your fault!"

"My fault?" His voice rose.

"How the hell was it my—"

He stopped himself, inhaling sharply and signaling for a timeout. Even he knew now wasn't the moment to argue.

"We'll talk about this later," he hissed, narrowing his eyes in warning.

Leah matched his intensity with a smirk. Hands on her hips, she leaned forward and stuck out her tongue in a defiant gesture.

Alec tried to hold in his laughter—and choked instead.

The tension between them shifted. It wasn't just banter anymore. Something deeper crackled in the air, as if energy was charging between them. The floor trembled slightly beneath Leah's feet.

Alec noticed too. His posture stiffened.

"We should go," he said, adjusting his stance, unease creeping into his tone.

"Yes, yes, let's… let's do that. Dungeons, this way." Her voice cracked slightly, and she turned quickly, leading the way down the hall.

Oh gods. What is wrong with you? He's married. To your friend.

The sound of her footsteps echoed against the black marble floor. She didn't dare look back, though she could feel Alec's eyes on her as they neared the spiral staircase of flat, worn stone. Voices floated up from below—proof the cells were occupied.

"Score one for the old man," Leah whispered, stepping aside to let Alec listen at the door. They exchanged a silent nod. He drew his sword, muscles taut, eyes steady.

They descended into the dark.

***

Marcus had found the children huddled beneath the trees near the short dock. With Ryanne's help, he'd calmed them, her presence easing their panic.

He knelt in the center of a circle formed by small, anxious faces. Gently, he took two hands in his—one of them nearly vanishing beneath his calloused fingers.

"Okay, guys. Leah said you'd know what to do," he said, searching each little face. "Let's go on a magic trip."

A girl, no more than nine, peered at him from behind thick spectacles. She looked like an owl perched in human form. She glanced around the circle, closed her eyes, and said softly, "Rigor Forum Transport Anta!"

Nothing happened.

Marcus blinked. "Is this everybody?"

The owl-eyed girl bit her lip. "We're missing Adam."

Marcus's chest tightened.

"You've taken trips when someone was missing before, right?"

"Yeah, all the time, but…"

The confusion on their faces twisted into something darker. Understanding set in.

"We've never taken a magic trip without Adam," she whispered. "He has to be here."

Panic surged through Marcus. This had been their only chance. There was no backup plan.

"Okay… new plan," he said, dropping to one knee. "We find Adam first."

***

Leah and Alec exploded through the dungeon door at the bottom of the stairs to find three priests circling a terrified Adam.

Without hesitation, Leah launched an energy blast that hurled the nearest priest into the stone wall beside Adam's cell. The boy screamed in shock.

Alec swung his sword in a clean arc, slicing the second priest open. As the man crumpled, Alec turned on the third, grabbing the priest's robe and pressing the blade to his throat with violent promise.

"Please! Please, don't kill me!" the man stammered, tears spilling down his cheeks. "I was just following orders—I swear it!"

Alec slammed him into the iron bars behind him.

"Oh, were you now?" he hissed, his voice low and venomous.

"Yes—I swear!"

"And what exactly were those orders?" Alec demanded, his sword biting just deep enough to draw blood, a thin line trickling down the priest's neck.

Leah knelt beside the body Alec had dropped, retrieving the keys from his belt. She unlocked Adam's cell and pulled the boy into her arms, wrapping him in a much-needed hug.

Behind her, Alec's interrogation continued. Leah didn't interfere—she knew better. Alec was just getting started, and she recognized the man in front of her. This priest had been one of the seven responsible for crafting the elixir. The cord on his robe marked him clearly—the lowest-ranking among them.

And the only one left alive.

"To find the boy and bring him here unharmed. Please, let me go."

The priest was beginning to sob uncontrollably, and Leah could tell it was starting to grate on Alec's nerves.

"I would stop crying if I were you," she said, rising to her feet and drawing both men's attention. "You're only going to make it worse," she added, gesturing subtly toward Alec by way of explanation.

"Why did they want the boy?" Alec snarled, eyes narrowing as he stepped forward.

"He's an offering! To the princess!" the priest sputtered through panicked gasps.

Alec's face twisted with confusion and rage. "Why would our princess want a child as an offering?" he demanded, his voice sharp with disbelief, pressing closer to the trembling man.

"I overheard them say… he is her son!" the priest screamed, fear cracking his voice.

"What?" Alec froze in place, just as stunned as Leah, who felt her stomach drop.

"The legend is a lie! The princess was taken by Ashur after the king and queen were executed! We made up the story—to explain the war!" The sudden revelation hit Leah like a slap, leaving her momentarily speechless.

"Why?" she asked, barely able to form the word.

"She's not what we thought she was. We're not even sure if she's the real princess or one of Ashur's creations. She's cruel, ruthless, and calls herself the Goddess now. We thought it best to give her the boy, hoping she'd leave us alone."

Alec let go of the priest's robes, stumbling back a step, horror dawning in his eyes.

"Then where is she now?" he muttered, the question barely audible.

"We don't know," the priest replied in a choked whisper. "But she'll be here soon. And if the boy isn't, she'll burn this village to the ground—with everyone in it."

Alec's expression hardened as he stared at the priest. "It would seem your priests have already beaten her to it."

The priest blinked in confusion. "That was an accident! He knocked over several lanterns before we caught him. Surely it's been put out by now?"

"No, it hasn't. The whole village is on fire," Alec snapped, advancing on the cowering man once more.

Before things escalated, Leah stepped forward and caught Alec's arm.

"I think we need to cage him before we leave. If what he says is true, then we need to get Adam as far away from here as possible."

Alec gave a curt nod and wrestled the flailing priest toward the cell. The man pleaded pitifully the entire way, but neither of them responded. With a final shove, Alec locked the cell and left him behind. As they exited the dungeon, they extinguished all the torches, plunging the priest into a suffocating blackness deeper than any he'd ever known.

Leah froze at the sound of footsteps echoing up the stairs—a man's voice followed by what sounded like a dozen others. Her heart quickened, adrenaline flooding her limbs. But then a familiar girlish voice answered, and without hesitation, she shoved open the door.

Marcus and the entire class stood in the hallway, wide-eyed and screaming in startled fear.

"What are you doing here?" Leah shouted, staring in disbelief.

"We couldn't leave without Adam," Ryanne said simply. Then, spotting Alec, she squealed, "Daddy!" and launched herself into his arms.

Alec caught her midair, pulling her close in a crushing hug. Leah marveled again at how quickly a child's emotions could shift—from terror to joy in a heartbeat—as she watched Alec examine his daughter, gently brushing her hair back to check for any injuries.

"That's very sweet, but it's too dangerous for you to be here," Leah said sternly, her words more directed at Marcus than the children.

"No—we literally couldn't leave," Marcus explained. "Apparently, Adam is the only reason these magical excursions of yours even work with other kids missing."

Leah sighed, rubbing her forehead. "Well… that explains a lot."

She reached for Adam's hand, gripping it tightly. No matter what, they had to get out of the palace.

Just as they turned to go, a chilling voice rang down the corridor.

"The boy stays."

Everyone spun toward the source. A woman in white approached, her presence commanding, her steps light yet deliberate. Her features were fierce and strangely familiar—her eyes glowed like the sea under moonlight.

She was identical to Leah.

The resemblance stunned everyone. Alec, Marcus, and even the children exchanged bewildered glances, unsure of what they were seeing. Leah stood frozen. It was like staring into a living mirror—but one twisted, wrong, and utterly foreign. Fear clawed at her chest. This woman hadn't just mimicked her appearance. Leah could feel it—she had taken something more.

Alec drew his sword and stepped in front of the group, standing protectively between them and the imposter.

"Who are you?" he demanded, his voice laced with disgust.

The woman smiled—broad, amused, disturbingly calm. She turned slightly, as if trying to stifle laughter, then returned her gaze to Leah.

"You really don't remember, do you?" she asked softly, her tone condescending, like a teacher addressing a slow pupil.

Leah clenched her fists, a chill crawling down her spine. "What exactly should I be remembering?" she asked, slowly nudging the children and Marcus back toward the entrance to the great hall. Her fingers brushed Marcus's arm—move.

"Why, your heritage, of course." The woman smiled, watching Leah intently as if expecting recognition.

When none came, she tilted her head and continued, "Well, either way… give me the boy, and I'll let you live."

She raised her hand slightly, like she was offering a gift instead of a death sentence. "For old time's sake," she added with a smile that never touched her eyes.

Leah felt irritation spark beneath her fear. She didn't trust this woman—would never trust her—and the ease with which she feigned kindness was almost more terrifying than her presence.

"And if she refuses?" Alec asked, his voice low, his body tense like a drawn bowstring.

The woman's bright smile curdled into a sneer. In an instant, the illusion of charm vanished, revealing something darker, something monstrous beneath the skin of a familiar face.

Leah subconsciously wondered if she had ever looked so wicked— so utterly devoid of empathy—as the sorceress turned on Alec with a glare that could strip paint. The expression she wore was one of pure disdain, as though Alec were nothing more than a speck of horse manure on the heel of her boot.

"Do be quiet. The adults are talking."

With a flick of her hand, she sent Alec flying backwards. His body slammed against the wall just beside the group of children, drawing horrified screams. Panic rippled through the room as the children bolted for the open door, their little feet slapping against the stone. Marcus scrambled to gather Alec, hoisting him up and rushing after them.

Leah remained in the hallway, body tense, heart hammering, ready to defend their escape.

She didn't have to wait long.

The sorceress lunged forward with frightening speed, tearing down the hall after the children like a predator who had locked onto its prey. Her eyes were fixed on Adam. Leah moved to intercept, but the impact of the sorceress's body slammed into her like a battering ram, knocking her sideways. The two women crashed to the floor in a tangle of fabric, limbs flailing and teeth bared.

"Let go of me, you traitorous bitch!" the woman shrieked, rearing her head back and slamming it into Leah's with skull-jarring force.

Stars exploded behind Leah's eyes as her grip slipped. The woman scrambled to her feet, attempting to sprint after the children. But Leah lashed out, grabbing her ankles just in time, and yanked.

This time, Leah transported.

Air howled past her ears as the two of them plummeted toward the fast-approaching forest. The trees below looked like a spiked sea of green rushing up to meet them.

A sharp, burning yank to her hair jolted Leah back to the moment—the witch was still conscious, still fighting. Clawed fingers clawed at the collar of her dress, ripping the fabric down its neatly stitched seam. Leah twisted violently, slipping free of her grip just as those awful hands sought her throat.

But she was too late.

The witch's fingers clamped down on her neck like iron vices, crushing her windpipe. Leah thrashed, her vision swimming, her limbs growing weaker by the second. Panic flooded her system as her body betrayed her.

Her fists flew blindly, striking what she hoped were vulnerable spots, but her strength was draining fast. Then, from deep within her chest, she felt it—a building energy, raw and instinctual. It surged upward, gathering behind her ribs like a storm.

A pulse tore through her.

The pressure around her neck vanished.

Darkness was already closing in as Leah, gasping what little air she could, whispered a phrase that might yet save her life—just as the world faded to black.

***

The children, along with Marcus and Alec, landed roughly near the Great Oak. Earth scattered beneath their feet. A crowd of nearly twenty villagers rushed toward them. Healers immediately began assessing injuries. Parents pushed past one another, frantic to locate their children in the chaos.

Marcus handed Alec off to Ketria, whose eyes darted across the boy's battered frame.

"Where's Leah?" she asked, voice tight with urgency as she examined Alec's condition.

"She stayed behind to give us more time," Marcus said, the words leaving his mouth thick and heavy. He wasn't sure how to explain what had happened—wasn't even sure he understood it himself.

"We need to get moving," Alec interrupted, still catching his breath.

"What?" one of the nearby villagers asked, alarmed by his tone.

"We have to go," Alec insisted. "There's a woman down there who looks exactly like Leah. She's searching for Adam."

A hush fell over the gathering. More villagers pressed closer, drawn by the tension in Alec's voice.

"If we wait for her... there's a chance the wrong Leah could find us."

Even as the words left his mouth, they sounded absurd. Unreal. But they were true.

"You're sure?" asked Freya, stepping forward from the crowd, her face creased with worry.

Marcus nodded slowly. "It's true, Maja Freya. We all saw her."

A small voice piped up from somewhere near the back—Ryanne.

"We can take everyone somewhere safe, but we can't let the mean lady find Adam. Maja Leah has to stay behind."

Though young, Ryanne spoke with eerie clarity, her voice soft but unwavering. It silenced the adults as her wisdom cut straight through their fear.

"She'll understand. There's no other way."

A single tear tracked down her cheek as she looked toward the horizon, knowing in her heart that she might never see her beloved teacher again. Leah had taught her to be brave. To think of others. To do what was right, no matter how hard it was.

And so, they obeyed.

The surviving villagers packed up their wounded and gathered what few belongings they had managed to salvage. One last time, they turned to look at the burning remains of their village. Their homes. Their memories. The lives they'd built.

They whispered farewells to the dead.

Then, with heavy hearts, they followed Ryanne into the forest—eighty souls, bound together by loss, fear, and the quiet courage of a child.

Chapter Five

Layla appeared before Ashur. The god barely looked up from the scroll he was reading.

"I told you she'd kick your ass."

Breathless and fuming from the unwanted rescue, she stomped toward him, anger radiating from every step. Without thinking, she swung. Layla hadn't expected to make contact, but the sting in her palm and the sharp snap of Ashur's head told her she had.

He was leaning casually against the massive bed in her new palace chambers. The pale skin of his cheek was already blooming with the red imprint of her hand. For a moment, he simply stared, stunned by her audacity.

Her eyes widened. Fear crept into her chest, tightening her breath as she waited for the storm she was sure would follow.

Ashur's jaw flexed slowly as he looked up at her.

"Thank you for saving me, Ashur. I would never have survived the fall if you hadn't helped me," he said, mocking her voice in exaggerated sweetness.

"Why, you're very welcome, Layla. Why don't you smack me again to show how grateful you are?"

Sarcasm hadn't been what she expected. She smacked him again.

"Thanks," she spat, turning away in a huff. She didn't know how else to respond. Nothing in their strange, dangerous history had prepared her for a meeting where he spared her. It was too strange to process.

The familiarity returned quickly. A strong hand wrapped around her throat and pulled her back until her body collided with his chest.

"I was being sarcastic, dear."

She felt the low growl vibrate against her spine as his grip tightened—not enough to cut her air, but enough to remind her of his control. His thumb tilted her face toward his. Then, unexpectedly, his lips brushed the corner of her eyelid in a soft, almost reverent kiss.

The tenderness startled her. Gentleness was not in his nature. She shut her eyes, bracing for cruelty, but nothing followed.

A deep sigh escaped him. Only then did she realize she'd been holding her breath. She risked a glance at her narcissistic lover, unsure of what to expect.

"I think you're finally ready, my love."

His smile was startling—broad, genuine, almost joyful.

"What the fuck happened while I was gone?" she asked, baffled.

He giggled. Ashur—God of the Air, Lord of the Skies, creator of so much cruelty—was giggling at her.

"No, seriously, what the fuck happened?"

Still smiling, he handed her a slip of parchment.

"Find the girl and gather these items. You'll need them for the next part of the plan."

While she read the paper, Ashur crossed the room to pour himself a glass of whiskey. The amber liquid caught the light as he replaced the stopper and perched on the arm of a powder-blue chair beside the dark mahogany bed her parents had once shared.

The room had changed over the years. Once painted a deep royal blue—her mother's preference—the walls now glittered with a gold fleur-de-lis pattern, perhaps a concession to her father's dislike for heavy darkness.

"This is a hosting spell," she said. "What the hell is this for?"

He chuckled again. "It's for you."

Her blank stare made him roll his eyes.

"Gods, you're vapid. I'm going to use you as a host vessel. Why else have I tolerated you for the last thousand years? You didn't think I cared for you, did you?"

His words landed like a blade between her ribs. She had never truly believed he loved her, but somewhere deep down, she had hoped—hoped that his attention, his keeping her close, had meant something.

Her gaze dropped to the parchment.

A Willing Vessel

Liquid Wolfsbane

Stardust of a Supernova

Salt

Cornmeal

Dragon's Blood of an Innocent

An Offering of Natural Magic Taken by Force

Her hands trembled. "Some of these will be difficult—if not impossible—to find."

"Is that going to be a problem?"

His casual posture didn't fool her. The cold focus in his eyes over the rim of his glass told her he was deadly serious.

"You really don't care about me at all, do you?" she asked before she could stop herself.

He looked briefly amused. "Not particularly. You're pretty annoying, now that I think about it."

The words stripped her bare. Centuries of service to him—spilled blood, brutal battles, lying in his bed, even giving him a son—meant nothing. She had endured his abuse, twisted it into some warped proof of affection, and now...

Her heart cracked. The sob tore out of her before she could swallow it. She felt foolish, betrayed, and utterly disposable.

"You have four days to execute the spell," Ashur said flatly, standing and finishing his drink.

"That's impossible! It could take a month to gather the ingredients!"

"Pull yourself together, Layla. I expect you to make it happen—or I'll kill your son."

Her stomach lurched. "What?"

"I will kill your son."

He said it as though remarking on the weather, then vanished before she could respond.

"But… you wanted him…"

She stood frozen in the cold silence, his threat echoing. Then, slowly, a fire lit in her chest.

Your son, he had said.

Her spine straightened. Her grief hardened into resolve. Without another thought, Layla set to work.

Chapter Six

Leah woke to a raw, burning dryness in her throat. The sound of a brook just south of the palace pounded in her skull like a war drum. Her breath caught, triggering a violent fit of coughing that wracked her body.

Cold droplets of rain had soaked her clothes through. A groan shuddered from her lips as she forced her eyes open, searching for the source of the sound.

Water.

The thought came with primal urgency. She dragged herself toward the embankment, every movement sending fresh waves of pain through her battered body. Her muscles screamed, ribs flaring in agony.

Finally reaching the edge, she plunged forward, pulling herself into the cool, life-giving current. She drank desperately, greedily—until her stomach clenched like a fist. Pain gripped her belly, and she vomited the water back into the brook in a bitter mix with bile.

Still coughing, she fought for breath. It was a cruel trick of the body—to crave what it could not yet hold.

When the spasms eased, she leaned forward again, this time taking careful sips, letting the cold liquid soothe her cracked lips and parched throat.

She stayed there, her cheek pressed to the damp earth, letting the sound of the water fill her ears.

The stabbing pain in her shoulder told her it was dislocated. Her right leg screamed with every shift—likely broken. Several ribs throbbed in protest; she prayed they were only bruised.

Alec's voice echoed inside her throbbing head.

"Pain means you're alive. What do we say to death?"

It was a mantra she had heard him repeat countless times over the years. The first time had been at Gravin Raw, when their small scouting party stumbled upon a hidden supply cache—clear proof that enemy troops were receiving inside information about the army's movements. Alec had been ordered to destroy the supply chain and uncover the spy responsible.

As it turned out, the spy was none other than Alec's first choice when assembling his team—a choice that had nearly cost Leah her life. The jagged scar across her chest was a permanent reminder of that day. A swift jab of the traitor's sword had narrowly missed her heart.

Alec had dispatched the man without hesitation and then pulled her against him, holding her steady while whispering words meant to anchor her in the moment until help arrived. She had survived, but she never let Alec forget that his taste in men was, as she put it, *truly terrible.*

Gritting her teeth now, Leah answered aloud, "Not today."

The words were more than a defiance against death—they were a reminder of the battles she had fought and won before. Compared to those memories, the pain in her shoulder was nothing.

Gingerly, she stretched her left arm until the ache flared into something sharp and biting. She felt the pressure building at her empty socket, each breath quickening as her body braced for what she was about to do. Exhaling fully, she dropped her weight onto it with every ounce of force she could muster.

A searing grind of bone followed by a sickening *pop* ripped through her torso. Eyes clamped shut, she drew in a deep breath, thankful for the discipline that kept her from screaming.

Somewhere in the distance, the princess was likely searching for her. The stillness of the forest felt unnatural in her current helpless state, but the steady plop of rain against the earth sounded almost normal—comforting in its own small way.

She lowered herself to the brook, sipped the cold water, and forced her breathing into a rhythm. Her thirst clawed at her, but she took her time, allowing only small mouthfuls until she dared drink again.

The torturous pattern felt endless before she was finally satisfied. Propped up by trembling arms, her shoulders and neck burned as she fought to keep her head above the water. Closing her eyes, she listened to the hammering of her heart, inhaling deeply and exhaling slowly until her pulse steadied.

Rolling onto her back, she rested her shoulders against the bank, the warm current curling around her body from knees to chest. Safety was still a distant goal—the priests would soon be scouring the land for her—but she had nothing left to give just yet. She had spent the last of her strength ensuring she wouldn't drown. For now, she needed rest.

Her eyes drifted shut as she tried to form her next plan.

***

"Where is she?"

The furious scream rattled down the palace hall, followed by the deafening crash of something heavy meeting stone. Layla's wrath was relentless. In the last hour alone, she had cut down at least four of Joel's men, and still her fury had not cooled.

Joel stood silently in the corner of the grand, opulent study Layla had claimed for herself. Over the past days, she had nearly destroyed its once-delicate carvings and sturdy shelves. Yesterday he had thought she might finally be done and ready to move to a new room. This morning proved otherwise. If anything, the destruction had worsened.

He made a mental note to find her another study before this one was reduced to splinters.

"It has been three days, Joel! Where the fuck is she?" Layla snarled, her eyes bright with rage.

After Ashur had left her in a storm of tears and disgust, she had wasted no time setting Joel to work. Every scroll in the village had been gathered. Every priest who might offer answers about Leah's whereabouts had been summoned. She pored over the scrolls from Leah's hut, sending her men to search the Great Oak—a place the journals suggested Leah frequented—only to find nothing.

The sewers had been scoured, the palace grounds swept, the village combed inch by inch. Not a single trace of her sister had turned up.

Meanwhile, Joel had quietly secured several rare ingredients from Layla's growing list and prepared a functional restraint in the village square. Layla hadn't forgotten this, and it was the only reason she reminded herself that killing him now would be inconvenient.

She took a steadying breath, though her eyes still burned with murderous intent.

"We're looking, my lady," Joel replied. "The priests are combing the forest as we speak. They've cleared the Northern and Eastern sectors and are moving to the South and West this afternoon."

He indicated the marked areas on the tattered map hanging from the wall, the burns and tears speaking to Layla's earlier rage.

Stepping closer, Layla's fingers brushed Joel's cheek, her sigh long and deliberate. The dangerous light in her eyes made his blood stir.

"Well, they'd better find her, Joel. I'm beginning to like you—but we need a sacrifice, and I intend to have one."

Her tone was almost tender, but the threat underneath was sharp as a blade. Running her fingers through his shaggy hair, she kissed him softly.

"One way or another," she whispered before leaving the room.

Joel stood rooted in place, the weight of her words sinking in, when a knock came at the door. One of the lesser priests entered, visibly trembling.

"You wanted to see me, sir?" His voice wavered.

Joel nodded. "Find a new study for the princess and clean this mess. We'll be having guests soon."

The young priest's shoulders sagged in relief, but Joel's expression didn't soften.

"Also—here's a list of ingredients we need. Track them down. If you fail, I'll kill you myself."

Handing over the list, Joel strode from the room. His mind was already elsewhere.

He was going to find Leah.

Leah judged by the deep ache in her muscles that she had been unconscious for a long time—how long, she couldn't say. Every joint felt stiff, her limbs weighted as though they'd been buried in stone.

Slowly, she pressed her palms into the sodden earth, attempting to hoist herself from the shallow mud puddle in which she now lay. At some point, she had dragged herself—half crawling, half scooting— away from the icy brook. She could only hope her hands still functioned after the freezing water and the brutal fall.

Fragments of memory flickered behind her eyes, sharp and disjointed, and her worst suspicion took shape. She had been lying here for at least two days, perhaps longer, her body mending from an impact that should have killed her outright.

It was an old, nearly forgotten gift—her unnaturally fast healing— that had spared her life. During the war, that very gift had made her a terror to her enemies. A slash that would cripple the soldier beside her might close on her body within the hour. Now, once again, she owed her survival to it.

Stretching her neck, Leah realized just how close to death she had come and allowed herself a shaky breath of relief. She mentally assessed her injuries. Her shoulder throbbed but still obeyed her. Her ribs had begun to knit, and even her leg was healing—though when she lifted her skirt to inspect it, her stomach lurched.

From hip to knee, the flesh was a sickening wash of black and purple. At the center, an unnatural S-shaped curve distorted the line of the bone. The sight turned her nausea into violent retching. She knew instantly what had to be done.

She would have to re-break it.

Oh, gods… this is going to be hell.

Gritting her teeth, she crawled to the base of a nearby tree, dragging a heavy rock with her. She gathered three sturdy sticks from the ground and tore strips from the hem of her skirt for bandages.

Once she had everything she needed, she placed one stick between her teeth and gripped the rock with both hands. Lifting it high above her head, she focused on the break, willing herself not to miss.

The rock came down with a sickening crack. Pain exploded through her thigh, blinding in its intensity. Leah screamed into the stick clamped between her jaws, then forced her trembling hands to set the bone. She splinted it quickly, binding it tight to keep it in place as her breathing came in sharp, shallow bursts.

When the worst of the agony dulled to a throbbing burn, she found a forked branch sturdy enough to serve as a crutch and stripped away its foliage. Bracing herself against it, she pushed to her feet, waiting for the cramps in her stiff limbs to ease until she could stand nearly straight.

She had lingered here far too long. It was a wonder no one had found her yet. Still, she needed shelter to heal.

To the south, a network of caves beneath the mountains would give her a defensible perch until her strength returned and she could begin searching for survivors. But getting there with a broken leg would be slow, and her magic was already draining the last of her stamina.

That left one other option—heading north to the village sewers. The priests' presence there would likely be minimal, especially if Adam remained their main target. They would be out searching for him. That would give her a chance to slip in unnoticed.

Neither path was appealing, but the city was closer, and her body was failing fast.

The sewers it is.

Leah tucked the makeshift crutch under her arm and started toward the village, silently praying it had been abandoned.

An hour later, she realized she had made the wrong choice. Ahead, a trio of priests tromped through the woods, their loud voices carrying on the wind. If they'd been quieter, she might have stumbled right into them.

Fortunately, she had more than enough battlefield sense to avoid that mistake. She crouched behind a boulder, using it to support her aching knee. For a moment, she wished she had paid more attention to Lydia all those years when the woman had mended her broken bones. Then she wouldn't be hobbling like a wounded goat, praying she stayed unseen.

Her luck didn't last.

The priests found her before long, and in a twisted way, she was almost grateful. At least she wouldn't have to drag herself all the way to the village.

They rendered her unconscious and levitated her over the forest floor until she was brought here—chained in the village square, limbs spread in four opposing directions, secured to two massive, cigar-shaped pillars by thick iron links.

She knew her capture was her own fault. Carelessness had led her here.

From the broad steps of the Dragon Fold's communal hall, the High Priest's second-in-command, Joel, emerged with a wide, almost boyish smile.

"Ah, good day, Leah! I heard you caused a bit of trouble earlier." His eyes shone with a peculiar excitement, as though he were a child seeing the stars for the first time.

Leah said nothing, forcing him to fill the silence. His smile dimmed, just enough for her to feel a sliver of satisfaction.

"Where did they go, Leah?" he asked, almost kindly.

"Where's the High Priest? Isn't he supposed to be here for things like this?" she countered, her chin tilting up just slightly.

"Oh… well, he's dead. Sorry, did I forget to mention that?"

The words hit her like a slap.

"In any case," he continued cheerfully, "I'm the new High Priest, and you'll be dealing with me."

He withdrew a ceremonial dagger from his robes, its blade gleaming. The smug grin he wore deepened, and a ripple of unease swept through Leah. That feeling sharpened when a figure in white entered the stone circle—the princess, her smile reserved for Joel.

"What are you doing?" Leah demanded, thrashing against her bonds as the woman stepped forward and laid a hand against her chest.

Searing pain ripped through her as her skin bubbled beneath the woman's fingers.

"They say the deepest pit in the blackest corner of hell is where a soul meant to endure utter agony and loss in the living world is forged," the sorceress murmured, withdrawing her hand to reveal a fresh burn: a circle with a large X through it, and the small figure of a sun at its peak.

"Those who commit unforgivable sins are thrown into that pit," she continued, her voice like ice, "melted into the fluid of Fate herself and hammered by the steel of the gods into new souls—broken, separated from themselves, cursed to wander in search of pieces that may never exist."

Her fingers traced the mark almost tenderly before her eyes hardened.

"You, dear sister, will never know peace. You will never cradle your child, nor feel the warmth of another human's touch. Death would be merciful compared to what you've earned."

Her glare was so sharp Leah flinched. She didn't even know what crime she was being condemned for.

"Joel, let's begin," Layla snapped. Her smile returned, and Joel seemed to melt under it.

The Dragon Priests began to gather, their black robes and downcast eyes giving them the look of shadows made flesh. Their slow, deliberate march brought them into the square.

Two priests at the front carried heavy brass pitchers. One poured a trail of cornmeal clockwise from south to north; the other followed with rum in the opposite direction.

Leah's stomach turned cold.

Black magic.

The reality of what was coming crashed into her with suffocating force.

"No… NO! You can't do this!" She pulled against the chains with renewed desperation.

Layla's laugh was almost girlish. "Leah, this is serious. Don't make me laugh."

The smile vanished from her face as she turned to Joel.

"Gag her," Layla ordered, her voice sharp as a blade. She took a small dragon—no older than a single season—from Joel, who muttered complaints under his breath.

Leah fought the only way she could. Like a cornered animal, she lunged forward, her teeth snapping onto the delicate webbing between Joel's thumb and forefinger. His scream tore through the night, raw and pained. Determined to make him pay for what he was about to do, she bit down harder, feeling the warm rush of blood fill her mouth. The metallic tang nearly made her gag—right before a vicious blow struck the side of her head, forcing her to release him.

When she lifted her eyes, the darkness swimming in Layla's gaze was so absolute that Leah felt death itself would hesitate to escort this woman from the stone circle.

The ritual markings were nearly complete—a ring of cornmeal and rum encircling the space like a prison. As the final line closed, the drums began, deep and rhythmic, each beat stoking the wildfire of her fear. Joel crouched low and began etching the darkest of sacred symbols into the sand, his movements precise and deliberate.

Leah strained against her restraints, desperate to break free, knowing all too well what would come next.

Nothing—no nightmare, no whispered threat—could have prepared her for the shrill, piercing death cries of the infant dragon. The sudden silence that followed hit harder than the sound itself, turning her stomach until she nearly wretched. Hot tears blurred her vision, her heart splintering in her chest. She screamed into her gag until her throat burned, thrashing wildly as Layla's voice cut through the air.

"Transfer your soul into this vessel. You will not have to wrestle, for I will make it easy; you shall make it fine. You need not search for a body—I offer you mine."

Arms raised high, Layla brandished the sacrificial knife, its blade slick with fresh blood. Dark clouds rolled and twisted overhead, the sky itself seeming to recoil. Her smile was almost disbelieving as she stepped toward Leah, finishing the spell with a brutal thrust, driving the dagger into the marked point on Leah's chest.

"An offering submitted in innocent blood to open the way. A second submitted to take your place so that you may stay. I invoke thee, Lux—RETURN!"

A jagged bolt of green light split the now-blackened sky, hurricane winds tearing over the mountains and flooding into the valley from all sides. Leah's scream was ripped from her as a force unlike anything she had ever felt wrenched her soul from her body, pulling it toward oblivion.

For an instant, Layla screamed too.

Then, as suddenly as it had begun, the storm stilled. Both women collapsed to the ground, panting and coughing, their bodies wracked with shuddering breaths. The circle of priests stood frozen, watching, until Joel stepped forward.

"Are you all right, my love? Did it work?"

"Oh, it worked all right," Layla replied with a smile as Joel helped her stand.

"How do you know for sure? You don't look any different."

"Because I'm over here…"

The voice was weak but clear—Leah's body lay chained on the ground, its lips curled into a breathless smile.

"Lux, Joel. Joel, Lux."

Joel recovered from his shock quickly, bowing deeply before taking the former Layla's hand and kissing it with formal grace.

"Pleasure to meet you, Lady Lux."

"Well, well," Lux purred, returning a small curtsy, "and here I thought chivalry had died eons ago. The pleasure is mine, good sir."

From Leah's body came a furious shout. "Now that the introductions are done, someone get me out of these gods-forsaken chains!"

The front row of priests rushed forward—then halted mid-stride, their legs stiff as though frozen in place. Lux stood with one arm folded across her chest, the other raised with two fingers extended. Her stance carried all the poise and authority of Layla's late mother—attitude sharpened by just enough righteous anger—before a polite smile softened her expression.

"It will not do to speak to my subjects in such a manner, young lady. As of this moment, you are, at best, their equal. If you wish to command them one day, earn their loyalty through respect. I doubt your mother would have taught you otherwise."

"And what makes you so certain of that?" Layla sneered, wincing as Leah's injured body betrayed her.

Lux's smile turned knowing. She stepped forward with a girlish bounce, twirling once before slowly closing her hand into a fist. Layla's breath caught as invisible fingers squeezed the air from her lungs.

"If nothing else," Lux said sweetly, "my sister was a master in the art of respect. Her first lesson: when in doubt—fake it. I suggest you remember the rest." She released her with a flick of her fingers, watching Layla gasp for air.

"Now… where is my husband?"

Her eyes scanned the gathered priests, her blood-stained skirt swaying as she spun with girlish delight.

"I'm here!"

A voice rang out over the crowd, and the parting bodies revealed Ashur, his piercing blue eyes bright beneath tousled blond hair. In one hand, he clutched a bouquet of wildflowers battered from the run; in the other, a small velvet box.

Lux squealed, rushing into his arms. He caught her effortlessly, spinning her in a circle before pressing a kiss to her lips.

"Oh gods, I've missed you," he murmured.

"And I you, my love. But you're late." She pouted, arms crossed, stamping her foot.

Ashur sighed, his smile warm. "I know. I'm sorry. I wanted to bring you something special and thought I had more time." He lifted the flowers and box for her to see.

Lux opened the velvet box, her breath catching at the sight of the golden band he had once placed on her finger. The memory lit her face with the same wonder it had centuries ago.

"Can you forgive me?" he asked, nuzzling into her neck.

Lux slipped the ring on, her smile playful.

"For you, darling, I'd do anything," she said softly. "But I am going to need a new dress. This one has blood on it."

"Of course, my pet. Many new dresses. But first—a bath. It's only been twenty thousand years since I've seen you naked."

"Well, aren't you romantic," she teased, brushing a kiss over his jaw before looking past him at Joel, who was helping a trembling, blood-soaked Layla sit upright.

"Layla, when you've finished, send word to our sister capitals. Their offerings are due within the month. I'm sure they remember what to bring."

Joel stiffened at her tone. "And if they refuse?" he asked carefully.

Lux looked genuinely puzzled, glancing at Ashur. "Would they dare?"

"It's possible," Ashur admitted.

"Well," Lux said, her voice dropping into something dangerous, "I will not be insulted in public." She stepped away from him, power rippling off her in visible waves. Turning back to Joel, her eyes were cold. "If they refuse, I'll remind them why they pay tribute."

With a lazy twist of her fingers, screams erupted across the village. Buildings collapsed in clouds of dust. Villagers' cries deepened into guttural howls as their bodies twisted and expanded, transforming into massive, mindless giants—beasts driven by hunger and bloodlust, slaughtering anything in their path.

"After all," Lux said, smiling like a child offered a new toy, "killing with kindness is my specialty."

Joel tightened his grip on Layla, every instinct screaming at him. He knew madness when he saw it—he'd lived with it in his mother's house. This queen was worse.

"Yes, Goddess," he murmured, bowing awkwardly before carrying Layla away toward his chambers.

Chapter Seven

Laying her gently on his bed, Joel welcomed the quiet of the chamber—the only sounds were the shallow, ragged breaths rattling from Layla's lips. She had lost an alarming amount of blood.

On the way here, Joel had counted six sets of footsteps trailing them down the corridor—members of his priesthood, likely flight guards. Their faint echoes had followed them all the way into his private quarters. It was impressive, in its own way, if they still held loyalty to him. That loyalty could be an advantage. But right now, Layla's life took precedence.

Joel crossed to the desk beneath the wide window beside his bed. He scribbled quick notes, scanning them once before giving a curt nod of approval. Turning back to the room, he finally addressed the supposed flight guard—only to realize his miscalculation. Not six, but eight priests stood scattered throughout the chamber, their eyes wandering over the richly furnished space.

"I need clean bandages, hot water, and these herbs from the garden." Joel held out the list to the nearest priest, adding with a slight shrug, "I'd fetch them myself, but I doubt you'd let me leave."

The subtle shift in the air—tension draining from the room—confirmed his suspicion. These men no longer served him.

The priest took the list without a word, scanning it briefly before hurrying out. He returned minutes later with everything Joel had requested.

By then, Layla's breathing had worsened, each inhale shorter, quicker—desperation replacing strength. Joel kept her still as best he could, pressing firmly against the wound in her chest. But her fragile body jerked with a sudden fit of coughing, tearing the wound open further. The wet, gasping sound that followed sent ice into Joel's veins. Her eyes widened in silent panic as she clawed at him for help.

Rolling her to her side, Joel barked over his shoulder, "Get the surgeon in here—now!" His voice carried a sharp edge of fear. As one priest bolted for the door, Joel's stomach twisted with an unwelcome truth: he bore part of the blame for this.

"Joel…" Layla whimpered between gasps, her trembling hands clutching the front of his robes. Tears welled in her eyes. "Don't… let me… die… like this."

Each pause came with a sickening, sucking sound from her wound, sending her into another brutal coughing spell. Blood flecked her lips. Joel swallowed hard, shushing her with forced calm.

"Don't talk. You're going to be fine. Just a little longer, alright? Can you do that for me?"

Her gaze locked on his, as wary as a wounded doe sizing up a farmer—unsure whether to trust him. Another cough wracked her frame before she gave the faintest nod. Whether it was true trust or simply resignation to her only chance of survival, Joel didn't know. He'd take it either way.

The door burst open. Two priests returned, half-dragging a short, round man between them.

"Let go of me, you madmen! I will not be manhandled like a com—" His words broke off when he saw Layla. The sight of her bloody, limp body snapped him instantly into the role of a seasoned surgeon.

Shaking off his escorts, he waddled forward with surprising speed, nearly losing his balance in the process. He knelt beside the bed, rolling up already bloodstained sleeves, and examined the wound in brisk, practiced motions.

"What happened? How long has she been like this?" His eyes flicked sharply to Joel, demanding answers.

"She was stabbed. Started coughing blood a few minutes ago," Joel replied carefully, keeping his details sparse.

The surgeon gave a curt nod, then called to one of the priests. "You—here. See my hands? Keep pressure right there until I tell you otherwise. Do not move."

Gathering some of Joel's herbs and supplies, the surgeon barked orders for additional items, dismissing everyone but three priests and Joel. Then he set to work.

Joel was left pacing the hallway, barred from his own room. His gratitude that the surgeon had arrived so quickly was dulled by the frustration of being rendered useless. The need to protect Layla gnawed at him, but all he could do was wait while others fought to save her life.

He slumped against the wall, then stood again, unable to stay still under the constant watch of the priests stationed outside. Their eyes tracked his every movement. In this moment of helpless agitation, Joel could almost understand why his predecessor had been prone to public outbursts of rage.

The chamber door opened at last. The surgeon emerged, wiping Layla's blood from his hands.

"How is she?" Joel asked immediately.

"She's resting. Bleeding's stopped, stitches are holding. The main concern now is fever and infection."

Joel exhaled a breath he hadn't realized he was holding. "But she's going to be alright?"

"If she makes it through tonight, she'll be in the clear," the surgeon replied. "She'll need someone watching her constantly—keep her temperature down, wound clean, and bandages changed every hour until the sweating stops. After that, change them every three to four hours for the next few days. I'll be back in the morning."

Joel clasped his hand. "Thank you, doctor. Truly."

The priests followed Joel back into the chamber, keeping quiet as Layla slept.

***

By morning, the surgeon returned.

"Her fever broke earlier," Joel reported softly, careful not to wake her.

"Good, good," the man murmured, checking her over. "Any new symptoms? Twitching, sudden bursts of power—anything unusual?"

Joel looked down at her. Her breathing was stronger, the wound already beginning to scab. She had stopped tossing in her sleep. The night before, during her fever's worst grip, she had murmured one name again and again—*Colton.*

Joel assumed he was a former lover. A strange, unwelcome jealousy had stirred in him. He wanted her for himself. The thought of being her second choice sat bitter in his chest.

Forcing the thought aside, he answered, "No. Nothing like that."

"Good. I'll need to wake her for a moment—check her responses, run a few more tests—but she's healing well."

"I'll step aside," Joel said, moving just far enough to give the doctor room while keeping himself close.

The instinct to protect her ran too deep to walk away completely. Arms crossed, Joel stood watch as the doctor lifted Layla's arm to take her pulse, his large frame moving with surprising precision. Years of practice, Joel guessed.

He had only visited a physician once in his life, and it had been unpleasant. Yet watching this man handle Layla with such care eased some of his tension. The doctor checked her limbs for fractures, scanned her skin for signs of internal bleeding, and listened closely to her breathing.

Layla stirred with a faint groan. The doctor pursed his lips, making a low, thoughtful hum. Joel's patience thinned as he waited for him to speak.

"Hmmm."

The longer the silence stretched, the tighter Joel's nerves wound. He paced back and forth, trying to keep his hands busy—anything to stop himself from wrapping them around the man's thick neck out of sheer impatience.

At last, the doctor looked up from his examination.

"She's OK. It's mostly bruising, from what I can see, but she does have a broken femur and inflammation in her shoulder. It's nothing that time won't fix, but she will need to keep still until it heals properly."

"How long do you think that might take?"

"Well, based on how quickly the wound on her chest is healing, I'd say no more than a week and a half—but it's tough to say. The majority of my patients take months, even years, to recover from wounds like these, but Layla… she seems to have a gift."

Removing the bandage from her chest, the doctor let out a low whistle and gestured for Joel to see for himself before tossing the bloodied cloth into the nearby garbage bin.

"It's almost gone."

Joel stared in disbelief at the faintly reddened patch of skin where, only the night before, there had been a gaping hole.

"How is this even possible?" he asked, unable to wrap his head around the impossible speed of her recovery. The sheer amount of power it must take for her body to mend itself like that was staggering.

"I don't know," the doctor admitted, "but she's… very special."

Joel nodded, reluctantly agreeing. Yet even as he did, a thought flickered through his mind—one he instantly pushed away. This was Leah's body. There couldn't possibly be that much residual power left in it. This had to be Layla's own strength.

"I'm Dr. Calvin, by the way." The man extended his hand.

"Joel. Nice to officially meet you," he said, shaking it.

"You've got quite the entourage here." Dr. Calvin's eyes drifted toward the eight priests who had been tracking Joel's every move since Lux had arrived.

"Yes," Joel replied dryly, "seems I'm not to be trusted anymore. A problem I'm sure will sort itself out soon enough." He sighed, feeling the weight of his commanders' lack of faith in their proven disciples.

Dr. Calvin nodded sympathetically. "From what I've heard, this guard isn't for you—it's for her." He inclined his head toward Layla. "There's talk they're worried she might slip away to search for her son."

"She has a son?"

Joel's surprise was genuine. "She's never mentioned a son. I knew she was looking for a boy, but I didn't realize…"

His voice trailed off. The revelation rattled him. They had only just met, yes, but still—he had thought they were close enough for her to have shared something like that. In truth, he realized bitterly, he knew almost nothing about her. Not even her surname.

How could he have ever convinced himself they were close? Their "relationship," if it could be called that, had consisted mostly of her giving orders and him following them. The only intimate thing they had done was share a bed—and even then, he had woken to find she'd left him behind without a word, making him feel like an arrogant fool. A disgusting one. He had treated her as if she were a prize to be claimed, never stopping to consider she might not have wanted him.

Joel's stomach churned, and his skin prickled as he looked at the broken woman lying in his bed.

"What's his name?" he asked quietly.

"Oh, I don't know. I just overheard someone mention she had a son." Dr. Calvin shrugged.

"Anyway, I need to check on other patients—and maybe get some sleep. It was nice meeting you."

Shaking Joel's hand once more, the doctor left, closing the door behind him and leaving Joel alone with his thoughts—and with the question of how he could possibly make right his earlier mistakes.

Layla stirred, her eyelids fluttering before she quickly squeezed them shut again with a groan. She shielded her face with a hand as if she could swat the light away.

"No… sleep, come back," she mumbled, rolling onto her stomach and burying her face into the pillow with another loud groan.

The button-down shirt Joel had dressed her in the night before had twisted around her body like a deep green snake. She lay still for a moment, her face smashed into the pillow, then made a muffled sound.

"Fud…"

Joel tilted his head, puzzled. This was a side of Layla he hadn't seen before, and a faint smile tugged at his lips when she repeated the noise. It was… cute.

That is, until she suddenly sat up and hurled the pillow at him.

"I said *food*, you asshole! I'm starving."

Grimacing at the pain caused by the sudden movement, Layla's stomach rumbled in emphatic agreement.

Joel, caught off guard, fumbled to intercept the pillow, eventually clutching it to his chest. The sound of the flight guard's stifled laughter made heat creep up his neck—until Layla's own chuckle reached him, melting away his embarrassment.

"I'm keeping this," he told her, holding up the pillow with a grin.

"No, give it back. I'm sleepy."

Layla crawled toward him on all fours, stretching one arm out while keeping her balance with a look of exaggerated focus. She stared at the pillow as if sheer willpower could make him hand it over—something Joel suspected she could actually manage if she tried.

After a theatrical sigh, she said, "Oh crap, I'm falling!"

Her stretch collapsed into a clumsy scramble to save herself from the short drop, leaving her tangled in limbs and dangling precariously off the side of the bed.

"Joel! Help!"

Joel burst into laughter, joined by the flight guard, as she slipped lower with a squeak.

"It's not funny! Get me up!" Layla protested, laughing despite herself.

Joel hooked an arm under her legs and around her shoulders, lifting her easily.

"You can let go now," he murmured into her ear. She released her death grip on the bed with an exaggerated sigh of relief.

"Woosh—touch and go there for a minute. I'm pretty sure I could have died." She nodded at him with mock solemnity.

"Oh really?" Joel teased.

"Yes, really. That's like a two-foot drop. Could have killed me," she insisted, crossing her legs and tugging the shirt down over her knees. She scanned the room with the same exaggerated seriousness, making sure everyone understood the gravity of her "life-or-death" moment.

"So… I take it you feel fine?" Joel asked.

"Yep. But I wasn't joking about being starving. And since I doubt our little entourage is going to let me leave the room anytime soon… if you don't mind—meat would be preferable."

"Just meat? Not a cheeseburger with fries? Not a pork steak with vegetables? Just… meat?"

"Yes," Layla replied flatly. "As long as it's not human, I don't care."

Joel turned toward the flight guard. "You mind?"

The guards exchanged uncertain glances, shuffling their feet.

Layla rolled her eyes. "Come on—you're here to make sure I don't run away, not starve me to death. You three go with Joel, the rest stay with me. It's so simple it actually hurts my feelings that you haven't figured it out."

The guards obeyed, splitting into two groups just as she'd instructed.

"You could be a little nicer," Joel remarked.

"Shut up. I'm hungry. Now go—food! Now!" She shoved at his back, her small frame straining against his weight.

He laughed as she grunted, "Go, you big jerk!" and gave him one final push out the door.

Joel made his way down the dim corridor of the compound, his boots echoing faintly against the stone. Through the open windows, he caught glimpses of the charred remains of the village. Wisps of smoke still curled into the air from the blackened debris. The fire had been extinguished in time to spare most of the buildings surrounding the compound, but the rest of the settlement had been reduced to ash.

A small price to pay in times of war, he mused grimly, though the thought rang hollow in his mind.

A sudden scream tore through the air—raw, high, and terrified. Joel froze mid-step, his body tightening in instinct before pivoting toward the sound. It had come from outside, not from within the corridor.

"What the hell was that?" he demanded of his escorts.

Neither man seemed eager to answer. Their expressions held the stiff resignation of men who had seen this before.

"Ashur and Lux have us… snuffing out survivors," one of the priests muttered at last, his voice low, as though speaking the words aloud left a bitter taste. "Only the loyal ones remain that way."

Joel stiffened, repulsed by the casual cruelty.

"A small price to pay in times of war, I suppose," he forced himself to reply, the lie scraping his throat. Every instinct screamed against the practice—this senseless slaughter disguised as strategy—but he masked his disgust. If they sensed his dissent, it could prove costly.

Eager to divert suspicion, he forced a lighter tone.

"So, what does a guy have to do to get some chow around here? I'm starving."

The priests gestured him toward the cafeteria. They followed close behind, speaking in hushed tones, likely discussing which weaknesses they might report back to Ashur. Joel told himself they'd find none.

Inside the cafeteria, the scene almost could have belonged to an ordinary day—the sunlight spilling through the high windows, the murmur of voices, the faint scent of roasted meat and vegetables. But the moment Joel stepped in, the room went silent. Conversations cut off mid-sentence. Every eye turned toward him, the weight of his diminished status hanging in the air like smoke.

After a moment, the tension eased. A few bowed their heads in respect before resuming their meals. Joel's shoulders loosened slightly. He wasn't entirely obsolete, then—some of his priests still held loyalty to him, and for now, that was enough to keep hope alive.

A heaping mound of potatoes dropped onto his plate with such force that the dish nearly slipped from his hands. He caught it just in time, a growl rumbling in his chest before he managed to smooth his expression. Offering the server a polite nod, he held up a second plate for Layla.

Hopefully, she likes potatoes.

At the end of the line, he waited for his entourage to gather the remaining plates—five more for the guards assigned to watch over Layla. One minor priest at the rear struggled under the weight of too many dishes, so Joel relieved him of one before they made their way back toward his chamber.

He thought of Layla's shift in demeanor. This morning, she had been almost playful—something he hadn't realized she was capable of. Then again, he didn't know her well. They had spent only a handful of days together over the past week. It was hard to tell whether her lightness earlier had been natural or a rare glimpse into a side of herself she rarely showed.

He also recalled the ferocity she had displayed during their search for Leah—how violently she had destroyed the palace. Joel had never sought the company of women with such fire. Before taking his vows to Ashur, he had envisioned a partner soft, gentle, pliable. Layla was none of those things—and that intrigued him.

Perhaps, he thought, they could start fresh. This time, he could take his time instead of stumbling like a fool.

The memory of the night they had spent together struck him like a blade to the gut. His spine stiffened under the wave of shame. He would redeem himself. That silent vow lingered in his mind as he stepped through the doorway into the chamber— —and froze.

Ashur struck Layla hard enough to send her sprawling to the floor.

Joel's escorts halted beside him, shock etched across their faces. None of them had expected this.

Rage flared through Joel's chest, his gaze snapping to Ashur. The flight guards in the room, who had been seated, now stood with tense readiness, their attention fixed entirely on the confrontation between Ashur and Layla.

Layla rose to her feet, fists clenched, murder in her eyes. The air in the chamber thickened, the tension almost physical.

Ashur's gaze flicked to Joel, sharp with warning. He turned slowly, sweeping his attention over the room before giving a short, derisive scoff.

"Mind yourselves, boys. You really don't want to get into this."

Power gathered around him, an almost tangible current in the air. One by one, the other men backed down—until only Joel remained, glowering at Ashur with the unspoken promise of retribution.

Then a voice—small but cutting through the tension—drew their attention.

"Don't," Layla breathed.

Whether it was meant for Joel or Ashur, he couldn't tell. He hesitated, his jaw tight, before forcing himself to lower his gaze and step back. Shame washed over him again.

The charged energy in the room dissipated as Ashur reined it in, his lips pursing with irritation. He crossed the short distance to Layla, looming over her.

"Understand this, Layla," Ashur said, his tone heavy with possession. Joel saw her flinch at whatever she read in his expression. "These men may be yours—but you belong to me."

Joel surged forward, the plates in his hands clattering to the floor, but Ashur seized Layla by the arm and vanished before Joel could reach them.

He landed hard on the marble, the impact sending a sharp pain through his face.

"God dammit!"

Pounding his fist against the cold floor, Joel seethed. His mind filled with the horrors Layla would endure until she was found—or until Ashur had had his fill. Based on her reaction, it was clear she had already suffered at his hands.

Darkness crept into Joel's thoughts. Forcing his voice into a level, icy tone he barely recognized, he ordered, "Find them."

The stillness of the room shattered as the eight former guards sprang into motion, searching every corner for any sign of Ashur's departure point.

The youngest guard hesitated before speaking.

"Um, guys? You don't think he just took her to his temple, do you?"

His uncertain glance around the room earned him nothing but grim looks before he quickly joined the others in the search.

There was little doubt Ashur had taken her to his temple.

The problem was, no one knew where it was. It had been cloaked more than three millennia ago, and those who built it had either vanished or died soon after its completion.

They worked through the long night, pulling scroll after scroll from the towering shelves of the library and from the cramped crawl spaces of the restricted section—an area reserved for the most dangerous spells and the most guarded pieces of intelligence.

The air was thick with dust and the faint scent of aged parchment. By the time the first pale streaks of dawn touched the high windows, their efforts had turned up only a handful of mythical accounts describing the temple's construction, along with early blueprints of the structure itself. Yet none of it offered a single concrete clue to its location.

Frustrated but unwilling to waste the momentum, Joel instructed the oldest of the guards to organize a sleep rotation. He took on at least two of the men's waking shifts himself, reasoning there was no point in waking exhausted men just to replace someone who couldn't sleep anyway. They needed their rest as badly as he did, he mused, though his own mind refused to quiet.

By daylight, the operation ran like a well-oiled machine. One of the elders brought in a large steaming vat of an inky-black drink—brewed from ground coffee beans aged until they were almost sweet, with a faint note of hazelnut. The scent drifted through the room like a warm current, lifting the heavy fog from the priests' eyes. Those who had been scheduled to rest instead powered through their sleep shift, gifting their counterparts a stretch of deep, uninterrupted rest.

Two days passed in this relentless rhythm. The priests combed through nearly every scroll the library possessed, yet they remained no closer to locating the temple. Then, without warning, a sharp crack echoed above them.

A heavy thump followed, and a shower of scrolls rained down onto the large table they had dragged to the center of the room.

When the last scroll rolled to the floor, the priests saw her—Layla—dumped unceremoniously across the tabletop.

Every man not already beside her lunged forward in a startled rush. She stayed still for a moment, catching her breath, before pushing herself upright with a sharp wince.

"Oww," she muttered, her voice edged with indignation. She cradled her ribs with one arm. Her left eye was swollen completely shut; bruises bloomed across every bit of exposed skin, and shallow cuts had only just begun to scab.

Joel stared, struck utterly silent. The shock of her sudden return cracked through him, sending his mind reeling. Relief that she was alive twisted together with anger—fueled by the sight of her injuries and the sickening knowledge that if he had acted sooner, she might not be in this condition. That anger clashed with guilt, and guilt gave way to a cold, hard vow: he would never allow this to happen again.

When he finally found his voice, his expression had already shuttered into cool composure. He didn't know how she would react to open concern, so he kept his tone even.

"Are you alright?"

Even to his own ears, the words sounded hollow.

Layla looked at him as if he had taken leave of his senses. Then, without a word, she backhanded him—hard enough to knock him a step backward.

"How's that for an answer?" she wheezed.

A few priests stifled their laughter at her not-entirely-undeserved response. She scooted toward the end of the table Joel had just vacated, and the priests beside her helped her down with as much care as they could manage—then quickly stepped back, out of range of any further swats she might feel inclined to deliver.

"What was that for?" Joel snapped, gingerly touching his cheek where the sting still burned. His fingertips only made the throbbing worse.

"You made it worse, Joel! I told you to back off, and you practically dared him to do something. Guess what? He did!" Her voice dripped with fury. She gestured sharply down her battered body, her good eye blazing with a look that plainly told Joel he was an idiot.

Baffled, Joel felt a flicker of regret—maybe he was partly to blame—but he shoved the thought aside. He could not, would not, stand by and do nothing when it came to Layla's safety.

"You let him take you, Layla. We were ready to help you, and you refused. So explain to me how it's my fault when you told me to do nothing!" His voice climbed until it was almost a snarl. "You didn't want to be saved."

The words struck something in her. A brief flicker of surprise crossed her face before her expression hardened into steel.

And she knew—he was right. She hadn't wanted to be saved. She was exactly where she had chosen to be.

Ashur had abused her for centuries, and she had learned to endure it without calling for help that would never come. If a few more weeks, decades, or centuries of that pain was the cost of finding her son, then so be it.

Colton was worth it.

After Leah had spirited him away and handed him over to a near stranger—like lending out a garment she didn't care to keep—he'd even been stripped of his name to hide him from his own mother. It had taken Layla centuries to piece together that Colton was Adam. The truth had blindsided her.

When Leah arrived at the temple unannounced, Ashur had greeted her with an almost alien politeness. Layla, overjoyed to see her sister alive, was nonetheless wary of Ashur's sudden hospitality; he was rarely anything but cruel, even on his best days. Eventually, after relentless questioning that not even his beatings could silence, Ashur admitted he'd known Leah was alive for some time. He'd sent for her—on Layla's behalf.

For a time, the sisters got along better than they had in centuries, often taking Colton to the Great Oak for picnics several times a week.

Layla remembered the last day she had held him as if it had been etched into her bones.

A soft coo announced that he had woken from his nap. Smiling, she rose from the table where she'd been sipping tea. Leah giggled across from her as the sound of Colton's gurgling carried from the nursery.

Layla opened the door to find him bouncing in his cradle, pudgy arms waving in wobbly triumph. His toothy grin pushed his cheeks into the faint shape of a heart. His once-dark hair had lightened to a pale brown and already needed trimming.

He squealed when he saw her, filling her chest with the warm rush of joy she clung to on the darkest nights after Ashur's punishments. Sometimes she would slip into the nursery in those hours just to hold him, rocking him until dawn and whispering promises that she would never let him come to harm.

Colton reached for her, and she gathered him close, kissing his cheek and feeling the impossible softness of his skin beneath her lips. His blue-grey eyes locked with hers, full of quiet intelligence, and he cradled her face in his small hands. His smile never wavered.

If she had known it would be the last time she ever held him, she would have clung to him longer, kissed him more, told him she loved him a thousand times over. But she hadn't known.

Hours later, he was gone. Leah, too.

That loss pulled her back to the present with a renewed, razor-sharp determination to find her son—the boy they now called Adam—before more years were stolen from them.

So yes, she had no intention of being saved. Not yet.

"I don't need saving." The words felt good, almost liberating, on her tongue.

"What I need," she continued, "is an entourage I can trust. I'm not sure you fit that description yet, but we're going to do some recruiting."

The priests shifted uneasily, exchanging glances heavy with curiosity.

"Pack light," she said, her voice firm. "We leave within the hour."

Chapter Eight

Alec paced the length of his tent, his thoughts circling the events of the past few weeks like vultures over carrion. The first rescue mission had been a disaster. They had gone in half-prepared and came back half-dead.

By the time he woke after the ambush, the villagers had already made it to a safe enough place to finally rest from their endless wandering. They told him he had been unconscious for three days. Ryanne had been beside herself with worry and threw herself at him the moment his eyes opened, clinging to him with a tearful embrace. Her sobs went on for what felt like hours, her grip so fierce around his neck that she nearly choked him back into unconsciousness. When she finally pulled away, her large magenta eyes locked on his with a stern, trembling intensity.

"Don't ever do that again. We're safe now."

With a huff, Ryanne slipped from his arms and stormed out of the tent, leaving Alec stunned. For all her youth, she reminded him so much of her mother—fire and brimstone when angered, quick to fury, likely cursing him under her breath for days to come.

But it wasn't long before she came tearing back into his tent.

"What part of 'don't ever do that again' did you miss?" she demanded, her voice sharp enough to silence the men gathered inside. The raiding party had convened to plan that evening's assault, but every head turned from her to Alec and back again as they instinctively parted like the Red Sea before her wrath.

Alec couldn't deny it—he was proud. Watching his daughter cow a room full of hardened warriors was both impressive and unnerving. He crossed his arms, torn between scolding her for her insolence or laughing at the dumbstruck expressions around him.

"Give us a moment," he ordered, gesturing to Marcus. One by one, the men filed out, their eyes still flicking between father and daughter. Ryanne stood by the flap, seething in silence until the last man slipped through. Then, the moment the tent closed, she whirled on him.

"You can't go."

The audacity of her words hit him like a slap. Anger uncoiled inside his chest.

"And why is that, Ryanne?" His voice rose, firm and unyielding. "You don't get to tell me what I can or cannot do. I am your father—not your ward. So tell me why you felt the need to humiliate me in front of my men, just to throw a tantrum."

Tears welled in her eyes, instantly puncturing his anger. Guilt twisted like a knife in his chest.

"You won't come back," she whispered, her voice cracking. "You're all I have left, and it's a stupid plan. You're all going to die."

"Come here, baby." Alec's voice softened as he pulled her into his arms. She crumbled against him, sobbing so hard his shirt became soaked with tears, snot, and the ragged breaths of her fear. He didn't care. He stroked her hair, rocking her gently as if she were still the baby he once cradled through midnight storms.

"It's going to be all right, Ryanne," he murmured. "I'll come back. We have a plan."

"It's a dumb plan!" she snapped through her tears. "You shouldn't attack from the North. You should come from the West—at least then you'd have the sun behind you."

Her outburst startled him—not because of her anger, but because she was right. He hadn't considered the position of the sun. By the time they reached their target, dusk would be falling, and their approach from the North would put them at a disadvantage. His stomach dropped.

"Damn," he muttered. "You're right. That would be better." He leaned back, studying her tear-streaked face. "Why don't you show me how you'd do it, huh? Would that make you feel better?"

Ryanne nodded into his shoulder, then grimaced at the damp patch she had left on his tunic. "You should change your shirt."

She sniffled, wiped her face, and squared her shoulders with a maturity that always left him startled. "I'll be right back."

***

When Ryanne returned, she wasn't alone. Adam, Catria, and the entire raiding party trailed behind her as she carried a rolled scroll in her small hands. Determination sharpened her features, her earlier tears burned away by purpose.

She spread the map across the floor with Adam's help. Catria and Adam anchored the corners with stones, then began arranging additional markers. The men muttered in confusion until Marcus snapped, "What are you doing?"

"Wait, and we'll show you," Ryanne cut in, her tone icy enough to silence him. Alec nearly laughed aloud at the sight of Marcus—one of his most seasoned men—shrinking under his daughter's glare.

Together, the three children laid out their plan. To Alec's surprise, it was meticulous. Ryanne delegated roles with precision, Catria adjusted positions with careful logic, and Adam marked out secure checkpoints around the village perimeter with small stones. Their strategy emphasized subtlety—using a smaller infiltration team to remain undetected, while the bulk of the raiders held overwatch positions and supported evacuation. Marcus and four others would lead evac teams, guiding survivors to safety. Alec himself would take command of the infiltration unit.

The most impressive part came when Ryanne produced a set of scrolls.

"This is a communication spell," she explained, striding around the circle. "When you're in position, focus on the person you want to speak with. They'll hear you, and you'll hear them. But don't let your concentration slip. Even for a second. If your thoughts wander, whoever crosses your mind will hear everything."

The raiders shifted uneasily but nodded. Ryanne placed her hands on her hips, her gaze sweeping the room before landing on Alec.

"So. What do you think?"

For a moment, Alec was stunned into silence. This—this was the proudest moment of his life. His daughter, still so young, had shown wisdom and foresight beyond her years. Like her mother.

He studied the map once more, hunting for flaws, but there were none he could see. Finally, he looked back at her and let a smile spread across his face.

"I think this is the best damn plan I've ever seen."

Ryanne's stern mask cracked as he scooped her into a crushing embrace. The men chuckled, watching their commander beam with pride as he pointed to his daughter.

"That's my girl."

***

Hours later, Alec crouched at the outskirts of Morro, waiting for word that the evac teams had reached their positions. Adam had been placed with one such team and was meant to report back once they were in place.

The village was quiet, but the silence felt wrong. The fires had long been quenched, yet the skeletons of burnt buildings sagged inward, unstable and broken. Pulling on his gauntlets and tightening the black armor he had made infamous during the Thousand Year War, Alec scanned the rooftops. Something moved in the distance.

"What the hell...?" he muttered, praying it was only a low-flying dragon.

"Marcus, give me the spyglass!"

Marcus blinked in alarm at Alec's sudden urgency. "What? Why?"

"Just give it to me!" Alec snapped, snatching the glass and raising it to his eye. What he saw froze his blood.

"Shit. Shit, shit. Halt the evac teams—now!"

"What? You can't be serious!" Marcus protested.

"I'm deadly serious." Alec jabbed a finger toward the rooftops. "See those shapes moving through the buildings? Giants. And there's only one way you get Giants—through dark magic. The kind that twists the dead and enslaves the living. I'd bet my dark fae soul that anyone who resisted in that village is already gone… or worse."

The wind shifted, carrying the acrid scent of smoke and decay. Marcus raised the spyglass, scanning the rooftops, his face blanching with each pass.

"No. No, it can't be…" His voice broke with denial, even as the truth stared back at him.

"It's not… not possible. Giants are walking corpses—necromancy, that kind of magic… you said…"

Everyone they had left behind was dead.

Marcus threw himself at Alec, swinging with every ounce of his considerable strength. Alec narrowly dodged the first blow before pulling Marcus to the ground. They grappled furiously, rage driving them more than reason. Even when the men tried to drag them apart, the two slipped free and lunged at each other again, hammering fists, grief spilling out with every strike.

It was the silence afterward that etched itself into Alec's memory. The forest, once alive with birds and rustling leaves, seemed to grieve with them. Every tree stood solemn, every shadow stilled, as if the world itself mourned what had been lost.

Alec sat beneath the shade of a towering pine, hands twisting restlessly as he fought back the truth—and the tears clawing at the edges of his resolve. Lydia was gone. Ryanne would be waiting, expecting her mother's return.

The sun slipped behind the mountains, sinking into darkness. All eyes turned to Alec, waiting. His voice broke under the weight of despair when he finally spoke.

"Fall back… there's nothing left for us here."

He rose, spine straight despite the heaviness in his chest, and turned toward home. He was not ready to break his daughter's heart.

Now, standing by the fire, Alec remembered that moment as though no time had passed. The smell of smoke curling into the night brought the memory crashing back, raw and sharp. Lowering himself beside Ryanne's sleeping form, he brushed a stray lock from her face. She looked so much like her mother in slumber that the resemblance stabbed at him.

A soft sob slipped from his chest. For a fleeting heartbeat, he let his grief break free, walls tumbling down around his shattered heart. But only for a moment. Then he forced the storm back inside, pulling it tight, sealing it away. There was no room for weakness. Not yet. Not until this war was over and Ryanne was safe again.

For now, he would be her foundation. If nothing else, he was dark fae. Stone, if he must be. And he had proven as much in the days that followed their loss.

The reports from the evacuation teams had brought little comfort. Adam, still just a boy, had confessed that they were forced to cut down several undead villagers just to reach safety. A child should never have to bear such memories. Yet, if he were to survive, he would need training. They all would.

***

The slosh of water pulled Leah from unconsciousness.

Darkness stretched endlessly around her, deep and suffocating. She strained her ears, desperate for any sound, while her eyes fought to adjust to the faint, eerie glow flickering at the edge of sight. A tremor ran down her spine, and she shivered, exhaustion heavy in her bones.

Why do I always land in the water?

If it was even water. The liquid lapped against her legs, ankle-deep, yet soundless. She sensed movement nearby—something stirring in the black—but silence pressed down like a weight.

Her body tensed, ready to strike. She waited, breath shallow, every heartbeat stretching into eternity. Then, from the nothingness, a pale light appeared in the distance, as if beckoning her forward.

Leah hesitated. Every instinct told her not to trust it. But what choice did she have? She was dead. She knew it. Her spirit had been ripped from her body, cast into this place. Yet nothing about this resembled the afterlife she had been taught to expect.

No ferrymen.

No river, unless this shallow pool counted.

No torment, no bliss.

Only light suspended in endless black.

She began walking.

At first, she believed the journey would be short. But the further she went, the more the thought crept in: perhaps this was her torment, her eternity—chasing a light she could never reach.

She called into the void, her voice breaking the silence.

"Hello?"

No echo. The darkness swallowed her words whole. The quiet was so profound her ears began to ring.

She cursed under her breath, shaking her head, trying to force away the battlefield memories clawing back from her past. Even in death, they haunted her. Her progress slowed as the ringing grew unbearable, splitting her skull with every step closer to the light.

Finally, realization struck—*the light itself was the source of the pain.*

She stumbled backward, retreating into deeper shadow until the agony dulled. Now, only blackness stretched around her, broken by water that carried no sound, no reflection. Unable to advance and unwilling to return to the tormenting brilliance, Leah sat in the silence, hands trailing in the water. Ripples spread outward but faded to nothing.

She did not know how long she lingered there, staring into oblivion.

When at last she leaned back, allowing the liquid to cover her ears, calm washed over her. For the first time in what felt like a millennium, she felt peace. Arms stretched above her head, she dragged them lazily through the water, creating ripples that kissed her skin.

Until her hand struck something solid.

Her body convulsed in terror. She scrambled upright, water splashing, before a large hand—decisively masculine—fisted the back of her dress and lifted her effortlessly, like a child's doll.

Leah screamed, thrashing violently, refusing to submit.

"Cease!" a voice boomed.

Her limbs weakened, suddenly heavy, yet she fought on, swatting at the darkness.

"Let go of me!" she roared, hurling a blast of wind strong enough to unseat a cavalry rider.

The grip held. Both were hurled backward into the dark, and Leah landed atop something warm, solid—someone's body. Her attacker sucked in air as she struggled to flee, but he was fast.

A massive hand clamped around her ankle.

She spun, kicking, summoning her power through the water. He grunted, wounded, but still he held fast.

"Dammit, woman! Cease! I'm trying to help you!" His voice carried a strained timber, foreign yet commanding.

Leah froze. Something slick and warm coiled around her ankle—blood. She had injured him, but by the smell alone, she knew it wouldn't stop him for long.

"Then prove it—and let me go!" she snarled, kicking harder.

To her shock, he did.

Breathing raggedly, Leah stared as faint green luminescence pierced the void. One bud of light drifted near. Then another. Soon dozens surrounded them, glowing like fireflies, illuminating her assailant.

He lay on his back, groaning, blood pouring from a gash so deep his arm looked nearly severed. Yet, before her eyes, the wound knit itself closed, flesh mending beneath the glow.

A grotesque fascination pulled her closer.

"Fascinating," she whispered.

His golden eyes snapped to hers, wary.

"You cannot do this?" he asked. His voice carried tension, suspicion.

Only then did Leah realize she had leaned so close that her face hovered inches from his. She flushed, suddenly aware she had practically climbed onto him while studying the impossible healing. Clearing her throat, she scooted back, giving him space.

"Sorry," she muttered.

He sat up slowly, keeping his distance. Leah shook her head at the sight of his shoulder.

"To answer your question—no. I heal quickly, but that..." she gestured at him, "that's unnatural."

Her eyes narrowed.

"Who are you?"

"I am Ares," he replied flatly.

"I presume you are Leah of the Moro, correct?"

The question stunned her. Terror shot through her body so swiftly it felt as though the air had been ripped from her lungs. How could this man possibly know who she was—when she herself didn't even know where she was? Her chest tightened, her breath faltering until every inhale burned. Leah's reputation often traveled ahead of her, but this was something else entirely—something far more unnerving.

She steadied herself, forcing her lungs to obey, and asked the question that lodged like a thorn in her chest.

"How do you know me?"

Her breathing eased by degrees, her lungs finally taking air without struggle.

"Your mother told us of your plight," Ares replied evenly.

Leah blinked, stunned into silence. The words hit her like a stone to the temple, and for a moment she simply watched his lips move without registering a single sound. It was only when her hearing seemed to snap back that the full absurdity of his claim struck her.

Throwing up her hands, she cut him off.

"Wait! Wait, wait, wait, wait… You're telling me that my dead mother told you who I was, and what was happening to me, before I even got here?"

She stared him down, incredulity flashing in her eyes. His expression, however, was one of thinly veiled irritation, as if he thought she were slow to understand the obvious.

"Yes," he answered carefully, speaking with the patronizing slowness one might use with a child. His gaze swept her up and down as if searching for visible evidence of some deficiency. "Are you in some way defective?"

The insult left her reeling. Leah shook her head in disbelief before springing to her feet, startling Ares as her chair scraped sharply against the floor. Without another word, she spun on her heels and stomped away, her anger echoing in every step.

Confused but unwilling to let her go, Ares rose and strode after her.

"Where are you going?" he asked, lengthening his stride until he caught up. His long legs made the pursuit effortless, which only stoked Leah's fury further. She couldn't even outpace him if she tried.

She whirled on him, eyes blazing in the dim light. "Why are you following me? You're insane! What kind of man drags up a girl's dead parents, then calls her stupid when her natural reaction is not to believe him?" Her voice dropped into a mocking lilt, her head bobbing as she mimicked him cruelly. "'Yes, they're alive,'" she mocked, her tone sharp and dripping with derision.

For a long, tense moment, silence stretched between them.

"Is that supposed to be me?" Ares asked at last, his brow furrowed.

Leah threw her hands up in exasperation. "Why do I even bother—"

Her words were cut short by the low growl of her stomach, loud in the night air. The ache bent her slightly, a pained whimper escaping her throat.

Ares' expression softened. "Are you alright? You appear… uncomfortable."

Leah gave a reluctant nod. "I'm hungry. It's been a while since I've had a chance to eat. You wouldn't know where I could find something, would you?" Her voice was small, tinged with embarrassment. Heat flushed her cheeks. Not minutes ago she'd been screaming at him like a wild thing, and now here she was, forced to ask for his help. He was the only person she had encountered in this strange place, and she had nearly chased him off with her temper.

Her shame deepened when she met his gaze, drawn into the molten gold of his eyes.

"I should apologize for my behavior," she said at last, taking in a long, weary breath. "It was uncalled for—especially since you are, in some way, trying to help me. And the truth is, I need that help."

Ares considered her words, then gave a slight shrug. "Alright."

With military precision, he pivoted sharply to the right and began walking, his stride steady and disciplined. Leah sighed but followed, her odd, inscrutable companion leading the way.

The silence between them stretched for what felt like hours. Leah was too embarrassed by her outburst to attempt conversation, while Ares seemed perfectly content to march forward as though she weren't even there.

Eventually, out of sheer boredom, Leah snapped her fingers near his ear. His head tilted slightly, though he didn't fully look at her. She tried again, snapping sharper this time. This earned her an irritated glance, and she dropped her hand sheepishly, pretending to study the faint glow of the surrounding mist.

Finally, Ares halted. "This is far enough. You've done well, given your powers have yet to awaken."

For the first time, Leah took in the full measure of him. He raised his hands and began to pray.

"Darkness, open the doors, that I may be received home."

The words were answered at once. A swirling vortex bloomed into being before them, pulsing with shadows. Ares lowered his hands, murmuring his thanks before opening his eyes.

Leah stared in awe. She had read of such things—accounts buried in scripture and old texts—but never had she seen a true portal. Her hand reached out instinctively, fingers hovering inches from the shifting surface before hesitation rooted her in place.

What's on the other side?

Ares seemed to sense her pause. "You are wise to be cautious. Where we are going is no place for weakness. Brace yourself, for temptation there is great."

And with that, he stepped into the portal and vanished.

Leah closed her eyes, steeling herself. Her breath trembled, but she pushed forward. "Here we go."

She stepped through.

To her surprise, the world did not tilt or spin. She had braced herself for nausea or the stabbing ache she often endured after guiding children through their magic journeys. But nothing came. No sickness, no dizziness, not even a headache.

The lack of symptoms unsettled her more than any discomfort would have. It had taken centuries of training to reach a stage where travel left her with only mild pain. For this man to open a portal that left her untouched meant his power was beyond anything she had imagined.

A shudder ran through her as she realized just how differently their earlier argument could have ended had he chosen to harm her.

On the other side, a magnificent hall awaited her. Its walls were carved from luminous white stone, the columns stretching impossibly high. The ceiling was absent, leaving the vast chamber open to the radiant sky above. Sunlight poured in, yet its warmth was tempered, not oppressive.

Sconces cast a gentle glow, their flames more ornamental than functional, illuminating a lavish red carpet embroidered with golden leaf. The carpet stretched the length of the hall, splitting into two grand doorways that flanked the foyer.

Leah stood stunned, too rattled by her seamless passage to properly appreciate her surroundings until a light touch on her arm jolted her back to the moment. The contact sent a shiver coursing through her, warmth unfurling across her chest and settling low in her belly. She looked at Ares, startled to see him blush before he quickly broke away, retreating from her as though burned.

Her skin still tingled when movement caught her eye. A young man appeared, rounding the corner with easy confidence. He was strikingly handsome—dark hair, piercing blue eyes, and a sharp jawline carved to perfection. In one hand, he carried two goblets of wine; in the other, he dragged along a drunken, naked woman who clung to him weakly.

When his gaze fell on Leah, his jaw slackened. He dropped the woman carelessly to the floor like a sack of grain.

"By the gods, who is this beautiful creature!?" he exclaimed.

Horrified, Leah gaped at his callousness, her eyes darting between him and the discarded woman, who now struggled to sit upright, her expression furious. Leah hurried forward to help her, but the newcomer intercepted her with startling swiftness. His hand clamped firmly around her elbow, spinning her away from the woman with practiced ease.

He leaned close, his breath brushing her ear as he whispered, his voice pitched low for her alone—

"You should never close your mouth again. It's a very becoming feature on you."

The warmth from his grotesque touch surged aggressively up Leah's arm, spreading like wildfire across her neck and face as his aura pressed against hers. Unlike others before him, this man did not release her. Leah remained frozen, stunned by the intrusion. She had never been in such a situation, and her body betrayed her—reacting violently to whatever spell held her in place. The longer his hand lingered, the more a buried hunger stirred within her, needs she had not entertained in years.

This man was dangerous.

His smile remained fixed, just inches from her face. Leah, fighting the instinct to recoil, closed her mouth and glanced at Ares, silently pleading for aid. He hesitated, his expression carved from stone, until finally, after several tense seconds of inner debate, he spoke flatly.

"Let go."

Leah sensed the atmosphere shift like the crack of a storm between the two men. The stranger seemed to transform beside her, no longer charming but a wild predator snarling just out of sight. She realized then why Ares had delayed.

"Is that a challenge, brother?" The man's voice rolled low, and he turned slowly toward Ares. His grip on Leah's elbow tightened fractionally as Ares answered, his tone level but edged with steel.

"Leah, this is Zeus, ruler of Olympus. Zeus, this is Noctis' daughter, Leah."

At the introduction, Zeus stiffened. Surprise flickered in his eyes before he released her, his demeanor altering in an instant. Reappraising her with new weight, he straightened and, falling back on formal grace, stepped back.

"I see. My apologies, my lady. I did not realize."

Leah inclined her head, though her body screamed for distance. She edged closer to Ares, masking her unease with a carefully crafted smile as she dipped in a polite curtsy.

"None needed, my lord. I understand this must have been rather startling—finding us in your foyer unannounced." Years of diplomacy rose to her lips, smoothing her words.

"I was indeed surprised," Zeus admitted, his tone sly. "Ares does not usually visit The Menage." His mouth curved with a wink. "It makes him uncomfortable."

Leah gave a small nod, piecing together the truth—Ares had only brought her here because her body had given out earlier.

"It would appear my condition is to blame," she said softly, offering Zeus a shy, calculated glance. Inwardly, she steeled herself. This man was a predator, and until her strength returned, she would have to make him believe she was harmless prey.

"We need to stay until she has recovered from our journey," Ares declared bluntly. Subtlety had never been his strength; the weight of danger seemed lost on him. Zeus, however, took no offense.

"Of course," he replied with ease, gesturing toward the right. "Stay as long as you'd like. You'll find a feast in the dining hall at all hours. The vomitorium is opposite." He shifted his hand toward the left corridor, his tone turning sharp with distaste. "Hera and her ladies reside down that hall."

Leah caught the sneer. Whoever Hera was, Zeus clearly disliked her. That alone made Leah consider Hera her safest refuge.

"We'll go see Mother," Ares announced, already striding toward the indicated hallway. Leah gave Zeus one last curtsy before slipping quickly after Ares.

She felt like a child slinking away from a coiled serpent, her skin crawling as they turned the corner and left Zeus behind. Relief washed through her as the oppressive lust evaporated with distance. Ares remained silent, his focus sharp as he navigated the labyrinthine halls with ease. Though he clearly disliked this place, Leah could tell he had walked these paths many times before.

After a stretch of silence, Ares finally spoke. "My father is known for being a deviant. I should have warned you. I apologize."

He stopped before a large, unadorned door and turned to face her.

"My intention was to bypass The Menage entirely and bring you directly to the void pockets. Ideally, you would have entered at my own estate, but..." he gestured at her, his tone edged with disapproval, "I assumed too much of you."

Leah bristled at his dismissive air. A low growl slipped from her throat before she could stop it. Ares, instead of offended, nodded in satisfaction.

Barbarian, she thought with disgust.

"Mother won't be pleased," he went on, "but you will be safe here until you've rested." He reached for the door.

"I…I have questions," Leah interrupted, her thoughts spilling over in a rush.

Ares studied her for a moment. "I'll answer what I can—but you'll have to speak the words."

Leah huffed in frustration but gave in. "Why does Zeus call you brother?"

Leaning against the wall, Ares brushed his blond hair back from his eyes. "Zeus is my father, though never a good one. He prefers to call me 'brother'—saves him the trouble of admitting to his mistresses that I am his son."

A pang of sympathy pierced Leah's chest. He said little, and his face rarely betrayed his emotions, but she was beginning to discern the subtle shifts beneath his stoicism.

"So, if Hera is your mother…does that make her his wife?" she asked carefully.

"Yes," Ares said with a short laugh, "though they despise each other. My father calls her a buzzkill—mainly because she despises his constant affairs. Once, she even turned one of his mistresses into a spider to make her point."

Leah blinked, then smothered a laugh. It was shocking, but admittedly, she could not fault Hera's methods.

"She sounds like a resilient woman. I'm glad I'll get to meet her. But…how does she tolerate the endless orgy happening here?"

"She's probably aware," Ares shrugged. "Few true beings exist in these dimensions. The rest? Illusions. My father is essentially indulging in one giant fantasy. Mother intervenes only if a real person gets pulled into it. She's also deaf in one ear, so she usually keeps that side turned toward this door." His explanation was matter-of-fact, as though he were describing the weather. He pushed away from the wall, hesitating at the door. "Just…stay behind me."

The door groaned open, revealing a chamber utterly unlike the gilded halls they had left behind.

This room gleamed with glass and steel, sharp lines replacing marble and stone. Polished metal tables reflected light like mirrors. Strange devices sat beneath each desk, cords snaking upward to glowing towers that pulsed with energy. Women occupied the seats, their attire foreign to Leah's eyes, their attention fixed on luminous screens that flickered with unreadable symbols.

At the front of the chamber sat a woman whose presence commanded the room. Blond hair pulled high into a ponytail, dark cat-eyed glasses framing her sharp gaze, she leaned over her desk, tapping her lips in thought as the screen before her shifted with movement. Her white blouse and pinstriped vest were tailored perfectly, her black shoes marked with a dangerous spike jutting from the heel.

When she noticed Ares' movement, she did a double take. Snapping her gold pocket watch open, she checked the time before standing abruptly and sliding it back into her pocket.

"Sweetheart, what are you doing here?"

She swept from behind her desk with arms outstretched. Ares stepped forward, lifting her from the floor in a rare display of affection before setting her gently back down.

"I need your help," he said simply.

As he recounted the events, Hera listened, her face impassive save for the subtle rub of her fingers against her temple when Zeus' behavior was mentioned. She did not interrupt, not even when Ares explained how close he had come to losing his arm.

When introductions were made at last, Hera extended her hand.

"It is a pleasure to meet the progeny of our benefactor. You are welcome here for as long as you wish. I will see to it personally that your stay is safe and comfortable."

She guided Leah toward a door at the back of the chamber—one Leah had not noticed before.

"Come," Hera said warmly. "You may freshen up while I speak with my son."

"Take your time. I recommend you shower, change, and take a nap before you collapse. Honestly, dear, you look like you've been through hell. I expect you to give yourself ample time for a reprieve."

Leah stepped into the doorway, her eyes catching on the spacious chamber. A large in-floor bath was already filled to the brim with steaming water, its surface shimmering under the glow of unseen light. Across the room, a grand four-post bed dominated the space, draped in soft linens. One entire wall was made of glass, revealing a breathtaking view of the night sky scattered with endless stars.

Leah's gaze flickered nervously to Ares, uncertain, until Hera noticed and gave a reassuring nod.

"Ahh, I see. I will ensure Ares is here when you return," Hera said gently. Leah must have shown some visible relief because Hera smiled kindly before adding, "I'll have one of my ladies assist you with anything you desire."

She waved forward a young girl, Audra, who looked to be just stepping into adolescence. Hera instructed her to provide Leah with the best possible care before closing the door quietly behind them.

Audra moved with practiced efficiency, testing the bathwater and gathering a basket of petals and oils. She sprinkled lavender and eucalyptus in generous handfuls, the rich herbal scent filling the air until it felt as though the room itself breathed calm. Rose petals scattered across the surface of the water, while an otherworldly glow rose from beneath, casting the bath in a soothing, magical light.

Audra helped Leah remove what remained of her tattered clothes, though the girl tried valiantly not to reveal how shredded and scant they had become. Leah, however, insisted. Only then did she realize just how exposed she had been during the sacrifice, how much of her body had been laid bare before Ares, Zeus, and Hera. Embarrassment flamed hot across her skin. Mortification drove her to sink beneath the steaming surface, wishing she could disappear completely into the water.

Eyes closed, she released a muffled scream beneath the waves, expelling the pain, fear, and frustration that had been building since the dragon priests had stormed her village.

When Leah surfaced again, gasping, she froze. A swan now perched at the edge of the pool, its snowy feathers glowing against the backdrop of the night. It slid gracefully into the water and circled her playfully, its movements so fluid it seemed woven from the very water itself.

Despite herself, Leah smiled. The creature was beautiful—its feathers glistening silver where the light from beneath the water caught them. But her admiration turned to terror in an instant. The swan dove sharply toward her just as Audra reappeared carrying a set of fresh robes.

The girl shrieked, dropping the garments in horror, and bolted for the door screaming for help.

The swan's form twisted, melted, and in its place emerged Zeus, rising from the water with a mischievous grin. Leah shoved at him in shock, trying to scramble away, but he gripped her by the elbows. Heat flared up her arms and shoulders, the same scorching pull she had felt earlier, overwhelming her senses as panic rose in her chest.

The doors burst open. A flood of Hera's ladies poured into the chamber, skirts whipping as they dove into the pool to reach her. Thrashing desperately, Leah struggled against Zeus's hold, but he forced her under. Water filled her lungs as her limbs thrashed wildly.

Bubbles erupted around her, splashes breaking the surface as the women fought to free her. Leah used the last of her breath to whisper the words of her transportation spell. In a flash, she reappeared on the cold floor beside the pool.

Zeus followed, his elbow slamming into her diaphragm. The force expelled the water from her lungs in a violent cough that sprayed directly into his face. He laughed, unbothered, mimicking her gasps and flailing arms.

"Holy cow, you should have seen your face!" he jeered, his tone more like a frat boy's prank than a god's jest.

Something inside Leah shifted. The smell of blood rushed into her nostrils though none had been spilled, and her teeth felt sharper as a snarl tore from her throat.

"You think this is funny?" Her voice was a low growl. Rising to her feet, she felt the darkness inside her surge, stronger and more consuming with every heartbeat.

For the first time, Zeus's cocky grin faltered. His eyes widened, and he took a step back, raising his hands in surrender.

"Whoa, easy now. It was just a joke," he stammered.

But Leah's rage was bottomless. She had been tricked, beaten, murdered, dragged into another world, and now mocked. No apology could erase that.

The tranquility Hera had promised was shattered, replaced with fear, humiliation, and fury. Leah stepped forward, snarling, but her strength gave out as suddenly as it had surged. Darkness closed in, and she collapsed.

***

When Leah finally woke, she learned she had been unconscious for several days. Though her body still felt weak, her appetite returned quickly. A tray of fruits and meats was placed before her, and she ate hungrily, as though she hadn't eaten in weeks.

Ares was there when her eyes opened. He sat silently in the corner, unmoving, watching the wall as if carved from stone. Even when Hera's ladies fussed over Leah—bathing, tending, and dressing her— Ares didn't stir.

One attendant in a bright red jumper dragged a folding screen across the chamber, blocking Ares from view. Three more surrounded

Leah, stripping her nightgown away and dressing her in a new outfit: a brilliant white pantsuit fastened with gleaming gold buttons, nearly identical to the one Hera herself had worn. For shoes, Leah was given a choice—shimmering gold heels or black ones. She selected the gold, marveling at their strange, elevated shape.

Her hair was fussed over for nearly an hour until the attendants finally stepped back, satisfied with their work.

When all was finished, Leah and Ares were escorted to an exterior banquet hall where Hera awaited them for lunch. The table was small, meant for only four, but adorned with pure gold dishes and cutlery that gleamed against the snow-white cloth. At its center sat a vase shaped like a cow, filled with a bouquet of lilies in every color.

"You look much better without the gore all over you," Hera said matter-of-factly, spearing a piece of chicken with her fork.

Leah managed a nod as she devoured her food with the desperation of the starving. She reminded herself to slow down, to chew, but her hunger was unrelenting. Hera waved for another plate to be brought when Leah finished her first.

It was then Leah spoke.

"Your majesty, can you fill me in on what happened last night? I seem to be missing time."

At once, Ares set his fork down, his expression unreadable. He wore only a simple shirt and pants today, but something about his restraint unsettled Leah. His gaze lingered on her, cautious, as though he was measuring every word.

Hera, however, continued eating without pause. She rested her chin lightly on the backs of her wrists, looking thoughtful.

"Why don't you tell me what you remember first? Then we can fill in the blanks."

Leah hesitated, then nodded. "I remember taking a bath. There was a swan... but it wasn't a swan. Zeus almost drowned me. I teleported out of the pool. And then I remember getting angry. Really, really angry."

She trailed off, struggling to describe it. "I felt something... strange. In my chest. It was like a color—black. That's the only way I can explain it. I was so angry I thought I..." Her words failed, and she shook her head with a frustrated sigh. "I'm sorry. I must sound ridiculous. Saying I felt like the color black."

Hera reached out and touched her arm. "It's not as ridiculous as you think, considering your parentage."

Pushing away her plate, Hera stood gracefully. "Follow me. There's something I'd like to show you."

The trio left the dining hall and turned immediately into a passage swallowed by shadow. The air grew moist and cool as they stepped inside, and the light from behind them faded.

"Where are we going?" Leah asked, gripping Ares's arm tightly as the darkness consumed them.

"The beginning," he said flatly.

The silence pressed on her ears until it felt deafening. Leah's head rang with the sharp high-pitched squeal that had haunted her since her years as a soldier. The quiet was unbearable. Clearing her throat, she loosened her hold, letting her hand brush lightly against Ares's arm just enough to keep her bearings in the dark.

"Sorry," she muttered. She could almost feel his golden gaze on her even without light.

Her senses sharpened. The air was damp and chilled. The echo of rippling water grew louder with every step. Shadows wrapped around her like a heavy cloak, stifling, until the faintest shimmer of the doorway vanished completely.

Ares halted abruptly. Leah, distracted by her thoughts, walked straight into Hera's back with a startled "oof."

"Oh gods, I am so sorry!" she blurted, her face flaming with embarrassment.

Hera only hummed softly.

"We're here," Ares whispered.

"Stay silent; Hecate can be aggressive."

Leah hadn't been worried when they first entered the chamber, but Ares had a way of fucking that up for her.

A sudden light flared in the corner, startling her out of her rising irritation. Hera appeared, standing beside a torch mounted against the wall. Ahead, Leah noticed they had come upon a small pool of water feeding into the roots of a dead tree. The tree, petrified with age, stretched its roots into the water. Gentle ripples stirred as the pool shifted against them, carrying an eerie stillness.

Leah was overcome with an ache of longing—powerful, extraordinary, though she couldn't name what it was for. The scene held her, heavy and moving, like something half-remembered from a dream.

Movement flickered behind Hera. Leah's breath caught, then burst into a scream as two glowing yellow eyes emerged over Hera's shoulder. She had only a heartbeat to think *swamp witch* before the petite figure shrieked—an unearthly, piercing cry that shook the cavern—and lunged for her.

Ares and Hera moved instantly. The witch barreled past Hera, who snatched at her wrist, slowing her only for a moment. Ares shoved Leah behind him just as the woman's face twisted into grotesque flickers of rage.

Her appearance was feral. Her tangled hair had been knotted into a crude headdress woven from bones and twigs. Her only covering was mud, thick and clinging, caking her from head to toe. The grime made her wrist slick, slipping easily from Hera's grip. Then, in a terrifying rush, she turned to smoke and embers, phasing through Ares' body. He dropped to the floor with a cry of pain.

Leah froze as the witch reappeared before her, eyes pulsing with malice. A crooked smile curled across her lips as time itself seemed to slow. With Hera and Ares caught outside the spell, Leah was alone.

The woman's eyes gleamed with cruel delight. She looked down on Leah as though she were nothing more than an insect to be crushed.

Something inside Leah snapped. A spark of rage ignited in her chest, surging upward, overtaking her fear. It rose like a flood, spilling out in a guttural scream.

The cavern shook with the force of her release. Power erupted from Leah, blasting the witch across the chamber and hurling her into the wall she had come from—dragging a helpless Hera with her. The wall buckled and collapsed inward upon impact.

For an instant, horror ripped through Leah at what might have happened to her friend—then the world went black as she fainted.

***

Leah awoke with the painful crush of air being forced from her lungs. Forcing her eyes open, she saw chaos: stone crumbling, walls collapsing. Hera blasted a surge of power against the debris, shielding a mud-caked, limping, snarling Hecate from being crushed.

Ares stepped forward, seizing Hecate from Hera's grasp, knocking her unconscious with practiced force.

"How long has she been in there?" Ares asked, his tone sharp with accusation.

"A couple of days. She said she would be right back, but I must have lost track of time." Hera sighed.

"You should be more careful." Ares' voice was cold.

Hera bowed her head, properly chastised. Locks of hair had fallen loose from her immaculate bun, and streaks of mud and blood stained her torn clothing. Leah watched as shallow cuts across Hera's exposed skin shimmered and sealed, the wounds knitting closed on their own.

Hera knelt to examine Leah, while Ares inspected Hecate.

"I'm sorry about my cousin," Hera said softly. "She's drawn to magic, and you carry an incredible surplus. Normally, she's far more levelheaded, but it seems we interrupted a ritual. She's intoxicated with the power of it." Shaking her head with exhaustion, Hera gently probed Leah's arm, checking for internal injuries.

"Conversely," she added, "you're stronger than I anticipated. We won't need to delay your training."

"Training?" Leah pulled her wrist away, rubbing at the tingling sensation Hera's touch had left behind.

"Yes." Hera nodded firmly. "Your mother asked us to escort you to Hades. His realm stands between life and death, the very place you now exist. If anyone knows how to bring Lux back across the veil—and how to send you home—it will be him."

The ground trembled as the last of the cave-in settled. Over Hera's shoulder, Leah noticed the shattered columns that had stood watch over the chamber entrance only minutes before. Hera's attendants swarmed into the hallway with shovels, buckets, and charms, working with both muscle and magic to clear the way.

Leah sat up fully. A woman in a bright yellow jumper, golden waterfall earrings swaying at her ears, approached and draped a thick blanket around Leah's shoulders. Without a word, she turned back to help the others.

None of them are dressed for manual labor, Leah thought. Yet the blanket was warm, a small mercy against the biting chill of the cavern. Shivering, she pulled it tighter around her shoulders and forced herself to stand, wobbling slightly on one broken heel.

"My mother is dead. I've said this before." The bitterness in her voice stung, making her cringe inwardly. She chanced a glance at Hera, still crouched before her, and met an unyielding golden gaze.

"But she is alive, Leah." Hera gestured to her attendants, who worked tirelessly to pull stone after stone from the wreckage. The progress was startling in such a short time. "She is just beyond the rubble. She has been waiting for you."

Leah blinked, her breath faltering.

"She is not bound by death. Your understanding of it is final—on the other side of the veil. But your mother is no ordinary being. She existed long before Death ever came to be."

Hera rose, wrapping an arm around Leah and turning her back toward the dining chamber they had come from.

"I want to see her," Leah whispered, glancing over her shoulder toward the wreckage.

"My ladies will need time to clear the passage," Hera replied gently. "Until then, we begin your training." She gave Leah a reassuring squeeze, her smile warm, almost motherly, as she opened a glowing portal before them.

Leah stepped through without hesitation.

Chapter Nine

Hades was an unexpectedly pleasant man—jovial, even. Since her arrival with Hera, Leah had grown accustomed to the evening routine: long, winding conversations with the two of them after an extravagant dinner that would put mortal feasts to shame. The Underworld was nothing like she had imagined; dark, yes, but steeped in a haunting elegance that mirrored its ruler.

During these talks, Hades often spoke with a gentleness that surprised her, especially when the subject turned to the grief she had endured. On one poignant evening, when her composure finally shattered, he embraced her as she sobbed bitter tears over the sheer magnitude of her losses. His voice had been steady, his words almost tender as he tried to reassure her that her pain was not insurmountable. And in that moment, he succeeded—at least a little.

The embrace reminded her of her mother's: strong, grounding, and difficult to pull away from. But something essential was missing. It wasn't warm. Leah realized with a shiver that Hades felt as cold as the grave—a chill that seeped through her bones like water through cracked stone.

When she first heard about his wife, she had expected Persephone to be the same. The goddess of spring—the bringer of life itself—had been away visiting her mother when Leah arrived. Hades, however, spoke of her often, his words brimming with devotion. Her beauty, her vitality, her warmth—he praised them all without hesitation. He assured Leah that once Persephone returned, she would be in the best possible hands for training.

He hadn't exaggerated. When Persephone finally appeared, Leah was struck breathless. The goddess's hair fell in waves of deep chestnut streaked with blond and amber, framing a sharp, angular face. Her eyes were an arresting shade of green, vivid and alive, like the first shoots of spring breaking through frost. She wasn't tall, but her body was sculpted into an effortless hourglass shape—strength tempered by elegance, the kind of figure that spoke of resilience and fertility alike.

But for all her beauty, Persephone was also—Leah realized quickly—a wildly jealous, venom-tongued tyrant.

Her training began the very next day.

***

"You're fat. You're slow. You're completely out of shape. And you crumble under the slightest pressure!" Persephone's voice cracked like a whip across the arena as she slammed the flat of her blade against Leah's back, driving her face-first into the packed dirt.

Leah spat grit from her mouth as her body throbbed from the impact. It had been weeks of this—relentless drills punctuated by verbal lashings—and she was sick of it. Sick of the bruises. Sick of the jeers. Sick of the goddess's unrelenting scorn.

"You can barely get out of bed in the morning!" Persephone stalked in a slow circle around her, boots grinding in the dust. The leather of her battle armor creaked with each measured step. When she passed behind Leah, she gave her a sharp smack on the hip with the flat of her blade, the sting blooming hot across her skin.

"Life is pain!" Persephone roared, voice echoing across the empty coliseum. "You need to embrace all of it—make it part of who you are! Stop running like a coward. Death will not save you."

Leah clenched her jaw until her teeth ached, swallowing down the growl clawing its way up her throat. *Jealous cow,* she thought bitterly, but she knew better than to let the words slip. Losing control now would be worse than defeat.

Sucking in a deep breath, she pushed herself upright, trembling but defiant, and raised her sword to guard. Today's lesson was simple: hold your ground. But after half a day of brutal sparring, her muscles screamed for mercy. Persephone didn't look the least bit winded.

"Who are you to challenge me?" the goddess snarled, her blade already descending in a blur. Leah parried, barely, steel ringing in her ears as blow after blow rained down.

"Better!" Persephone barked, driving forward in a vicious assault. "But dodging isn't enough!"

Sweat stung Leah's eyes as she twisted to meet an attack from her left. Her heart thundered, her breath ragged. A slashing strike skimmed her side, the force jarring her arms to the bone. Persephone pivoted low, dropping to one knee, and swept her blade in a brutal arc toward Leah's legs.

Leah leapt instinctively—then cursed herself an instant later. The goddess seized the opening, snatching Leah mid-air by her belt. With inhuman strength, she flung her like a ragdoll, slamming her to the ground. Cold metal kissed her throat before she could recover.

"Close," Persephone hissed, eyes flashing, "but never sacrifice stability for safety. Or you'll lose both."

She straightened, stalking back to her starting point with lethal grace. "Again."

Leah didn't move. Flat on her back, chest heaving, she stared at the bleak expanse of sky above the arena. Her limbs trembled with exhaustion. Tears burned behind her eyelids, unbidden and hot. She couldn't do this anymore. Her heart felt like a shattered thing bleeding in her chest, and all she wanted was to stop.

Persephone lowered her sword, lips curling in disgust. "We're done here," she muttered, shaking her head before striding away without another glance.

***

From the stands, Hera watched in silence. Draped in a white fox-fur shawl, a wide-brimmed hat shading half her face, and oversized square sunglasses perched on her nose, she looked every inch the queen—even here, amid the dust and blood of the arena. Gold hoops gleamed at her ears as she adjusted the shawl against the chill breeze.

Her gaze flicked toward Ares, lounging far too casually beside her. The God of War sat sprawled with his feet propped on the row ahead, face half-buried in a bag of popcorn like this was a mortal spectacle for his amusement.

Persephone approached, armor clinking faintly, expression thunderous. "If we don't find a way to break her out of that"—she jerked her thumb toward Leah's crumpled form—"she'd be better off dead."

Hera inclined her head with regal composure. "Thank you for your candor, Persephone. We'll take it from here."

The goddess of spring offered a curt bow, muttering under her breath about weak women as she stalked away.

Hera's patience snapped. She jabbed an elbow into Ares so sharply that the popcorn bag flew, scattering kernels like golden hail. He toppled sideways with a grunt, sprawling on the steps in a shower of salt and oil.

"Could you be any more imbecilic?" she hissed.

"What?" Ares blinked up at her, genuinely baffled, still clutching the mangled bag. "What did I do?"

"Do something about this—now!" Hera threw an imperious hand toward the arena, where Leah lay motionless.

"I'm the God of War," he said flatly, brushing crumbs from his black leathers. "I don't *do* feelings."

"Then make her go to war!" Hera snapped, her voice slicing through the air like a whipcrack.

For a moment, he just stared, then shrugged slowly. "I could do that," he murmured, almost to himself.

Hera rolled her eyes heavenward, muttering what sounded very much like a prayer for strength, before stalking off in a storm of clicking heels and gold.

***

Ares descended into the arena, calling out as Leah finally dragged herself upright. "Hey!" His voice boomed like thunder across the empty space. "Do you want to die?"

Leah froze mid-motion, staring at him like he'd grown a second head.

When she didn't answer, he cupped his hands around his mouth and bellowed again, louder: "DO YOU WANT TO DIE?"

This time, there was no mistaking it.

Her blood simmered with irritation. *This fucking idiot.* Did he seriously not see what had just happened?

"No!" she shouted back, shoving hair from her damp face. "I do not want to die!"

"Then why did you quit?" Ares roared, closing the distance in a few long strides.

"I didn't quit." Her voice was flat, brittle.

"Yes, you did," he shot back without missing a beat. "I watched you. You laid right there and quit." He stabbed a finger at the dirt where her outline was still visible, dark with sweat.

"Could we not do this right now?" she snapped, exhaustion fraying her last nerve.

"No need to get hostile," he said lightly, now standing inches away, infuriatingly calm. "Your sparring partner's gone."

"You can be such an ass," she muttered, snatching up her sword. She turned it in her hands, checking for nicks, already dreading the hours she'd spend sharpening it—and praying she wouldn't have to share that time with *him.*

"I'm the God of War," Ares said with a shrug, flashing a grin that was equal parts charming and infuriating. "Prickly comes with the job."

"Did you not see what just happened?" Leah burst out, her voice rising. "I've been getting my ass kicked by that jealous bitch for a month, and it's not getting better!"

His laugh rang out, low and amused. "You think Persephone is jealous? Of you?"

Leah stared at him, heat climbing her cheeks as his laughter ebbed into a chuckle.

"That's ridiculous," he said finally, eyes glinting with dark humor. "Persephone has never been the jealous type. She's harder on you than the rest of us, sure, but jealous? No. Hades worships the ground she walks on."

Leah shook her head, shoulders slumping. "It's the only thing that makes sense. She found out I hugged her husband, and she lost her shit."

That killed his smile. His gaze sharpened, his jaw ticking. Before she could turn away, he caught her arm—not hard, but firm enough to halt her.

"You've grossly misjudged the situation," he said, voice like a blade drawn slow from its sheath.

A chill rippled through her, crawling down her spine. She met his eyes, startled by the sudden steel there.

"Then explain it to me," she demanded softly, defiance threading her words even as her pulse stumbled.

He studied her for a long beat before speaking. "We gods aren't just vessels of power, Leah. We are what we represent. I am not merely a relic of battle—I *am* war. Entirely. It lives in me, as unyielding as stone."

His grip loosened, but his voice only deepened, thrumming with something primal. "You embraced death in its entirety before life had the chance to teach you her lessons. That's why Persephone hates you. She isn't jealous of you." His eyes burned with cold certainty. "She's jealous of him."

Ares released her and turned away without another word, his silhouette cutting sharp against the sunlight as he strode from the arena.

Leah stood frozen, his words reverberating through her skull. Slowly, shame bled into her exhaustion, thick and heavy. He was right. Gods help her, he was right.

Persephone hadn't been trying to destroy her—she'd been trying to reach her. And Leah, blinded by her own assumptions, had missed it all.

She clenched her fists, resolve hardening like tempered steel. Words wouldn't fix this. Only action would.

Without another thought, Leah ran after Ares. She would need his help.

Over the next few months, Leah committed herself to an exhausting routine, training twice a day without fail. At dawn, she began with Persephone, mastering precision and grace under her watchful eye. By dusk, after Persephone retired, she faced the relentless drills of Ares.

Ares demanded she live like a soldier. Leah pitched her tent near the training grounds, a lonely shelter against the harsh elements. Her meals were stripped down to the bare minimum—hard bread and tangy cheese, three times a day. Gone were the comforts of warmth and ease; complaints had no place here. Her world became steel, sweat, and discipline.

But as the days bled into weeks, Leah noticed something unexpected—a softening in Persephone's manner. The sharp edges of her words dulled. The relentless punishment of the early days gave way to a rhythm Leah could almost endure. Slowly, impossibly, she began to keep pace with the Gods.

Ares urged her to push harder, to embrace the warrior within. Persephone, in contrast, spoke of life—how power, when balanced, could shape destinies instead of destroying them. Leah listened, soaking in each word, trying to weave those lessons into the fabric of who she was becoming.

Yet something darker stirred beneath the surface. That familiar tug of power in her chest grew stronger with every session, clawing its way up whenever her temper frayed. Each time, it took longer to shove it down, to keep it chained. She knew this was a battle she could not win forever.

How can I stop this? The question haunted her with every breath.

The breaking point came after a day that felt endless—a blur of grueling drills and merciless blows. Exhaustion weighed on her like lead when Persephone struck again, sweeping Leah's legs out from under her for the third time in an hour. She hit the ground hard, the impact rattling her bones as the breath tore from her lungs.

Again.

Something inside her snapped. Rage surged like wildfire through dry brush. Leah sprang to her feet in one violent motion, charging at Persephone's unguarded back with all the force she could muster.

Steel met steel as Ares intercepted her blade. Persephone spun at the clash of metal, eyes wide.

"It seems we've overlooked something!" Ares bellowed, straining as Leah twisted around him. She drove a fist beneath his ribs with brutal precision, forcing a grunt from his lips.

Then came the storm.

Leah's eyes blazed, twin orbs of light against a backdrop of darkness that swallowed her shape. The air howled as a gale ripped through the arena. Power poured off her in violent bursts—wild, chaotic shockwaves that cracked stone and bent iron. Each pulse was accompanied by her scream of agony as if her very soul were tearing apart.

Ares fought to hold his ground, every surge battering against him like a hammer blow. "Leah!" he roared over the tempest, dodging her feral strikes. "You must listen to me! This power is yours. Stop fighting it—or it will destroy you!"

But Leah couldn't hear him. Pain and fury ruled her now. A fresh convulsion of energy sent Ares tumbling across the floor. Persephone caught him mid-flight with a whip of vines, anchoring them both before the next wave hit.

"We're not leaving her!" she shouted, voice raw over the wind.

"It hurts!" The cry came from the heart of the swirling blackness—a sound so broken it twisted Persephone's chest.

"Please... make it stop!"

The arena floor shuddered. Jagged cracks tore through the ground like veins of ice. Another pulse ripped free, splintering stone beneath their feet.

"She's crushing it down!" Ares yelled, struggling to rise. "If she keeps forcing it back, it'll kill her!"

"I've got her!" Persephone snarled. Roots burst from her wrists and ankles, anchoring her body to the quaking ground. She crawled forward, weaving through debris, her green eyes locked on the flicker of Leah within the darkness.

"Leah!" she called, her voice a lifeline against the chaos. "I'm coming! But you have to breathe, do you hear me? Stop fighting. Let it go. We can take it."

Vines lashed ahead, coiling for stability as Persephone plunged into the storm.

Above, the stands trembled. Hades appeared in a ripple of shadow beside Hera and Hecate, his expression tight.

"Think they can stop her?" Hera asked, twisting her gloves in nervous hands.

Hades grimaced. "If I'm here… then it's close."

Hecate, eyes glittering with hunger, extended her fingers and began drawing the raw magic bleeding into the air. "So much," she whispered, thrilled. "Too much for me to take… but I'll keep what I can."

With a snap, colossal vases materialized across the grandstands. Streams of power funneled into them like rivers of light. Hades and Hera stepped aside as Hecate worked, laughter bubbling at the edges of her lips.

Below, Leah writhed in torment. Her skin split under the pressure, peeling away in strips before regenerating in a grotesque loop of agony. Persephone's heart clenched at the sight. She lunged, seizing Leah's wrist and binding them together with living roots. Pulling the trembling girl against her, Persephone cradled her close, whispering fiercely into her ear.

"You're going to be okay," she murmured, rocking her through the storm.

"You can't hold it in forever," she pressed on, her voice breaking with urgency. "Breathe, Leah. Let it out."

Leah tried. Gods, she tried. But every breath dragged fire through her lungs. Wind screamed around them, and needles of power burst from beneath her skin. The pain was unbearable, yet Persephone's voice anchored her, soft but unyielding.

"Find it," Persephone urged. "Find the source."

Through tears and terror, Leah reached inward. She traced the storm's origin, following the pins and needles from her fingertips, up her arms, to the numbness masking her eyes.

"I... I think I found it," she gasped.

"Good. Give it a path out," Persephone urged. "Draw a line from the source to your hand. Concentrate."

Leah lifted her arm, palm trembling skyward. Power screamed for release as she inhaled deeply, her mind flashing back to a different time—a gentler time.

Adam. The boy who once believed he would never master magic. She remembered the day he nearly gave up, despair carving hollows into his young face. She had knelt beside him then, steady and patient. *Draw the line. Take a deep breath. Let the magic flow as you exhale.* And when he tried again—when that spark of triumph lit his eyes—it had filled her with pride so fierce it burned.

Be brave, she had told him. *Don't back down.*

Now it was her turn.

Leah smiled faintly through the haze, inhaled once more, and unleashed it.

The orb formed instantly—a black sun suspended in air, swelling with lethal promise. Terror clawed at her chest, but Persephone's arms held her fast.

"Now shoot it!" Persephone cried.

Leah obeyed.

The blast ripped across the arena like the wrath of a god. The orb streaked forward, carving a crescent trench through the earth, heat so intense it fused sand into molten glass. It slammed into the far wall with an explosion that birthed a miniature sun.

The shockwave screamed, tearing stone benches from their roots and hurling them into Hades' distant dominion. Somewhere beyond sight, devastation bloomed.

And then—silence.

Leah sagged in Persephone's arms, her strength spent. The goddess held her close as applause rolled through the stands, wild and deafening.

Persephone bent her head, whispering into Leah's tangled hair, voice tender with awe.

"I wish I had the words to tell you how beautiful that was."

Leah tilted her face up weakly, meeting Persephone's radiant smile before glancing back at the chaos she had wrought. Her voice was a rasp.

"You're... not mad?"

Persephone laughed softly, eyes glimmering with pride.

"Gods, no."

"No one in this realm or the next could have created and controlled that much power without leaving a trail of bodies. Except maybe your mother. That young lady was… breathtaking!"

Hera, Hades, and Hecate appeared out of thin air, their faces etched with concern. They circled Leah one by one, checking her over with practiced precision. Hecate murmured an incantation, her fingers tracing glowing sigils over the containment vessels, ensuring no residual magic leaked out. Hera, frowning at the pallor in Leah's cheeks, manifested a soft wool blanket and draped it over her trembling shoulders. Meanwhile, Hades stood silently at her side, eyes dark and calculating, as if weighing her odds of survival in real time.

Ares, however, took his time. He emerged slowly from a dune of sand, only a few feet from the glittering, newly formed sheet of glass. Shaking himself violently like a dog after a bath, grains scattered in every direction. The sight was so absurd that Leah let out an involuntary snort. It was only then the others seemed to notice Ares was still in the arena.

He stalked toward them with a pronounced limp that made Leah wince. His expression was thunderous, his jaw tight with fury. The other gods stiffened as he drew near, and for the first time since the chaos ended, unease curled in Leah's stomach. She caught Hera casting quick, nervous glances between Ares and herself. Leah's mind raced—she couldn't defend herself in this condition if he decided to make good on that murderous glare.

Persephone, silent until now, tightened her grip around Leah's waist, lending her strength as Ares closed the last few feet. Leah's breath hitched when he finally stopped, squatting down to her level with slow, deliberate ease. His molten eyes burned into hers.

"If we ever go to war," he said, voice low and lethal, "I'm on your side."

Relief crashed over her so hard her knees nearly buckled, but before she could respond, the tension shattered. The group erupted in excited chatter, voices tumbling over one another as they gushed about what they'd just witnessed. Hera and Ares each took an arm, guiding Leah gently to her feet. Hecate collected the vessels of unused magic, vanishing in a ripple of black smoke.

Hades swept Persephone into a crushing embrace and kissed her with unrestrained passion. Leah watched, blinking in surprise, as the lord of the dead whispered something against his queen's ear that made her positively glow. Persephone's delighted laugh echoed in the space like chimes. Leah couldn't imagine what could soften the stubborn goddess so completely—and she had no intention of prying—but it gave her a new perspective on the pair.

That night, Leah finally let herself collapse. Hera refused to even consider letting her sleep in a tent after the ordeal she had endured. Persephone and Hades agreed without hesitation, and for the first time in what felt like a lifetime, Leah sank into a proper bed. The straw mattress beneath her felt like heaven itself.

A feast appeared in her room—platters of fruits glazed in honey, roasted meats fragrant with herbs, warm loaves of bread that steamed when torn open. She tried to sample everything, but there was too much, and her body ached with exhaustion. Eventually, she shooed the attendants away with a sheepish apology about her "poor constitution." Eight uninterrupted hours of sleep later, she woke before dawn feeling lighter than she had in ages.

Padding softly into the kitchen, Leah stopped short at the sight before her. Persephone stood at the wide wooden counter, elbows dusted in flour, her dark hair braided loosely down her back as she kneaded dough with firm, rhythmic motions. The scent of yeast and ripening fruit perfumed the air.

"Oh! Good morning!" Persephone exclaimed, startled by Leah's sudden appearance. She flashed a smile over her shoulder before returning to her task, deftly tossing a ball of dough from palm to palm in a smooth circle.

"How are you feeling?" she asked casually, though her tone held a trace of concern.

"I feel… pretty good," Leah admitted, sliding into a chair. "Lighter somehow."

"Ah." Persephone nodded knowingly, her hands never still. "That would be the release of pent-up magic. Normally, when magic isn't used regularly, it seeps out in tiny, harmless ways. But you…" She slammed the dough against the table with a sharp crack, rolling it out beneath her palms before lifting and slapping it down again. "Something has been holding yours back for a long time. Now that you're no longer chained to a mortal body, that power's breaking loose in chunks—like a clogged artery finally bursting free."

Leah blinked, absorbing the analogy as Persephone rolled the dough into a perfect sphere and dropped it into a wooden bowl to rise.

"The good news?" Persephone grinned. "The hardest part is over."

"We did?" Leah tilted her head, confusion knitting her brow.

"Of course! You broke through your fear yesterday." Persephone shrugged as if it were obvious, punctuating the statement with another emphatic thud of dough.

"Starting tomorrow, you'll begin training with Hecate. She understands raw magic better than I do. You're still welcome to join me in the stadium, but trust me—" She brushed flour from her fingers with a satisfied sigh. "You're well on your way to being strong enough for what's coming."

Leah hesitated, her stomach twisting. "About that… what exactly does 'what's coming' mean?" She tucked a loose strand of hair behind her ear, watching as Persephone's hands stilled mid-motion.

"No one told you?" The goddess stared at her, dumbstruck.

"Nope." Leah popped the 'p,' brows lifting.

Persephone muttered something under her breath—something sharp and colorful—and dropped heavily into the chair beside Leah. For a long moment, she just sat there, massaging her temples.

"Those assholes," she hissed finally. "I thought someone had explained… Ugh. Fine. I'll tell you."

Leah braced herself.

"There's a war coming," Persephone began quietly. "We—the new gods—have been tasked with stopping it. But here's the problem: we can't break through to the mortal plane alone. We're strong, but not that strong. We need help. We need a mother."

Leah's pulse spiked. "A mother?"

"Yes." Persephone's gaze locked onto hers. "You were supposed to meet her first. We were going to offer you a deal then. But when Hecate lost her mind and sealed the tunnel… well, that never happened."

Leah leaned back, the wooden chair creaking under her weight. Her eyes roamed the room, tracing the gentle curves of the river-stone walls, the hanging herbs swaying in the kitchen breeze like green whispers. Anything to steady herself.

"We have enough power to send one person to the physical world," Persephone continued, voice tightening. "Since your body is still alive, we believe we can reverse the ceremony that brought you here. But in return…" She exhaled slowly. "We'd need you to give five of us physical forms."

Leah stared at her, words caught in her throat. It took several heartbeats before she managed, "Would we win?"

Persephone nodded slowly—but her silence after that made Leah's skin prickle.

"There's a catch," the goddess said at last.

"There always is." Leah gestured for her to go on.

"Hades would be the key to victory. But…" Persephone's voice softened, a tremor curling through it. "You cannot give life to Death without taking a life in return."

The silence that followed was suffocating.

Finally, Leah blew out a shaky breath. "Okay… one question." Her gaze drifted over the kitchen again—the woven baskets, the clay jars, the greenery spilling from every corner—before landing on a peculiar sight.

"What's with all the mint?"

Chapter Ten

Seven Centuries Later

The clang of metal rang through the village, sharp and rhythmic, mingling with the tang of sweat and the earthy scent of trampled dirt. Each strike echoed like a drumbeat of endurance as Alec pushed Adam to his limits, testing everything the boy had absorbed over the centuries of hard-earned lessons.

Alec had volunteered for nearly every recruiting mission since their exile, throwing himself into the fray until Catherine herself had chastised him for abandoning Ryanne during her darkest days. She was right, of course, but Alec couldn't deny the truth—he needed the distraction. The weight of stillness was too heavy to bear.

In his rare moments of downtime, he had even begun building them a home beyond the ragged sprawl of tents they now called a village. To him, it was a gesture of permanence, a promise. To Ryanne, it was surrender. She had refused outright, claiming the construction was an admission that they would never return to the Morro. Deep down, Alec knew she was right. Without Lydia, without Leah, what reason did they have to go back?

Adam lunged, seizing on Alec's wandering thoughts. His effort was bold—but sluggish. Alec pivoted smoothly, spinning out of reach, and with a quick flick of the wrist, slapped the boy's backside with the flat of his blade.

Adam stumbled forward, arms flailing, before crashing face-first into the dirt with a resounding *"Harrumph!"* A puff of dust billowed around him, clinging to his hair and lashes.

"Dammit! I had you!" he bellowed into the ground, earning laughter from a handful of onlookers as he pushed himself up, cheeks flushed with embarrassment.

"No," Alec corrected, his voice calm but firm. "You *thought* you had me. But you're still too slow—and you forgot your balance."

Planting his boots in the earth, Alec demonstrated the proper stance, adjusting his shoulders and shifting his weight with deliberate precision. Adam mirrored the pose, awkward at first, until Alec circled him like a hawk and made several minor corrections.

Finally, Adam managed to execute the lunge correctly. Alec gave a satisfied nod.

"Fifty times. Every day. Until it feels like breathing," he instructed before leaving the boy to his drills.

He paused at the river on the way home, kneeling to wash the grime from his clothes and the sweat from his brow. The cold water bit into his skin, but it cleared his thoughts. He lingered there longer than necessary before heading back to Ryanne. It wouldn't be long before she demanded her own space in the village—a thought Alec wasn't sure he was ready to accept.

A sharp knock on the tent's wooden frame broke through his reverie. Alec kissed Ryanne's forehead gently before slipping out and pulling the flap closed behind him.

Marcus stood waiting, pale and drawn, his eyes darting anywhere but Alec's face.

"Sorry to bother you," Marcus began, his voice low and strained. "We've got another mission coming up. The elders want to know if you're going…"

Alec's gut tightened. Marcus hadn't met his gaze since the raid. Part of Alec wondered if he preferred it that way.

"When?" Alec asked, keeping his tone quiet so as not to wake Ryanne. She had barely slept these past weeks, and he feared that if the pattern continued, sickness would follow.

"Day after tomorrow."

Ryanne would rage at the news. He had no idea how to soothe her anymore. The villagers could offer their help—he could not.

"I'll ask Catherine to watch her while we're gone," Alec said at last. "We'll talk details in the morning."

Marcus nodded but didn't move. His silence stretched between them like a taut rope until finally, his eyes lifted.

"How is she?"

Alec exhaled slowly, dragging a hand down his face.

"As good as can be expected," he admitted. "Truth is…I don't know. She barely speaks to me anymore."

Marcus shifted, his expression softening. "I was the same when I lost my mother. Shut everyone out. It was hell, but Da' and I got through it. She'll come around, Alec. Just be patient. Keep trying."

The words landed heavier than Alec expected. He'd always known Marcus had lost his mother, but it had never occurred to him that Marcus might understand Ryanne's grief better than anyone.

"Thank you," Alec said quietly, clapping Marcus on the shoulder.

Marcus gave a noncommittal shrug, his gaze sinking back to the ground before he mumbled something about rabbit stew and shuffled away.

The next day came too quickly. Alec absorbed the mission details, packed his saddlebag, and sent word to Catherine about his departure— half-dreading her response. The last time she'd seen him, she'd flayed him alive for neglecting Ryanne. And now, he was leaving again.

Breaking the news to his daughter had been worse.

"It's only for a few days," he promised softly. "Nothing dangerous. I'll be back before you know it."

Ryanne stared past him, her exhaustion dimming the fire in her eyes.

"Fine. Go."

It was all the fight she had left. Maybe space would help. Lydia had been the same after a quarrel—silent walls that no words could breach. Ryanne had inherited that same stubborn streak.

A couple of days won't break us, Alec told himself as he strapped the saddlebag to his horse and mounted up with the small troop. He rode away with a sense of relief blooming in his chest, the first he'd felt in weeks.

The rhythm of hooves and the camaraderie of his brothers-in-arms washed his burdens clean—for a little while.

***

Layla's band rode hard for Altrious, the last of the great strongholds to bend its knee to Lux. Perched on the windswept edge of the Northwestern Morro, the kingdom was rumored to glisten with riches beyond imagining, its wealth a stark contrast to its remote isolation.

Twelve capitals had been called to pledge allegiance. Nine had bowed. Three had bled. The first kingdoms Lux conquered were broken by fire and giants, their villages crushed and their treasuries stripped bare before their rulers fell to their knees.

Altrious would not fall so easily—or so the whispers claimed.

Lux's patience was fraying. Time was a noose tightening around Layla's throat. She and her priests would have to ride without rest, storming through five capitals in three days just to meet his deadline.

Every neighboring realm had learned the truth: resist and die. Submit and live.

***

The pounding rhythm of Joel's horse jarred his bones and churned his stomach. They had been at full gallop for half the morning, the wind clawing at his cloak as the animal strained beneath him. Foam flecked the mare's bay coat, her sweat slicking the leather saddle, yet she thundered onward without complaint.

That was what Joel loved most about horses—no quit in them. They would run until their hearts gave out, trusting their rider to know when to stop. That kind of loyalty deserved reverence. It was the kind of trust he wished Layla would one day place in him.

He caught her silhouette ahead, a dark banner whipping in the wind, and lifted a hand in signal. A stable lay just beyond the ridge. They had to stop. His mare's stride had grown uneven, her breath a ragged rasp that clouded the chill October air like smoke.

Joel reined her in, easing her into a walk. She had been his for weeks now, a steadfast companion on their relentless march to bind Lux's will across the land. The thought of trading her for a fresh mount made his chest tighten, but he would not see her suffer.

Provided the stable had enough horses, he would make the exchange.

They had been granted an extra two weeks after Ashur's impulsive kidnapping, but even with that mercy, the clock was still ticking. And time—time was a blade.

"We need to keep going," Layla panted as she slid from the back of her chocolate-brown stallion. Her boots sank slightly into the packed dirt as she reached up, fingers brushing along the white blaze that streaked down his forehead, soft against the coarse hair of his forelock.

"Thank you, my friend," she murmured, pressing a kiss to his velvety snout. The stallion answered with a short whinny, pawing the ground as if to acknowledge her gratitude. Smiling faintly, she patted the breadth of his cheek, lingering for a heartbeat before leading him to a waiting stable hand.

"Fresh horses for the group," she instructed, slipping the boy a neat stack of coins.

Behind her, Joel gave his mare one last affectionate stroke, his hand gliding down the elegant curve of her neck.

"Sorry, girl. This is where I leave you," he whispered. With a soft pat, he swung down and strode toward the tavern, the weight of their task pulling at his shoulders.

Inside, the air turned heavy and foul. Joel claimed an empty table, lowering himself onto the splintered bench as his eyes roved over the surroundings.

The tavern was, at best, decrepit—a place where time had not just lingered but rotted everything it touched. Thick, age-blackened beams groaned overhead, petrified and hollowed by years of neglect. The crossbeams looked brittle enough to give way at any moment. The few windows scattered along the walls were pathetically small, almost mean in their design, allowing in neither light nor relief from the suffocating stench.

Joel's nose wrinkled at the mix of vomit, sour ale, and human filth that clung to every inch of the space. He would have wagered—more than a shilling—that the floorboards sat directly on bare dirt, and no broom had touched them in years. If this was gambling, it was the kind worth taking.

How the owners managed to keep the room dimly lit was a mystery. Candles, flickering and stubby, burned low in their wax puddles, casting warped shadows that stretched like claws across the warped tables. Joel imagined there must be a cellar beneath this place—though if there was, it reeked as badly as the tavern above.

His thoughts were interrupted by the approach of the tavern keep. The man was short and thick through the middle, a bloated figure whose weight likely topped two hundred pounds. His beady eyes glittered beneath the oily sheen of his forehead, and his snaggle-toothed grin spoke of illicit dealings—services offered for the right price.

The stench that rolled off him was enough to kill Joel's appetite outright. It was a cloying mixture of rot and decay, and when the man opened his mouth, Joel swore he could smell infection in his breath.

The tavern keep set three bulging sacks on the table with a grunt, each landing with a dull thud. Grease smeared across the coarse fabric where his hands had gripped them, leaving behind prints that looked like stains from something long dead.

"I'll be back with the rest," the man rasped, teeth flashing yellow as his foul breath spilled into the air.

Joel didn't respond. His stomach had turned too sour for words, and instead, his gaze lingered on those greasy marks as a new thought struck him—if whatever plagued this man was contagious.

"I don't believe those bite."

The voice pulled him back to the present. He turned, startled, and met the amused gaze of Layla. Heat pricked his neck as he realized how long he'd been staring at the sacks like a man sizing up a beast.

"At least… that's what I've heard." Her dark brows dipped briefly as her expression shifted to one of mild suspicion, as if she was considering the possibility that these odd burlap lumps could, in fact, bite.

Layla's ignorance of common things in The Morro had become glaringly obvious in the short time they'd been among its people. For all her power, for all the centuries she had lived, she was often more like an inquisitive child than the deadly sorceress Joel knew her to be.

Just that morning, she'd tried to drink tea from a lantern, charmed by its glasswork. Joel had barely intervened before disaster—and had been forced to stop her again when she nearly decapitated a glassmaker for selling what she considered "defective wares."

She was chaos wrapped in grace, his Layla. And for all the headaches, she was still something to behold.

A faint shake of her head broke her inner debate. She slid the gloves from her hands with deliberate care, each movement as elegant as a court dance, and took the chair Joel had pulled out for her. A small smile ghosted her lips as she settled in.

"Either way," she said lightly, "I think you can manage them."

Joel smirked, leaning back in his seat. "I certainly hope so. I don't think I'd be much good to you if I couldn't defend you from a few sacks of supplies."

"No. You wouldn't, would you…" Her voice drifted off, the weight of that truth lingering in the air.

"Damn." The word slipped out as a thought rather than an answer. For a fleeting moment, she considered what use he could possibly be if such a simple task bested him. And yet… she liked this one. Her gaze lifted, catching the curl of his smile—the faintest quirk at the corner of his mouth. Those sinfully hazel eyes glittered with humor, teasing her without a word.

Scrunching her nose, she swatted at him with her gloves. "You brat!"

He dodged easily, laughter warm and low, before sliding into the chair across from her. Layla tried—truly tried—not to fidget under the weight of that look, but it was like being set ablaze from the inside out.

He was fire, and she'd been warned never to play with matches. Yet here she was, yearning for the burn.

If he kept looking at her like that, she was going to melt. Desperate for distraction, she pressed a hand to her brow, peeking at him from between her fingers as she asked, "What are those fire-stick-thingies called again?"

Joel's grin widened. "You mean candles?"

"No, no—the other ones! The sticks with the red thing on top. You know, the ones you can't put too close to the lantern or it goes… boom." She mimed an explosion with her hands, and Joel's composure shattered.

Laughter tore from him so hard and sudden that his chair nearly toppled. Within seconds, he was bent double, choking on his mirth, color flooding his cheeks until it deepened to purple. Layla stared in disbelief.

"Pick a side, Joel—get up or die. You can't do both! It's not that damn funny!"

But it was. Gods, it was to him.

When he finally managed to pull himself off the floor and collapse back into his chair, tears streaked his face, and his grin was so bright it hurt to look at. His laughter was still trembling through him when the priests came in, fresh from the stables, their heavy boots echoing on the warped planks.

Joel's attempt to explain only reignited his hysteria, and soon the men were laughing too, their deep chuckles rumbling like drums. Layla could only roll her eyes as they reenacted her innocent gestures with exaggerated flair.

And yet… something inside her softened. She hadn't felt this in so long—not laughter, not warmth, not this strange, fragile thing her father once called a *bonding moment.* She hadn't understood it then. She did now. And she clung to it like breath.

"Holy Gods, she does smile…"

The words shattered the quiet joy blooming in her chest. Layla's smile slipped as her gaze snapped to the speaker—Christian.

"And it's gone," he muttered in mock lament, earning a sharp swat from the towering man beside him.

"Ouch! What was that for?" Christian whined, rubbing his head.

"Apologize," Micha said flatly, his scarred face brooking no argument.

Christian opened his mouth to protest, but Micha's look cut him short. It reminded Layla of her father—that same silent, unyielding authority. She remembered a day long ago when she had unknowingly insulted a foreign emissary in her father's throne room. The man had worn a sweeping gown of greens, golds, and browns patterned like a jungle cat. Intrigued by what she assumed was a daring new trend, she'd asked brightly where he had purchased his *dress.*

Her father's glare had been the same as Micha's now.

Christian, like that emissary, wilted beneath it. He mumbled, "Sorry. Didn't mean to offend," his face folding into an exaggerated pout.

Layla's sternness cracked just a little. Gods help her, but he was almost… adorable.

She inclined her head in cool acceptance and rose to her feet, unwilling to expose any further emotion. The men scrambled to follow, all gallant deference. Chivalry, she was beginning to learn, was oddly convenient.

"I think I'll go find the tavern keep," she announced, smoothing her skirts. "See what's keeping our supplies."

She slipped away before anyone could argue, catching Micha's dry murmur—"Now you've done it…"—followed by the familiar thwack of brotherly discipline.

***

A short meal later, their mismatched band was back on the road, driving hard toward Altrious. For five relentless days, they pushed through dust and wind, Layla's urgency spurring them long past dusk. When the city's towers finally rose from the gloom, night had settled thick and black around them.

They arrived well past the hour of courtesy—an offense she knew she would pay for if matters weren't resolved quickly. The neighboring kingdoms had folded with barely a whisper, giving her just enough time to dispatch a note to Ashur declaring their success.

But the cost of delay would come due soon, and Layla was no fool.

The palace gates groaned open, and guards led them through echoing halls to a grand study at the heart of the keep. Her claim of royal blood had stripped away most of the waiting, but the king's temper was far from soothed.

Layla felt the weight of it in the air as she shoved the doors wide.

"Well, you haven't changed a bit, have you, darling!"

A curvaceous, red-haired servant stood frozen in the doorway, clad in an almost sheer nightgown that clung to her from the remnants of recent activity. She had clearly been caught off guard, hastily tugging at the thin fabric in a desperate attempt to appear somewhat decent. Her movements were tense, each gesture betraying her mortification as she tried to retreat into the narrow shadows cast by the oil lamp.

Her face burned a deeper shade of crimson with every passing second, her humiliation mounting under the weight of seven pairs of wide, unblinking eyes. At last, mercy came when she was dismissed and hurriedly ushered out by the gawking onlookers.

The king remained silent, his expression impassive as he listened to the fading shuffle of boots and whispers retreating down the hall. Only when the latch clicked firmly into place did he release a long breath.

Moving toward the sideboard, he reached for his crystal decanter, the amber liquid within catching the flicker of lamplight. Pouring himself a generous measure of scotch, he took the glass in hand, slammed the drink back with practiced ease, and poured another without hesitation.

"Why are you here, Layla?" His voice was low, tinged with exhaustion. "I thought our business ended after the war."

He raised the decanter in silent offering. Layla stepped deeper into the room, her heels clicking softly on the polished floor, and accepted the glass.

"It was," she replied simply, before taking a sip.

Her tone held a quiet resolve, though her presence carried an air of unease. "I know this isn't what you wanted to hear," she continued after a pause. "But I don't have a choice. I've been ordered to recruit allegiance for the risen Goddess Lux."

The weight of her words hung in the air, heavy and unreal.

"She's demanding the neighboring rulers attend a banquet within the month. They're to bend the knee… and bring tribute, of course."

Layla raised her glass in a mock toast, offering a wry smile with her curtsey, a gesture dripping with irony.

***

Alec's official stance was that the reception at Altrious had been anything but expected.

When their small riding party arrived at the gates of the summer palace, they were met with grandeur—and then humiliation. A short, flustered butler, all pomp and propriety, loudly demanded they leave the front approach at once. Minutes later, the same man hustled them through a narrow servants' passage, ushering them like contraband through dim back corridors.

Alec, leading the group in silence, couldn't shake the sense that they weren't nearly as welcome as the elders had promised. The butler offered no explanation, only ushered them through winding halls and servant stairwells until they were crammed into a tiny antechamber, the door closing sharply behind them.

"Roberts… that better be your sword in my back," Marcus muttered, breaking the oppressive silence. The remark sparked a ripple of laughter among the men, their unease spilling into rough humor.

Marcus pressed his ear to the door, shoulders hunched as the rest shifted impatiently in the cramped space.

"He's coming," Marcus hissed.

The door creaked open, and there stood the butler again, parchment in one hand, a heavy leather-bound book in the other.

"Take these." His voice was clipped, formal, betraying no emotion. "The king has heard your request, and this is all the aid he can safely provide. He wishes you well in your endeavors."

He handed the book and sealed scroll to Marcus, then met each man's gaze in turn. When his eyes locked with Alec's, they softened, just for a heartbeat, before clouding again.

"Should you require anything further… we cannot help you."

A single tear glimmered at the butler's eye as he turned away. Leading them swiftly back through the palace, he paused only long enough to clasp Alec in a brief, firm embrace before sending them into the night.

***

Marcus was the first to break the silence.

"What the hell, man? Three days on the road, and we don't even see the guy we came here for? And you're not even pissed? You hugged the guy who locked us in a closet!"

The raw edge in his voice mirrored the disbelief on every face in the group.

Alec exhaled slowly. "That man we came to see is Lydia's father," he said, his voice hollow. "And he hates me."

The words landed heavy in the cold night air.

What they had received tonight—cryptic as it was—was a gift, a final gesture wrung from grief. Lydia's father had given them all he could without betraying his crown.

Alec's thoughts wandered back to the day Lydia left for war. Her father, a scholar as much as a king, had expected his daughter to follow his path—quiet diplomacy, the safety of courtly walls. But Lydia had chosen the battlefield, alongside Leah.

Her father's fury had been legendary. He stormed her first battalion, shouting before the ranks, trying to drag her home by force. The whispers had been merciless. Alec had stepped in, shielding her from the humiliation, silencing the laughter that lingered long after. That moment had changed everything—for her, for him. His life had been brighter ever since.

And now she was gone. Both men bore the weight of that loss like iron chains.

The scroll and book were not tokens of courtesy—they were all he could spare without dooming his throne.

Alec stared down at the book in Marcus's hands. Its title glinted in the moonlight.

The Sword in the Stone.

Alec barked out a bitter laugh. "The man's lost his mind."

The men crowded around, puzzled.

"Care to explain?" one asked.

Alec sighed and began walking, the group falling in behind him.

"The story goes like this," he said, voice low, half amused, half resigned. "A long time ago—when the universe first breathed life into itself—two beings were born. One of light, one of darkness. Perfect opposites.

The being of light grew bored and created life. Creatures of every kind. The other, bound by balance, answered with death and the shadows cast by those creatures.

Light fell in love with a mortal. Darkness, bound by law, was dragged into balance again—forced into a union neither wanted.

Light wanted to gift their beloved immortality, but Darkness demanded a failsafe—a way to end them if eternity drove them mad. So together, they forged a weapon. A blade to strip an Initial from existence.

They hid it where no mortal could find it and created a guardian beast to ensure none unworthy could wield it.

No one's ever seen the sword. Most believe it's just a myth."

Alec shrugged as they reached camp, tossing his sword down beside the dead fire.

Adam broke the silence first. "What if it's not?"

Alec turned sharply. "Of course it is. You'd have to be insane to believe that fairy tale."

Adam's reply was quick, biting. "You mean the same kind of insane where we all believed a princess would come back from the moon to drink with us before heading back to her shiny cage in the sky?"

A ripple of laughter broke the tension. Alec smirked despite himself.

"My father-in-law's been chasing this story for centuries," Alec muttered. "Millennia, maybe. The man's obsessed."

Adam held his ground. "Maybe so. But he's a king. He can't be completely mad. And in a world full of magic, why write anything off as impossible?"

The murmurs of agreement sealed it. Alec sighed in defeat.

"Fine," he said, rubbing his temples. "But if we find nothing…" His grin cut through his fatigue. "Adam owes me a drink."

The men chuckled as they scattered to their duties. Marcus clapped Alec on the shoulder with a grin. Adam beamed with pride, though Alec gave him a stern look.

"Don't let it swell your head," Alec warned. "You've earned respect tonight—but you've still got a lot to learn. Leaders don't have the luxury of staying quiet, but they also don't skip chores."

"Yes, sir," Adam said quickly, already reaching for the herb satchel.

***

Back at the palace, Layla turned as the butler reentered the study. His expression was grim.

"I apologize, Your Majesty, but this is urgent." His eyes flicked toward Layla, distrust plain in his gaze, before he leaned in to whisper feverishly in the king's ear.

For a fleeting second, the king's mask cracked—panic flashing in his eyes—before the steel returned.

"You'll find the items under my desk in the study," he said calmly, slipping a chain from his neck and pressing a key into the butler's palm.

"Ensure that I am not disturbed again."

The butler bowed deeply before vanishing into the shadows.

"Yes, Your Majesty," he said before leaving the room.

Layla watched the man's retreat, noting the deliberate slowness of his steps and the feigned boredom etched across his face. Through the open doorway, her gaze caught Christian's. A subtle flick of her eyes, sharp as a blade, commanded him to follow. The butler's polished shoes disappeared down the corridor, and the heavy doors closed with a muted thud behind him.

The remainder of the evening unfolded in layers of false pleasantries and hollow laughter. Layla played her part flawlessly, masking every shred of suspicion behind a veneer of charm. She allowed the king of Altrious to revel in his imagined triumph, giving him enough space to believe he had outwitted her. When the last toast had been made and the fire in the great hall had burned low, she gathered her men under the guise of exhaustion and excused herself.

Though the king had graciously offered them quarters in the castle, Layla declined with polite insistence. Better to disappear before dawn's first light—before he realized two of her men were unaccounted for.

They regrouped at a modest tavern tucked on the outskirts of the city. The room smelled of stale ale and old wood, but it was safe. Joel had already sprawled across her bed, boots kicked off and mouth slack as a soft snore escaped him.

Layla sat at the desk by the single window, pen scratching across parchment as she drafted her final report for Ashur before their return. The candle flickered, shadows dancing across the walls when a faint knock sounded at the door.

She froze. Rising slowly, the exhaustion in her limbs clung like chains. Her fingers slipped into the slit of her nightdress, curling around the hilt of a blade hidden there. Quiet as a whisper, she moved to the door and cracked it open an inch.

Micha stood on the other side, hood drawn low over his brow. His voice was barely audible.

"The butler passed off a scroll to a small group of men outside the city," he murmured. "We believe they're survivors from the Moro."

"And the scroll?" Layla's tone was measured, her words a thread of sound in the stillness. She cast a glance over her shoulder; Joel remained undisturbed, chest rising and falling in steady rhythm.

"They were careful. No talk of plans in the open. But…" Micha hesitated, his jaw tightening. "The fact that survivors are seeking Altrious' aid? That alone calls for investigation."

Layla gave a curt nod. "Go. Take Christian. Report back with anything you find."

As Micha slipped away, the door closed softly, and Layla lingered in the quiet. Eyes and ears within enemy territory—she would need both.

***

Later that night, Alec turned the scroll over in his hands. At first glance, it looked like simple sheathing, but as his fingers traced its rough texture, he realized it was no ordinary parchment. It was animal hide, worn and scarred from age. The fur clinging to its edges had been rubbed nearly bare, like some relic from an age that refused to die.

For a moment, he considered taking it to Leah—then the thought twisted into bitter resignation. Leah and Lydia were gone. Likely forever. The weight of that truth never loosened its grip on him.

Which one had he loved more? He could never say. Leah had carved her place in his life early, shaping it like a blade on whetstone. And now, there was nothing but absence and regret.

Forcing himself out of that spiral, Alec unrolled the scroll. His eyes narrowed. A map. Crude, yet deliberate. If his oath meant anything— mad though it seemed—he would follow this path come first light. Assuming the sword even existed.

They would need provisions, but the route would take them past the village site. That, at least, was a stroke of fortune.

Alec scrawled a message for Ryanne and sent it with a courier. *Don't worry,* he wrote, though worry gnawed at him all the same. The girl was strong, yes, but softer than she realized. And Adam…

Adam was her weakness, though she would deny it until her last breath. She was far too much like her father. Alec smirked at the thought as he stepped out of his tent. The night air wrapped around him in a chill embrace, sharp with the scent of smoke and pine. Perhaps he should speak to Adam directly. The image of the boy squirming under his scrutiny amused him.

And if Adam disappointed him? Well, that would be a shame. Alec rather liked the lad. Killing him would put a damper on things.

The savory tang of game stew pulled him from darker thoughts. The men clustered around the fire, their laughter mingling with the crackle of flames. Alec wove through the throng, ladled himself a generous bowl, and settled among the circle.

Marcus caught his eye, then jerked his chin toward the shadows where Adam sat hunched over a chaos of scrolls. Marcus threw up his hands in silent defeat. Alec chuckled, filled another bowl, and strode toward the boy.

Adam was so buried in his work he didn't notice Alec until the bowl landed on the makeshift table. Startled, the boy flailed, sending parchment and ink scattering like startled birds. He toppled backward with an undignified thud.

"That is not the reaction I'd hope for from a future son-in-law," Alec said dryly.

Adam froze, eyes wide, his face draining white before flushing crimson. "I… we aren't—"

"I'm teasing, lad," Alec cut in with a laugh.

The commotion drew chuckles from the men, though they soon returned to their stew. Adam scrambled upright, still flustered. Alec dropped onto a cool stone near the log.

"I know you two wouldn't keep something that important a secret," Alec added with a grin.

"No," Adam muttered, sinking back down. Suspicion flickered in his eyes. "Besides… I'm pretty sure she doesn't like me anyway." The words carried a note of sadness, but before Alec could speak, Adam seized on a distraction.

"I found something you should see." He thrust a parchment into Alec's hands, then reached for the stew, shoveling it down with ravenous speed.

"Oh gods," Adam groaned between mouthfuls. "I didn't realize how hungry I was. Is there more?"

"Help yourself. Then you can tell me about this." Alec gestured to the scattered papers. Adam nearly sprinted toward the pot, drawing laughter and taunts from the men.

Alec watched him with quiet pride. Adam had grown—not just a boy of the village, but a warrior in his own right.

***

Joel woke in a cold sweat.

The images clung like chains: Layla's body arching in agony, her screams slicing through the roar of fire. He stood again beneath the towering columns of Ashur's temple, the marble gleaming white under the unnatural blue glow. Below, the Moro burned—a sea of flame and ruin. Giants stalked through the inferno, crushing soldiers like insects as they surged toward the sanctum.

Layla knelt before the god, a rusted sword trembling in her hands. Joel tried to hear the words, but the sound warped, muffled as though his head were underwater.

Then Ashur laughed.

Joel's breath seized as the god plunged the sword into Layla's stomach. Her body jerked violently, blood spilling as Ashur pulled her close, lips grazing her ear in a whisper Joel could not hear.

He tried to run, to reach her. His feet refused to move.

Blue fire erupted across the marble floor, encircling her fallen form. Layla writhed, choking on her own blood, her screams piercing the temple's vaulted silence. The sound ripped through Joel's soul.

And then—blackness.

Joel shot upright, trembling. The room was quiet, the only sound Layla's soft breathing beside him. His hand reached blindly, finding her warm body curled on the edge of the bed. She grunted as he pulled her close, her hair brushing his lips. He kissed her gently, burying his face in her scent, but the echoes of her death still clawed at him.

After seven centuries together, he could not imagine a world without her.

***

Morning came.

The company rode at a steady pace, the chill air crisp with the scent of wet earth. Joel rode in silence, his jaw set, his eyes distant. It did not go unnoticed.

Layla urged her mare forward until she was alongside him. "Joel!" she called, voice bright.

He turned, forcing a smile. "Yes, my lady."

That stung. He only used her name when his mood was light. *My lady* meant something was wrong.

"So, that's how it's going to be today?" Her brow arched in mock reproach.

"What's that supposed to mean?" His tone was sharper than intended, and he caught himself, wincing. "Ah. I hear it now. Sorry."

He looked at her then, really looked—at the overcloak tossed carelessly behind her shoulders, the thick black braid gleaming like silk in the morning sun, freckles dusting her high cheekbones. A smudge of dirt streaked her flawless skin, and her lips—soft, full, and pink—curved into a patient line.

"What's bothering you?" she asked.

He hesitated. The nightmares. The unease gnawing at him like rot. But she bore the weight of the war council on her shoulders. Did she need his fears added to hers?

He wasn't sure.

"It's nothing of concern," he lied smoothly, forcing his tone to remain casual. Joel's fingers reached for her braid, idly twisting the thick rope of hair between them as the two rode in silence. He felt her eyes lingering on him—searching, questioning—and silently prayed she wouldn't press the matter.

"I like your hair like this," he said finally, the words meant as an easy distraction from the guilt gnawing at his chest.

Layla glanced down with a soft smile tugging at her lips.

"Ah yes, the maid insisted this was the best way to travel. I figured it couldn't be worse than the rat's nest I arrived with." A faint blush colored her cheeks, blooming delicately against her skin.

Joel grinned, lifting the braid and brushing it against his face. With a mischievous growl, he pretended to take a bite.

"Gross!" Layla squealed, swatting at his chest in mock outrage.

Laughing, Joel released the braid and pulled a face, tongue out dramatically as if purging the taste.

"You're right—it tastes like soap."

Layla's laughter spilled into the cool morning air, bright and unrestrained.

"Serves you right," she teased, eyes sparkling.

Joel's own brown hair bounced lightly with his chuckle, his mulberry-colored eyes glowing with a warmth that made Layla's heart flutter unexpectedly. His jaw flexed as he held her gaze; the whiskers shading his face caught the light, revealing a strange reddish glint that made his eyes burn even brighter.

Something about his stare felt different today—charged somehow—and Layla's body reacted before her mind could make sense of it. A tingling warmth spread through her limbs, awakening something deep and unspoken, as though anticipating the brush of his hands. Her gaze traced the scar along his cheek, nearly hidden beneath the stubble, and she reached out instinctively.

Before her fingers could graze the mark, Joel leaned into her touch, nuzzling her hand gently. The intimacy in that simple act startled her—it was tender, unexpected—but she didn't pull away. It was nice, she thought, having someone to share these days with.

"Ahhh! How cute!"

The voice shattered the quiet like a blade slicing silk. Layla and Joel jerked in surprise, their horses dancing nervously to an abrupt halt in the middle of the dirt road.

From the opposite direction, Lux approached. Layla's scowl flashed like lightning before she schooled her expression into something flat and polite.

Lux's gown—or what little could be called a gown—was a whisper of deep violet fabric clinging to her like water. The breeze teased it mercilessly, revealing the full silhouette of her naked form beneath. From behind her came low murmurs of lust from her entourage of men—murmurs that died instantly when Layla's sharp glance swept back like a blade.

The midmorning sun sat behind Lux, casting her figure in a radiant halo, making the sheer fabric nearly disappear against her skin.

Joel reacted first. Steering his horse away from Layla, he urged his mount toward the Goddess with deliberate haste.

"Your Benevolence! What a pleasant surprise! We were just returning to the temple to pay homage to the Lady of Light."

Sliding down from his saddle, Joel offered her his horse with a reverent bow.

"You are too kind," Lux purred, her lips curving as Joel dropped to one knee and guided her upward. She swung gracefully into the saddle with an elegance that was almost painful to watch.

Her gaze flicked lazily toward Layla.

"I can see why you enjoy this one," she said, smiling down at Joel like a buyer appraising prime livestock. "He is quite fetching."

Turning the horse, she trotted a few steps back toward her followers, her eyes sweeping the men over Layla's shoulder like one choosing the ripest fruit.

"How may I assist you this morning, Your Divinity?" Layla's voice was carefully stripped of all emotion. She had learned early that Lux was dangerous beyond reason—a creature who could slaughter an entire company without so much as wrinkling her smile.

"You're late, darling," Lux said lightly, circling Layla's mare like a predator. "I came to check on my favorite niece. The least I could do, since you so generously donated your body to me."

The words fell sharp and poisonous, disguised as silk.

"I was worried about you."

Lux's fingers plucked at Layla's braid, lifting it as if inspecting an inferior trinket before letting it fall. Her gaze cut toward Joel with naked distaste.

"Men can be so disgusting," she muttered.

The remark stung, though Layla couldn't explain why. Straightening her spine, she forced her voice to steady calm.

"I appreciate the concern, Your Grace. However, this band has my utmost confidence. They've proven themselves competent time and again."

Lux tilted her head, amusement glinting in her eyes.

"Oh, really?"

"Yes," Layla replied, lips curving faintly. Pride swelled in her chest for the men who had stood by her without question, their loyalty unbroken even against the impossible. For them, she would fight—against anyone, even Lux.

Joel stepped close to Layla's mare, fingers brushing her cheek softly. Lux's eyes lingered on the gesture, narrowing slightly.

"Well," she said at last, "I suppose that settles it."

And then, without warning, Lux dismounted. With a casual snap of her fingers, the world erupted.

Blood, bone, and shredded flesh rained down in a grotesque torrent. Horses screamed and vanished in sprays of gore. Layla flinched but did not cry out, shoulders tightening as she tried to shield herself from the chunks of meat and viscera splattering across her cloak. She closed her eyes, waiting for the storm to end.

When silence finally settled, broken only by the whisper of wind, Joel stood frozen, horror carved into every line of his face.

Lux handed him the reins as though nothing had happened.

"Thank you for letting me borrow your horse. I'll see you two lovebirds at the temple in three days." Her gaze snapped to Layla, voice dropping to something cold and merciless.

"Three days, Layla. No later."

Turning to Joel, her tone shifted to a mocking sweetness.

"You really are adorable. I'll see you in three days, sweet cheeks." With a playful flick, she lifted his jaw, bopped his nose, and then—just like that—vanished into nothingness.

The road was silent but for the drip of blood sliding from leaves. The two remained motionless, statues in crimson, until Joel's scream tore through the stillness.

"What. The. Fuck!"

He stumbled backward, tripping over his own boots and landing hard on his rear. His wild eyes darted to Layla, begging for an explanation she did not offer. Her face was stone, Emerald eyes hollow and haunted.

Blood clung to her like a second skin—soaking her dark trousers from the knees up, saturating the forest-green cloak pooled behind her, staining the once-fawn tunic beneath. Bits of flesh clung to her raven hair like grotesque ornaments.

Joel looked down at himself and gagged—his own clothes drenched and sticky. Breath coming in harsh bursts, he started to hyperventilate.

Layla knelt beside him, drawing in a deep breath, then another. Her voice was soft but steady when she spoke.

"With me."

Her eyes locked on his, urging him to follow her pace. Slowly, painfully, Joel did—matching her breaths until the panic ebbed enough for him to rise on shaking legs.

"Holy shit," he whispered, horror still raw in his voice. "Holy fucking shit. She killed them. Snapped her fucking fingers and popped them like a boil."

"Yeah," Layla murmured, retrieving the wandering horses. "She does that... pretty frequently."

Joel dragged his hands through his hair, pacing frantically as Layla soothed her mare with a whisper, pressing her forehead to its warm muzzle. For a fleeting moment, she allowed herself the weight of exhaustion, the jagged edges of grief—then buried them deep.

"We need to get to the river before someone sees this," she said at last, leading the horses back to the road.

Joel stared at her in disbelief.

"Can't you just wave your hand and clean it up?"

Layla flicked her wrist. Joel's clothes were suddenly spotless—but his skin still crawled, the memory clinging like grease.

"Point taken," he muttered darkly.

"Don't worry," Layla said, mounting her horse. "You'll get used to it."

They rode hard, faster than Joel thought possible, the silence between them thick as iron. When they finally reached the river, they scrubbed away the blood in silence, and still, Layla pushed them onward—through the night, through exhaustion, until even the stars blurred above them.

Lux's voice haunted Joel with every pounding hoofbeat.

"I'll see you in three days, sweet cheeks."

She had threatened his life, and Layla was doing everything she could to keep him alive.

They finally stopped late the following evening. After three changes of mounts and hours of relentless riding, Joel could barely stay upright in the saddle. Layla looked almost as ragged as he felt, her hair wind-tossed and her shoulders slumped with exhaustion.

Dusk settled over the valley like a soft gray shroud. A tranquil forest framed the horizon, its dark silhouettes standing guard against the mountainside. Beyond, a half-moon cast its pale glow upon the lake that curled around the Moro like a silver ribbon. If they skipped breakfast, they could reach the temple a few hours after dawn.

Layla busied herself with trading the horses while Joel handled securing their room and supper. The tavern they found was a quaint log cabin, its rustic charm pulling weary travelers like moths to a lantern. Inside, the air was warm and humming with lively chatter as tourists sought respite from the road. The crackling fire drove away the mountain chill clinging to Joel's bones, and for the first time that day, he felt almost human again.

He bartered for two steaming mugs of spiced mead and a hearty serving of mutton. The cost, however, made his jaw tighten. Prices had climbed steeply since his last visit home, and while he had plenty of coin to cover it, the principle of the matter stung. Still, after a brief exchange—and a bit of his old charm—Joel secured the deal and settled into a corner table.

He hadn't been waiting long when an unusual hush fell over the room. Heads turned toward the door where Layla had just stepped inside, her cloak trailing like a shadow. The lively buzz stilled as though the tavern itself held its breath.

Joel's gaze swept the room, catching the wary stares aimed their way. He lifted a brow at her as she slid silently into the seat across from him. Without a word, he passed her the extra mug of mead.

"What's up with them, I wonder?" he murmured.

Layla scanned the crowd, her expression tightening. "My face, maybe?" she mumbled into the rim of her cup.

Joel smirked, trying to break the tension. "Yeah, if I had a face like that, people would stare too."

Her lips curved in a reluctant smile before she punched his shoulder. "Shut up."

Their brief laughter was cut short when the tavern owner approached cautiously, wiping his hands on a flour-stained apron. Behind him, the kitchen staff gathered at the doorway, peering out like curious birds. A stout woman in a brown dress and bonnet—likely the owner's wife—peeked over their shoulders, gawking openly.

"Your divinity," the man said, voice trembling, "what brings you to this humble tavern on such a fine evening?"

Joel felt the tension spike. Layla stood slowly, setting her mug on the bar with measured grace.

"I'm not who you think I am, sir," she said evenly. "I only share a striking likeness. Please—do not feel obliged to show fear or offer gifts. I'll be gone by morning and take nothing more than what my companion has already purchased."

The man exhaled sharply, relief flooding his features.

"Pardon my candor, miss, but thank the Gods. Last time she was here, she burned down my kitchen. You near gave me a heart attack."

Layla inclined her head, her tone softening. "My apologies. That wasn't my intent. If it's all the same, we'll take our meals in our room."

The wife nodded briskly, shooing the staff back into the kitchen as her husband turned to pass the message along.

"Thank you, miss. I'm sure that'll make the customers more comfortable," he added with a nervous chuckle.

Layla didn't respond. She simply moved toward the stairs, Joel following close behind, his eyes sweeping the room with silent warning. Only when the door closed behind them did he finally breathe.

The room was modest—a simple bed and dresser claimed most of the space, while a small desk sat beneath the lone window. On it rested a ceramic wash basin, a pitcher of water, and a generously sized mirror framed in polished oak. Two candles flickered warmly, chasing shadows across the walls as Layla pulled out the chair and sat down to wash her face.

"This is becoming a regular thing," Joel muttered, trying for nonchalance though unease coiled in his gut.

Layla's reflection met his eyes in the mirror. "It is," she admitted quietly. "I'll have to speak with Ashur when we return."

Her voice wavered, the crack in her composure brief but enough for Joel to feel the weight pressing on her.

"Do you think he'll ever let you go?" The question escaped before he could stop it.

Layla froze, staring into her own tired eyes. For a long moment, he thought she wouldn't answer. Then, so softly he almost missed it, she whispered, "I hope so."

Joel couldn't tell if he truly heard her—or if his weary mind supplied the words to fill the silence. Layla cleared her throat and rose, shrugging off her cloak with mechanical precision, resuming her evening ritual as though nothing had passed between them.

They had shared many nights like this before—wine and quiet conversation, the kind that made the world outside feel distant. But tonight, a black cloud hung over them. The warmth between them faltered beneath the looming truth: tomorrow they would reach the palace, and Layla would face Ashur and Lux alone.

Sleep came hard for Joel. When it did, it brought only nightmares.

The next morning, they rode for the Moro. Neither spoke. Their horses pounded over the trail, driven by urgency rather than leisure. The beauty of the land no longer mattered. The quaint village they once knew had long since fallen to ruin, swallowed by creeping vines and rot. Giants and other unnatural beasts now haunted the shells of homes that once held laughter and light.

Where the bakery had stood, a massive walnut tree now rooted, its sprawling trunk devouring what had been the ground floor. Joel's chest tightened at the memory—the baker and his boy setting out warm walnut loaves each morning. He never learned what became of them, but he wasn't naive enough to think the monsters had come from nowhere.

Until now, he had never questioned how it all began. Too many had died that day for him to dwell on the details. Too much blood on his hands to linger on ghosts. But the thought came anyway—sharp and unyielding: *If they ever come back, they deserve my head for this.*

The raw honesty of it startled him. Spurring his horse faster as they crossed the weathered bridge, Joel shoved the thought deep down where it belonged. For now, he needed to focus on Layla.

Joel woke up screaming—again.

The same nightmare haunted him every night: Layla lying lifeless on the floor, Ashur setting the world ablaze, and an unstoppable storm tearing everything apart. He could never escape it. Even now, as he jolted upright drenched in sweat, the images clung to him like shadows that refused to fade.

There was a war raging somewhere beyond these walls, fierce and relentless, though Joel still didn't know against whom. He rose from the bed and began pacing the length of the chamber, just as he had done nearly every day since returning to the palace. The silence here was suffocating.

When they had first arrived, Layla went straight to report to Lux and Ashur, while Joel stayed behind to settle the horses. He assumed she would return within hours. Two weeks had passed. She had not come back, and he had been confined to their chambers ever since that first night when he dared to search for her. The guards dragged him back before he could even make it past the main hall.

Each day stretched longer than the last, gnawing at his patience. There was nothing to do but eat, sleep, and skim through the same old books while waiting for her return. If it weren't for the updates sent from Christian and Micha, Joel would feel utterly useless.

A sharp knock interrupted the dead quiet. The door creaked open and a palace guard stepped inside, his stiff posture betraying discomfort as he held out a scroll.

"This came for the mistress, sir," the guard said.

Joel took the message with a curt nod, noting the man's unease. *Babysitting me—what a glorious assignment,* Joel thought bitterly. He envied their freedom, their ability to walk through these halls without chains of suspicion clamped around their throats. Shaking off the bitterness, he unrolled the scroll just enough to glimpse the writing. Even in the dim glow of dawn filtering through the curtains, he recognized Christian's neat script.

It was important—Joel could feel it—but he forced himself to stop. Layla should see it first. Rolling the parchment back up, he strode to the door and summoned the guard. "Inform their divinity—and Lady Layla—that I have a message. I'll deliver it myself."

It took insistence, but finally, they allowed him into the throne room.

The sight that greeted him stole the air from his lungs.

Ashur and Lux sat upon twin thrones like deities carved from light. Their garments shimmered with white and gold threads, mirroring one another in immaculate perfection. Lux's halo floated above her head in a delicate, interwoven pattern resembling a flattened crown, making her hair glow as though lit from within. Ashur bore a similar halo—a circlet of light, simple yet regal.

Joel scanned the room, searching desperately for Layla. He almost didn't see her at first. She lay crumpled in the king's shadow, sprawled across an oversized cushion like discarded refuse, a heavy iron collar biting into her bruised neck. Chains trailed from her throat like shackles of humiliation.

Joel's heart stopped.

Her face—nearly unrecognizable—looked like it had been through hell itself. Her left eye was grotesquely swollen, the skin splitting where it stretched too far. Dark bruises and mottled patches of purple and yellow marred every inch of visible skin, broken only by angry, raw cuts. One slash in particular carved across her right cheek, deep and untreated. When it healed, the scar would run jagged from brow to jaw. Her lips were split and blackened, and tufts of hair had been torn straight from her scalp.

She moved—slow, shaky, every motion an agony—and forced herself to sit up. Joel stared, frozen in horror.

Ashur noticed his silence. The king descended from his throne with a measured grace that only sharpened Joel's hatred.

"Ah," Ashur murmured, voice silk over steel. He gestured lazily for a guard to step forward. "The case of mistaken identity Lady Layla was so concerned about. Lux thought it prudent to… lend her to the barracks, so she might become better acquainted and settle those concerns."

Joel's stomach churned as the guard approached, unhooking Layla's chain with a grin that dripped malice. His eyes raked over her with naked hunger. Layla spat in his face.

The strike came fast—a savage backhand that split her lip anew, blood and saliva spattering across the polished floor. She staggered but didn't fall, clutching his cloak to anchor herself. Then, with a burst of defiance, she rammed her forehead into his nose. The crunch was audible. The guard reeled back as another soldier rushed forward to intervene.

Ashur gave a small shrug, his amusement barely concealed.

"They may have been… overzealous in their affections."

Layla straightened as best she could, limping past the second guard who knelt to check on his companion. Just as she neared Joel, Ashur cleared his throat. Layla stopped. Slowly—painfully—she turned back and bent low in a bow.

"Thank you for your consideration on this matter."

The acid in her voice was faint, but Joel heard it. Felt it.

She brushed past him with dead eyes, leaving the stench of blood and humiliation in her wake. Joel bowed quickly, then all but ran after her.

He found her leaning against the corridor wall, trembling from exhaustion.

"Here," he whispered, slipping an arm around her waist. "Let me help you."

She collapsed against him with a small, broken whimper.

"Take me home," she breathed, anger sharpening the desperation in her tone. "I need a bath. Then… the library."

Later, when Joel had settled her in the bath and shut the door, Layla wept—silent at first, then uncontrollably. The hot water bit at her raw skin, but nothing could scrub away the violation etched into her bones. Pain radiated through her body like fire, every breath a reminder. Even her soul ached. For the first time in centuries—though not the first time in her life—she wished she could simply die.

Hours passed before her tears ran dry and the water grew cold. In that stillness, something hardened inside her. Her heart turned to stone again.

She had softened over the centuries—found friends, love, a semblance of home. Ashur and Lux had twisted that into a weapon. They wanted her broken. This agony was their lesson: a reminder of her place.

But Layla prayed—silently, fiercely—to anyone who might hear. For an end. For retribution. For freedom.

When the maid arrived to help her from the bath, she rose without a word, steel in her spine even as her body trembled. Whatever came next, she would endure. She had to.

By the time Joel handed her Christian's message, the fire inside her was already rekindling.

Chapter Eleven

Leah jolted awake to find Persephone shaking her violently.

"It's time! I don't know how it happened, but we have an opening! We must move now!"

The urgency in Persephone's voice tore through Leah's drowsiness like a blade. It took her only a heartbeat to register the words before she launched herself from the bed. Bare feet hit the cool stone floor as she sprinted after Persephone, heart hammering against her ribs.

The warm glow of candlelight that had soaked into the stone walls—her sanctuary these past weeks—vanished behind her as they plunged into darkness, descending the spiral column staircase as fast as their legs allowed. Each step threatened disaster, the ancient stones slick beneath her toes. Leah tightened her grip on the wall, her stomach twisting with dread, and took extra care as they neared the bottom. The trick stair loomed, and she jumped, narrowly avoiding it as Persephone broke into a run.

The wide halls stretched ahead like veins of shadow, leading them toward the side entrance behind the kitchen. Leah's lungs burned, but she didn't slow.

It had been weeks—maybe longer—since they began preparing for this moment, for the circle that would change everything. Designed by Hecate herself, the spell circle was a masterpiece of precision and raw power, forged from the anguish of countless souls lost to Lux's army. Leah remembered the long nights watching Hecate hunched over parchment, her ink-stained fingers racing against time as she perfected the prototype.

The plan was simple in theory, devastating in practice: harness the overwhelming grief from the other side and use that energy to rip open a portal home. Yet only days had passed since Hecate had finally recovered enough strength to inscribe the circle in full scale—or had it been longer? Time here never flowed the same. Leah's stomach knotted as another thought crept in: *If the circle activated, something terrible must have happened. Something big.*

Sliding around the kitchen table, Leah spotted it—the light. A violent glow spilled through the doorway ahead, flickering against the walls like living fire. Persephone didn't hesitate; she flung the back door wide and stumbled forward, immediately buffeted by hurricane-force winds that hurled her against the wall.

Leah stopped dead in the doorway, her breath catching in her throat.

Before her stretched a storm of impossible beauty. A towering column of swirling emerald light reached so high it seemed to pierce the heavens themselves, streaked with ribbons of purple that twisted like serpents through green flame. The air crackled with energy, thick and alive, and it roared louder than any tempest.

Gods and Goddesses appeared in flashes around the circle, disoriented, summoned straight from their beds in varying states of undress to witness this raw eruption of power. Hecate stood among them, calm but intent, her sharp eyes reflecting the fury of the storm. A faint frown curved her lips as she extended one hand into the shimmering column, holding a crystalline vial—*a containment vessel,* Leah realized, a chill crawling up her spine. Of course Hecate would want to capture a sample of this. This was no ordinary magic.

Persephone gripped Leah's arm, yanking her from her reverie.

"You have to go!" she shouted over the deafening wind.

"What about my mom?" Leah screamed back, panic tearing at her chest. The thought slammed into her like a blow—this could be her last chance to see her mother. Hera's acolytes had barely begun the repairs needed to reach her chambers. Leah had always known it was a long shot, but somehow, foolishly, she'd let hope take root.

Persephone's face twisted with regret. She shook her head.

"I'm sorry. If you don't go now, we'll lose this chance. You have to go back."

Leah's throat burned as tears welled in her eyes. When had the longing become so sharp, so desperate? Maybe it had always been there, gnawing quietly beneath the surface. But now—knowing this was the end—it hurt in a way that hollowed her out.

She swallowed the ache, forcing it deep where it couldn't break her now. Later, she would let it consume her. For now, she straightened her shoulders, drew a long breath, and nodded.

Hecate intercepted her at the edge of the maelstrom, her voice as steady as the stone beneath their feet.

"When you get there, you'll be in enemy territory. Surrounded by foes. Watched every moment." Her obsidian eyes bored into Leah's. "Use what we've taught you. Trust the spells. Don't get caught unawares."

Leah managed a grim nod, nerves prickling across her skin like static. Her legs trembled, anticipation clawing up her spine. She bounced once on her toes, trying to shake the fear loose.

"Okay," she breathed. "I'm ready."

Drawing strength from the fire inside her, she let out a fierce, defiant cry and hurled herself into the circle.

Nothing happened.

Leah blinked in confusion—then Ares' laughter rang out behind her. She opened her eyes.

Inside the circle, the world was… silent. Still. The wind ceased, the chaos muted as if swallowed whole. Magic churned violently around her, swirling like a living tide, but not touching her. She looked down—and froze.

The runes etched into the stone were shifting. Climbing. Writhing like serpents, they slithered up her legs, glowing a pale, sinister orange. A faint tugging at her feet sent terror lancing through her chest. Magic—

her magic—was seeping from her skin, bleeding into the circle like ink into water.

"No," she whispered, yanking her foot back. It didn't move. The circle held her fast. Panic detonated in her chest as she jerked harder, fighting the invisible grip, but it was useless.

Persephone's scream tore through the air—the first sign anyone else had noticed. She lunged forward, but Hades caught her by the arm, stopping her cold as flames erupted up Leah's leg.

The agony was instantaneous. All sound vanished—there was only silence and fire. The Gods crowded the circle's edge, faces etched with alarm, their voices lost in the void that sealed around her.

The heat climbed higher, molten and merciless, and Leah's knees buckled. Magic poured from her in a torrent now, saturating the runes until they glowed like molten ore. Colors bled together—green, brown, orange—swirling in a dizzying spiral of raw creation and destruction.

Leah screamed. The sound tore itself from her lungs, ragged and primal, her body bowing under the weight of pain. It wasn't just heat—it was invasion. Like her very essence was being flayed, ripped apart thread by thread.

Tears streamed down her cheeks as sobs wrenched free, guttural and broken. Her heart felt like it was shattering, echoing the grief that had powered this spell to life. Her breath hitched—and then the world went white.

"Be still."

The voice was soft. So soft it barely brushed her consciousness, yet it cut through the roar of agony like steel. Her body quaked as blinding light consumed everything.

"Open your eyes, darling."

The words slithered through the wreckage of her thoughts, sweet as venom.

The pain was gone.

Leah blinked against the brilliance, shoving herself upright on trembling arms. Terror crawled through her bones. She was alone. Alone and hollowed out, just like the souls they'd left behind.

The ground vanished beneath her feet. She was falling—plunging into darkness with no end in sight.

What followed barely felt real. Disjointed flashes, like fragments of a dream. A hand, pale and elegant, gripped her shoulder with deceptive gentleness.

Leah looked up into the face of a stranger—a raven-haired beauty draped in blood-red silk. She hovered above the ground, robes flowing in an invisible current, her presence bending the shadows around her. And her eyes—gods, her eyes—one glimmered like a sapphire, the other burned green as emerald fire.

"You can't save her, find the sword buried in stone," the woman murmured and released her.

The darkness swallowed Leah whole.

She came to with a snap, consciousness slamming back as reality coalesced into horror.

She was in a throne room. A whip dangled from her hand. A body lay crumpled at her feet.

No—*not a body. A woman.* A maid.

Leah's stomach heaved, bile surging to her throat as she stared at the carnage. Skin flayed from bone, flesh a ruin of mangled stripes.

She barely had time to choke back the scream clawing up her throat when she felt eyes on her.

Ashur.

He stepped into view, gaze sharp and searching.

"Done already, my dear?" His tone was light, but suspicion flickered beneath.

Leah's pulse jackhammered. Forcing down the horror, she spat on what remained of the corpse, curling her lip in a cruel sneer. She even kicked at the shredded flesh, as if to scorn it further, while inside her soul begged for forgiveness.

Then she smiled. Bright. Dazzling. Deadly.

"I'm feeling a bit… what's the phrase?" She tilted her head, pausing theatrically. "Hangry!"

With an exaggerated flounce, she tossed the whip aside and plastered on a grin that didn't reach her eyes. "Shall we eat?"

Ashur's suspicion melted into a smile.

"Of course, my love."

His hand slid to her ass as he guided her toward the dining hall. Leah fought the instinct to recoil as his lips brushed the nape of her neck, sending a shudder racing through her body.

"What would you like for your meal, my dear?" His voice was silk, but there was iron beneath it. Possessive. Controlling.

Leah forced a giggle, tilting her head back in mock affection, summoning every ounce of charm Lydia had ever used on Alec.

"How could I not be alright," she purred, "when I have you?"

His arms cinched around her waist like a trap, pulling her flush against him as he nuzzled her shoulder. Heat pressed into her hip—a hard, insistent reminder of what he wanted. Before she could react, he bent her slightly over the table, grinding against her like a bull in rut.

Panic exploded in her chest.

She needed a way out. *Think, Leah. Think.*

Her mind scrambled for something—anything—that would shut him down.

"Let's make a baby!" she blurted.

Ashur froze mid-thrust, every muscle going rigid.

"Do… what now?" His voice cracked as he stepped back, clearing his throat.

Leah pounced on the hesitation, spinning to face him with wild-eyed enthusiasm. She clutched his sleeves, tugging him close, her voice high and fevered.

"Let's make a baby," she repeated breathlessly, wrapping her legs around his hips for emphasis.

Ashur recoiled like she'd struck him, wrenching free of her grasp.

"I just remembered—I have a few things to do this afternoon."

Nearly sprinting from the room, Ashur left her alone for the first time since her arrival.

Leah's lips curved into a victorious smile. A laugh threatened to escape her throat, but she swallowed it down as her eyes swept across the private dining hall. The grandeur of it felt almost foreign to her now. Once, this place would have been unrecognizable to her—but everything had changed since that catastrophic ceremony, the one that sealed her fate and destroyed her village. That single day had shattered the life she once knew and, in its wake, released memories she had long forgotten.

She recognized the hall now. This had once been part of her aunt's apartments in their youth. Back then, Leah was seldom allowed anywhere near her aunt or uncle, though no one ever explained why.

She knew why now.

They had been descending into madness, slowly, like a creeping rot, and her parents had feared they might harm her and her sister.

Layla.

Her heart clenched at the thought. Layla had been beautiful—radiant, even—with laughter that could brighten the darkest corridors and dreams as wide as the skies. She wanted to be cherished as one of the future queens, a desire her parents had encouraged. It was a destiny meant for both sisters: to inherit their mother's and aunt's thrones, ensuring peace when the elder queens inevitably passed on.

Leah could still remember the days when the world felt infinite. They would tear through the palace gates together, laughing as they darted into the farmers' wheat fields, hiding until their mother would rise into the skies and summon the dusk, sending the world to bed. They had shared everything—every secret, every smile, every sorrow. Their bond had felt unbreakable.

And then, one day, it broke.

They had learned diplomacy, arithmetic, etiquette, and even dance within these very walls. Yet, somehow, Leah had been kept apart from the heart of it all. Why? The question gnawed at her even now.

She remembered the moment she saw the light fade from Layla's eyes. That look had broken something inside her, something she could never mend.

A sound shattered her thoughts—footsteps echoing down the corridor.

Heart lurching, Leah darted toward the window. She was on the third floor, directly above the palace's front steps. From her vantage point, the grounds appeared empty, but she knew better. Ashur would never leave them truly unguarded. If she was going to escape, she had to move fast.

Throwing open the window, Leah drew on her power and leapt.

A blood-curdling scream erupted behind her. Whipping her head upward, she saw a maid leaning out of a higher window, shrieking for someone to help Her Majesty. Leah's shimmering blue gown snagged in the shrubs below, halting her momentum with a violent tug. She yanked at the fabric, teeth gritted, as a small group of dragon priests poured down the palace steps toward the commotion.

There was no time to waste. With a savage rip, she tore the dress free, clutching the trailing fabric in one hand as she sprinted toward the village bridge. Power surged through her veins as she gathered it in her core, unleashing it upon the bridge the moment her feet touched its planks.

The explosion shattered the air. Stone and timber crumbled in a deafening roar, sending shockwaves rippling across the river. By the time the dust settled, Leah was already across, the bridge reduced to rubble behind her.

She kept running—until she saw what remained of her home.

The ruins stopped her cold. Her chest constricted, grief clawing at her insides. Slowly, she tore at the hem of her dress, ripping away the excess fabric to free her legs.

At least I can move now, she thought grimly.

The sharp snap of a twig cut through the silence.

Leah froze. Her gaze darted to the tree line. Something was moving in the darkness—its silhouette shifting like liquid shadow, its eyes glowing faintly as they tracked her every movement.

Oh, that's not good.

The truth hit her like ice water: she might have just leapt out of the pan and straight into the fire. More shapes emerged from the gloom, creeping closer, circling her like predators.

Leah didn't wait to find out what they wanted.

Dropping the shredded skirt, she bolted down the narrow game trail—the remnants of what had once been the main road. Behind her, the forest erupted in chaos: crashing branches, guttural shrieks that sent a chill down her spine.

She risked a glance over her shoulder and immediately regretted it.

A horde of goblins poured through the underbrush, snarling and snapping, their jagged teeth flashing in the dim light. They screamed like rabid beasts, howler-monkey cries echoing through the night.

They were fast—too fast.

One vaulted across her path, claws slashing for her throat. Leah flung out her hands, fire bursting from her fingertips. Flames spiraled outward, engulfing her entire body in a blazing shield as she sprinted harder, searing the nearest goblins in an inferno. Their screams tore through the darkness, a symphony of agony and rage as the overgrowth around them ignited.

Then, just as suddenly, silence.

The surviving goblins melted back into the shadows, their courage singed away.

Leah released the fire reluctantly, unwilling to drain her reserves too soon. She forced her breathing steady and focused on the mission. She had to find the survivors.

Hera's voice echoed in her mind—a lesson from the void. One of the lesser goddesses had taught her to track prey, a task Leah had dismissed as busywork at the time. Just something to keep her from losing her mind while waiting.

Funny how useful it had become.

She stopped running. Lowering herself to the forest floor, she pressed her palm to the earth and summoned a pulse of power, letting it ripple deep into the soil.

The ground answered. Trees trembled, their leaves whispering in protest. Birds and even dragons burst from their perches, shrieking in alarm. The pulse returned to her like an echo, carrying knowledge.

There—a cavern due north, brimming with energy.

Leah's stomach knotted. She had no idea what awaited her inside. Maybe her allies. Maybe something worse—something monstrous and hungry for blood.

Shuddering, she pushed the thought aside and clung to the sliver of hope that it was uninhabited.

Either way, she would find out soon enough.

She rose to her feet, her mind whispering a single thought:

Thank you, Artemis.

Leah set off toward the cavern at a light run, her feet barely making a sound against the forest floor. The pace felt almost natural now. She had grown so accustomed to the relentless rhythm of the hunt that the strain on her muscles hardly registered anymore. Her time among the Gods had toughened her, built stamina she never imagined possible.

A flicker of pride washed over her, and she laughed under her breath at how absurd it seemed. Here she was, congratulating herself for keeping up with people who claimed to be lesser beings. Rolling her eyes at the irony, she pushed harder, lengthening her stride and aiming for the edge of her hunter's sight.

Artemis was a master of restraint—silent, patient, and deliberate. She never revealed herself to prey unless it was already too late. Leah knew the Goddess's methods well and had learned much under her watchful gaze. At this pace, if she ran through the night, she figured she could reach the cavern in a day and a half. Ares had warned her countless times during training about overexertion and the dangers of burning through stamina too quickly. Artemis, however, had an entirely different philosophy: less brute force, more precision. Leah knew she would need to slow eventually, but for now, she was determined to prove something—even if it was only to herself. Today, she intended to put that girl to shame.

The night stretched long and shadowed as she ran, the forest alive with whispers of unseen creatures. Every so often, she paused, checking her bearings and adjusting her course as the cavern drew nearer. Her lack of weapons was inconvenient, but not crippling. She had managed to skirt around the few creatures that lingered too close to her path, giving them a wide berth to avoid unwanted attention.

By dawn, the forest began to transform. Sunlight spilled through the canopy in fractured beams, igniting the undergrowth with splashes of color. Petals unfurled in the soft glow, eager to drink in the morning light. Vibrancy bloomed everywhere, and the air shimmered with a density that made breathing feel heavier. The magic here was palpable, thick enough to taste—an ancient presence that clung to every leaf and stone.

Leah slowed, senses alert. She didn't know what exactly waited inside the cavern, but she doubted it was empty. Experience told her that a power source this strong didn't go unnoticed. Something had claimed this place. Maybe she'd be lucky and find nothing worse than a cluster of small dragons—or, if fortune really favored her, just some delicate ethereal butterflies.

That hope shattered the moment a burst of white light seared across the cavern entrance, followed by an eerie, bone-deep howl that rippled through the morning air.

Well… that answers that.

Leah exhaled, silently questioning her own sanity for coming here in the first place. Still, she crept closer, each step a whispered prayer that she wouldn't end up as breakfast. *Please don't eat me, please don't eat me.* The mantra looped in her head, accompanied by her own inner voice scolding her: *This is dumb. This is really fucking dumb.*

Finding a shallow alcove in the rock face, she pressed herself flat, inching around the corner for a view inside. The cavern yawned wide and shadowed, its granite walls lined with dragons. Nests carved into the stone cradled sleeping giants, their scales glinting faintly in the dim glow that pulsed from deeper within.

Lowering herself carefully, Leah slid down from the ledge and eased inside, every muscle taut with caution. A few dragons wouldn't have concerned her, but this—this was a colony. Hundreds, maybe more. If they decided she was a threat, they would strip her to bone in seconds. She kept her movements slow, controlled, barely daring to breathe.

The passage curved sharply to the right, opening into a series of chambers where the glow intensified. Moisture dripped from the ceiling in slow, steady beats, the air thick with the scent of sulfur and decay. Stalactites hung like daggers, some so massive they dwarfed her, their shadowy lengths concealing hatchlings the size of lizards. Above, younglings tried their luck at spitting fire, bursts of orange and gold flickering against the stone like lightning. Leah muttered a curse as her sandal squelched into something soft and slimy. "It's just mud," she lied to herself, though the stench clawing up her throat said otherwise.

Ahead, a commotion drew her eye—a pair of reckless hatchlings darting from their cubby before a larger dragon swooped down like a living storm. Its teeth flashed, its prey vanished in a single snap. The beast didn't so much as glance at Leah before defecating into a steaming puddle near her feet.

Leah gagged, stepping into muck that swallowed her leg to the knee. She pressed on, forcing herself to breathe through her mouth as the stench of sulfur and ammonia grew so dense it coated her tongue. The glow now blazed so fiercely that she squinted against it, certain she was close to whatever source drew her here.

At last, the tunnel narrowed and veered into a hollow chamber. Life ceased abruptly. No dragons. No sound beyond the drip of distant water. The silence was heavier than the roar of a crowd. Power pooled thick in the center, wrapping itself around a jagged formation of stone. From that stone jutted a strange protrusion—waist-high, shaped almost like a hilt thrust into the wall.

Leah approached, scanning for traps. The stone around the object bore faint grooves, maybe once part of a mechanism, but time had swallowed whatever purpose it served. A few probing spells revealed nothing—no wards, no pressure triggers. The thing didn't want to be found, yet here it was, humming with magic so potent it prickled her fingertips when she reached out.

Her hand brushed the hilt. Warmth surged up her arm, thrumming like a heartbeat. Nothing else happened. Frowning, she gripped it fully and tugged. It budged—barely an inch. Bracing her foot against the wall, she yanked harder. Two inches. Huffing, she stepped back, weighing her options. She could risk magic, but that might rouse the entire cavern. Hundreds of dragons and razor-toothed hatchlings lay just beyond. No, this had to be done the old-fashioned way.

Setting her jaw, Leah wrapped both hands around what she now realized was a sword hilt. Her mother's words echoed through her, "find the sword buried in stone". It was, if nothing else, effectively buried. Planting her feet, she pulled with everything she had. Muscles screamed, veins burned—and the blade slid another inch. Again. Again. Her hands slipped. She toppled backward, cracking her head against the cold stone.

"Goddammit," she hissed, the sound bouncing through the chamber. A small dragon chirped from somewhere behind her. Anger flared, hot and irrational, twisting with her resolve. This wasn't going to beat her. Not a fucking chance.

Shoving to her feet, Leah seized the hilt once more. This time, something shifted—not in the stone, but in her. Power flowed through her grip, strength she hadn't felt since the trials with Ares. She heaved, every fiber straining, and the sword tore free from its prison with a grinding roar.

"Ah-ha!" The cry ripped from her throat before she could stop it. Triumph blazed—then horror as the echo slammed back at her, rolling through the cavern like thunder. Silence followed. Silence, and then… heads. Small at first, then more, necks arching, eyes glinting in the dark.

"Oh, shit." Leah clapped both hands over her mouth. Too late.

They didn't attack—not yet. She tiptoed, whispering, "I'm just gonna go," as if that would make a difference. She stepped over one, skirted another, clutching the sword like a lifeline. When the cavern mouth came into view, she bolted, and all hell broke loose. A young dragon snapped at her heels only to be snatched up by a larger version of itself. Within seconds, the cave turned into a feeding frenzy. Heart pounding, lungs burning, she didn't dare look back until the trees swallowed her. No dragons pursued beyond the entrance, but the sound of feasting followed Leah into the shadows.

Relief barely had time to settle before disaster struck. So focused on escaping, Leah didn't notice the man until the moment she collided with him.

"Layla?" His voice barely registered before impact. She hit him like a battering ram. The force knocked him flat, his ribs crunching under her weight. Leah went sprawling on top of him in a tangle of limbs and curses, her wrist smashing into something hard, pain lancing up her arm. Her grip on the sword broke, the weapon skidding out of reach as she slid over his head and into the dirt.

"Oh, fuck me, woman! What the hell?!" the man wheezed from beneath her.

"I'm so sorry!" Leah squealed, scrambling upright in a blind panic. "Are you okay?" Her voice trembled. Gods, if she'd actually hurt him—

Healing was never her strong suit. She could summon fire, command wind—but mend broken bones? Heal a ruptured organ? Not a chance.

Blood trickled from his nose as he muttered something into his hand. Leah pressed his face upward, trying to stop the flow. "What?" she asked, heart thundering in her chest.

"Can't you ever make a normal entrance?" he said, louder this time, his sharp gaze locking on her as he adjusted in his seat. Straightening, he shifted to get a better view, and in that moment, his expression changed.

Leah noticed the subtle shift immediately. She wasn't entirely sure how this man knew her sister, but it had to be well enough for him to sense something was off. The irritation in his tone melted into something colder—measured observation.

They stared at each other, eyes locked, silently weighing and calculating, like two predators deciding who would strike first. The moment an unspoken agreement was settled between them, Leah moved.

She lunged for the sword lying a few feet away, fingers brushing its hilt just as he yanked a dagger from his belt. Before she could gain leverage, his hand clamped around her ankle, yanking her backward with brutal force. She hit the ground hard, dirt biting into her palms as he dragged her toward him.

Leah kicked wildly, thrashing against his grip, her body twisting as his blows rained down—sharp, relentless, but sloppy. His strikes missed vital spots by inches, the blade grazing her ribs and tearing through the fabric of her dress instead of flesh. The metallic tang of her own fear mixed with the scent of sweat and earth.

Then, pain.

The dagger pierced deep into her abdomen, and Leah screamed—raw and guttural. Her vision flashed white-hot for a moment, but survival roared louder than agony. Summoning strength from sheer instinct, she slammed her elbow into his face with bone-crunching force. He reeled back with a grunt, grip faltering.

Leah seized the opening. She launched forward, pouncing on him like a wounded predator, pressing the edge of her sword hard against his throat. Blood trickled where steel kissed flesh as she shifted her weight, careful not to disturb the dagger still lodged in her gut. Every movement sent a spike of molten pain tearing through her body, but she refused to let it show.

"Who are you?" she snarled, voice ragged with fury.

"I could ask you the same question," he shot back through clenched teeth. His breath came fast as he tried to twist free, the muscles in his jaw twitching as the blade bit deeper into his skin.

"I won't ask again." Her tone dropped to a lethal whisper, and gods, she prayed he wouldn't realize how true that statement was. Her vision was starting to blur, dark shadows creeping at the edges. The dagger pulsed inside her like a heartbeat, every throb a cruel reminder of time slipping away. If she didn't end this quickly, she'd bleed out right here beside him.

He must have seen it—the fire in her eyes, the way her grip never faltered—because his resistance broke.

"Christian," he rasped. "My name is Christian. We were supposed to meet Layla here a week ago."

Leah's stomach knotted at the mention of her sister's name. "Who is 'we'?" she demanded, her gaze darting briefly around the forest floor. The risk of giving him a chance to break free was worth it. Better that than a blade in her spine from an unseen ally.

"Me and my brother," Christian said, his tone resigned now, his body sinking slightly into the dirt.

"Where is he?"

"He went back to the village a couple of days ago. People will get suspicious."

A village. Leah's pulse spiked. Considering the Morrow had been the only settlement in this valley two hundred miles wide—centuries ago—it stood to reason that any rebels would cluster near the ruins.

"I bet they will. Where is this village?" The question slipped out before she could mask her excitement. She cursed herself instantly. That reaction was all he needed—a bargaining chip served on a silver platter.

"How about I show you," he said with a thin smile, "and in exchange, you let me go."

Leah pressed the blade harder into his throat until his breath came in choking gasps. "How about you tell me, and I'll kill you quickly?" She leaned closer, too close. Pain exploded in her stomach as the dagger shifted, white heat searing her core. A broken sound escaped her lips, and her vision swam for an instant.

Christian noticed. His laugh was low, mocking. "I doubt you're going to last that long."

"Shut up." Her voice was ice. And then, with one swift, merciless motion, she slit his throat.

Blood sprayed warm across her hands. Leah shoved the lifeless body aside, forcing herself not to look at the dagger still jutting from her gut. She dragged him toward the cave entrance—the same one she'd emerged from—and left him sprawled there like an offering. With any luck, the scavengers inside would be too distracted by fresh meat to follow her deeper into the forest.

***

Layla had been preparing to advance on the village Christian mentioned in his letter when the doors to her chamber burst open. Joel stormed in, face pale and tense, a squad of soldiers thundering down the passageway behind him. The chaos outside had been building for over an hour—shouts, steel clashing in distant halls—and Layla had finally sent Joel to find out what the hell was happening.

"Lux is missing."

The words cracked like a whip in the tense air. Silence slammed down in their wake.

Layla dismissed the squad commander with a curt gesture, allowing him to resume his duties before her icy gaze cut back to Joel.

"What do you mean, missing?" Her tone was dangerously calm.

"She apparently jumped out the second-story window and ran into the ruins," Joel said, grim certainty in his voice.

Layla exhaled a slow, heavy sigh and lowered her eyes back to the maps spread across the table. Her fingers traced the inked symbols absently before tapping the marked point where Christian was supposed to meet them.

"Odd behavior, even for Lux," she murmured. "But it's not our problem."

Her voice was flat, but inside, something fractured—something raw and bitter. She wanted this war over. She wanted her son back.

Her mind drifted, unbidden, to the memory of Adam as an infant—the only time she had been allowed to hold him. To love him. To whisper hopes against his soft skin and imagine a future where happiness wasn't a crime. She remembered rocking him beneath his bedroom window for hours, watching dawn bleed into dusk, wishing time could freeze there forever.

Ashur hadn't liked it. He grew moody, jealous of the hours she spent with the child. So she'd tried—gods, she'd tried—to divide her attention, to keep him content. Back then, she thought they were happy. She thought that if she gave enough of herself, they'd survive.

But all of it—every fragile piece of her happiness—had been stolen. By her bitch of a sister.

The thought of Leah ignited a storm inside her chest. Rage licked her veins like wildfire. Layla remembered the day her sister appeared months after Adam's birth, a surprise arranged by Ashur himself. He'd pulled her from the battlefield, brought her here to the temple. Layla had never understood his obsession with war, but she learned early not to question him. Back then, she'd been young, naïve. His attention was enough to sustain her.

Now? The sight of him sickened her.

He was her uncle, after all—a truth her old friends once called monstrous. But they never knew the whole story.

She was a child when Ashur took her to her aunt's temple. She remembered the night vividly—the rush to leave under a storm-choked sky, Ashur's promise that Lux was waiting. But she never saw her sister after that night. "Too busy," they told her. "Too important for you."

Ashur filled the void instead. He visited daily, bringing sweets, playing games, spinning words like silk until the truth became chains—she could see them in the color of her eyes. Once a marvelous shade of sapphire like her father's, they now held an eerie quality, a faint glow of brilliant blue. Like Ashur's.

Heartbreak hollowed her. Ashur filled the emptiness.

Even now, after every punishment, every humiliation, she belonged to him. She hated him with a venom that burned, but the shame of leaving—of being unwanted again—rooted her in place. *Who could love you now?* The words slashed through her mind like a blade heated in flame.

Adam. That was the only answer. The only reason she breathed.

Leah had stolen that from her, and Leah would pay.

"We need to focus on locating the rebels," Layla said, voice sharpening like tempered steel. "We rendezvous near the cavern and wait for Christian to check in. Frankly, I'd rather be gone before Ashur decides to care enough to redirect his forces."

Joel nodded, fingers brushing her arm in a fleeting gesture of reassurance. "I'll go make sure the battalion's ready to move out. We can leave as soon as you're ready."

Layla rose, gathering her cloak with a flick of her wrist. "No need." Her tone was clipped, cold. "I'm ready now."

She tossed Joel his cloak, and together they swept from the room. Layla's boots struck the marble harder than usual as they crossed the palace halls toward the staging area. The acrid stench of smoke and sweat clung to the barracks beyond, and as her eyes fell on that section of the palace—a den of filth and loyalty bought with blood—rage coiled in her gut.

If she didn't leash it, she'd set the whole damn place ablaze.

"Let's move," she told the captain, her voice clipped with urgency.

Swinging her leg over a dapple-grey mare, Layla ignored the lust-filled jeers of the soldiers behind her and spurred the horse forward. The rhythmic pounding of hooves carried her out through the gate at a gallop, the bitter laughter of men fading behind her like an unwelcome shadow. Putting as much distance as possible between herself and her uncle was the only comfort she could hope for in a situation like this.

She knew the reality, though—once they were beyond the ruins of the village, someone would test her. Someone always did. And when that moment came, she would have to make an example out of them. The thought left a sour taste in her mouth. She wasn't in the mood for bloodshed, not tonight.

It should take the battalion two, maybe three days to reach the cavern, but Layla was confident she could make it in a few hours on horseback. The idea of the quiet forest night was tempting, almost a promise of solitude after weeks of chaos. She decided to seize it, to ride ahead and embrace the silence while she could.

Behind her, Joel followed, his face drawn tight with worry. The set of his jaw told Layla everything she needed to know: the visions had returned. They had been growing more frequent lately, and that unsettled him more than he dared admit aloud.

She had told him years ago that his gift—if one could even call it that—was tethered to her, to her power. Any fracture in her connection to Ashur sent ripples through him, and those ripples were becoming waves. His control was slipping beyond what stress alone could explain.

And stress was something they all had in spades.

Layla's connection to God was faint at best now, a brittle thread fraying more with each passing day. That weakness made Joel more liability than asset, and he knew it. In truth, he doubted he'd survive even a minor skirmish against the rebels, let alone an all-out war.

He bent low over his horse's neck as they tore through the forest, wind clawing at his hair. Ahead of him, Layla rode like a woman chased by ghosts. Maybe she was. Joel closed his eyes for a heartbeat, trying to swallow the sting rising in them.

He loved her. If there had ever been doubt, it was gone now. The certainty sat heavy in his chest, aching, raw. More than anything, he wanted her to find peace, to be happy—even if that happiness didn't include him. He wanted to tell her, to spill everything festering inside him. But the fear of his visions, the fear that speaking might make them real, kept his tongue tied.

By sundown, Layla wheeled her mare to a halt. The cavern loomed ahead, jagged shadows slicing across the clearing. She swung down from the saddle, muscles stiff from the hard ride, and tied the horse to a low branch. Joel entered the clearing moments later. When she looked up at him, she offered a smile. A sad one, perhaps, but a smile nonetheless.

Joel scanned the clearing before dismounting, his eyes sharp.

"Looks like there was a struggle," he murmured, pointing to the scuffed earth between them.

Layla followed his gaze and nodded.

"I noticed. Hopefully, the boys are alright."

Her words weren't a surprise, not exactly—Joel knew she cared for her men—but the vulnerability lacing them twisted something uneasy in his gut. She felt broken, and worse, she didn't seem to be hiding it well anymore.

He shifted awkwardly, kicking at a rock while she watched him with those heavy, mournful eyes. Then she exhaled sharply, the sound edged with frustration.

"Stop," she snapped.

Joel blinked at her, sheepish, but kept his silence.

"Look," she said, her tone softening, "I know this is… weird for you. Seeing me like this. But I'm kind of going through some shit right now."

Turning from him, she nuzzled her horse's muzzle, fingers threading absently through its mane. "So do me a favor—just pretend everything's fine until I figure out how the hell I'm supposed to act over here, okay?"

Joel turned his back to her, busying himself with removing his saddle.

"I have no idea what you're talking about," he said flatly.

The silence that followed stretched so long it felt suffocating. Layla stared at him, disbelief burning behind her eyes, until finally she let out a brittle giggle. It died on her lips as her gaze slid past him—past everything—straight to the yawning mouth of the cavern.

"Oh, Gods…" Her voice cracked on the words, horror flooding her features.

Joel spun just in time to see it: a man's severed leg dangling grotesquely from the rock face. The earlier signs of struggle now screamed for urgent investigation.

Joel's stomach knotted as his eyes swept the clearing. The body had been dragged toward the cave, leaving a dark trail that vanished into shadow. A lone boot, wedged in the underbrush, caught his attention— Christian's boot. Nearby, a set of smaller footprints led north.

Then came the sound—a sharp, birdlike chirp echoing from inside the cavern.

They didn't hesitate. Both melted into the treeline, crouching low in the brush. Moments later, the cave gave up its secret. A dragon emerged, scales glinting dully in the fading light. It clambered over the rocks with unnerving grace, clutching the severed leg in its talons. With a brutal jerk, it ripped a hunk of flesh free. Blood sprayed as it crunched down on the femur, its beak clicking like snapping bones.

"That's fucking gross," Joel muttered under his breath, inching toward the horses. He untied them quickly, shoving the reins of Layla's mare into her hands. Together, they slipped deeper into the forest, keeping the beast—and the grisly remains—between themselves and the cave.

Judging by the hollow look in Layla's eyes, Joel didn't need to say it aloud: Christian wasn't coming to the rendezvous.

***

Leah's trail was colder than she liked, but Christian's brother wasn't subtle. She traced his path with methodical precision, her hunter's eyes picking out the signs others would have missed—the heavy bootprints, the broken twigs, the faint drag marks.

It had taken nearly a week, but she had finally reached the edge of what passed for a village. Or rather, an encampment—hastily constructed, uneven, alive with the low hum of life beyond the treeline.

Leah crouched in the bushes, pain gnawing at her ribs where the dagger still sat lodged in her side. Every hour she waited brought her closer to death. The wound was festering, her body weakening. She clenched her jaw.

"Fuck it," she hissed, rising to her feet.

Staggering into the heart of the village, she knelt by the fire pit and struck a flame. The warmth bit at her chilled skin, though it did little for the blood loss. She sat heavily, letting the heat seep into her bones, waiting for the village to wake around her.

The reaction came as expected. The first villager to notice her froze, then slipped away like a wisp of smoke, no doubt running to fetch whoever was in charge now.

Leah placed her sword carefully across the fire from her and waited. They would come from the shadows; she knew their tactics as well as her own heartbeat.

The crunch of footsteps behind her drew her attention. She turned her head slowly, finding herself staring down the edge of a blade—a sword leveled at her throat.

"Oh, thank the Gods…" Her voice broke, thick with emotion as tears welled unbidden. She hadn't realized how desperately she had hoped for this—how much she needed to see that face again.

"Alec?" she whispered.

He stared at her like a man seeing a ghost, suspicion darkening his eyes.

"Leah?"

She nodded, her breath shuddering as her hand pressed against the dagger still embedded in her flesh. She was trembling now, though not entirely from fear. After all this time—after the horrors she had endured—she couldn't blame him for his hesitation.

It had been an eternity since they last stood together. By all rights, she shouldn't even be alive. In truth, she wasn't—not completely.

A flutter in her womb reminded her of that truth, sharp and sobering.

"There's something we need to discuss," she said quietly. "Privately, if possible." Her voice was steady despite the weight behind it. She couldn't risk startling him—not with that blade still so close.

"How do I know—"

"You have a scar," she interrupted, forcing a faint smile. "On your inner right thigh. From when I accidentally stabbed you at Cornwell's castle gate. It got infected because you were too damn stubborn to see the medics. They told you they'd have to draw the infection out by force, and you were so high on herbs you told the medic you'd never been sucked out by a man before—but he was welcome to come back anytime."

The murmuring crowd behind Alec erupted into laughter and scattered giggles.

Alec exhaled, lowering his sword with a look of exasperation.

Did you really have to tell that story?"

"It's one of my favorites," she teased, blinking hard to keep the tears at bay.

Then his arms were around her—strong, crushing, real. She clung to him, sobs shaking her as weeks of grief, relief, and failure poured out. For the friends she had lost. For the joy of reunion. For everything that still lay ahead.

When the storm passed, she pulled back, swiping at her wet cheeks.

"We need to talk strategy, Alec. There's a lot happening—and we need to be ready."

"Okay," he murmured softly against her hair.

"Let's go." Alec's tone was calm but firm as he guided Leah down the narrow pathway leading to a burgundy-colored tent nestled between two towering pines. The fabric flapped lightly in the breeze, a striking contrast against the muted earth tones of the surrounding camp.

Ryanne was waiting just inside. The moment Leah stepped through the opening, Ryanne froze in stunned disbelief. Then, without warning, she rushed forward and crushed Leah in a bear hug that spoke of unrestrained joy, nearly knocking the breath out of her.

Once inside and settled on a low cot, Leah began to talk—really talk. She told them everything, starting from the moment they were separated to the long, winding path that brought her to the camp. Her voice trembled as she spoke of her missing memories, how they had been gone until the awakening ceremony, and how she rediscovered who she had been before the war. She didn't hold back. Every secret she had kept locked away spilled out now like floodwater breaching a dam.

Alec said nothing at first. He let her speak as he moved about the tent with methodical precision, brewing a pot of rich, roasted coffee that filled the air with a comforting aroma. Ryanne tended to Leah's wounds, stitching her up with careful hands while insisting she rest once she finished recounting her story.

When Alec finally placed the steaming mug in Leah's hands, it was done silently. He only interrupted her once to clarify a few key details but otherwise listened without expression, his face as unreadable as ever, while Leah poured out what felt like a lifetime of pain and revelations.

When her voice finally faltered into silence, Alec rose from his crouch and turned to Ryanne.

"Bring Marcus—and Micha—to the tent. Quickly."

Ryanne slipped out without question. Alec returned his attention to Leah.

"You said the man you killed was named Christian? Shorter, kind of bulky, sand-brown hair?" His voice was even, but his eyes sharpened as he studied her face.

Leah nodded slowly. "Yes."

"And he had a brother here?"

"Yes."

"Did he give you a name?"

"No," she admitted, guilt tugging at her tone. "I'm sorry. I had to kill him before I could get any real answers."

Leah pulled the blanket Alec had draped over her shoulders tighter around her frame. She wasn't cold anymore, but the soft weight brought a measure of comfort she desperately needed.

"Now," Alec said, his gaze flicking toward the corner of the tent, "this sword you mentioned. Where is it?"

"In the corner," Leah replied, pointing to the dirt-coated blade propped against a small table.

"Do you know anything about it?" Alec picked up the weapon gingerly, turning it in his hands before setting it back with a deliberate motion.

"No. It just had a… strange power signature." She gave a small shrug, exhaustion weighing down her voice.

A sharp knock at the tent flap drew Alec's attention. His hand went to his dagger in one swift motion.

"Come in," he called, voice like steel.

The flap opened, and a man stepped inside—one who bore an uncanny resemblance to Christian. His brow furrowed in confusion as his eyes landed on Leah.

"What are you doing h—"

He never finished. Alec moved faster than thought, driving his dagger upward in a brutal arc. The blade punched through the soft palate and out the top of the man's skull. Leah didn't flinch. She'd seen Alec kill before, though it never failed to make her pulse quicken. Blood gushed in crimson spurts, pooling across the ground as the man collapsed in a graceless heap.

"What the 'ell Alec! Have you gone mad?" Marcus cursed.

Messy, but effective, Leah thought grimly.

"He and his brother came to us claiming they'd been attacked by bandits," Alec said matter-of-factly, wiping his blade clean on the dead man's tunic. "Kept to themselves mostly, but the fact that he knew your face tells me everything I need to know."

He tilted his head toward Marcus, who had just arrived.

"Give me a hand, big guy?"

Together, Alec and Marcus dragged the body out the back of the tent, disappearing into the shadowed trees. Leah was left alone with Ryanne, whose curious eyes burned with a question she could no longer hold back.

"So this plan to bring the Gods into the world…" Ryanne's voice broke the tense silence. "Does that happen the old-fashioned way, or are we talking magical intervention?"

Leah froze for a beat, truly understanding for the first time what the implications of her current condition were.

"Divine intervention," she answered softly, lifting the coffee to her lips. For a fleeting second, she wondered if Persephone—the presence stirring inside her—enjoyed the taste as much as she did.

"There are seven included in the pact," Leah continued. "Each one needs something different to enter the world. A totem, an act of service, a ritual—whatever ensures they stay intact through the transition. They needed a willing host to perform the rituals and carry their souls while they're… forming. It gives them added protection until puberty, when their powers mature. From what I've been told, it takes about a week for each. I provide the bodies, keep them safe, and when they're fully grown, they fight for us."

Ryanne tilted her head thoughtfully. "So how do you know what each one needs?"

"I can feel it," Leah replied. "Like a craving. It's hard to explain."

"And this one?" Ryanne's gaze flicked to Leah's stomach.

Leah smiled faintly. "She likes the coffee."

Ryanne burst out laughing, mercifully dropping the line of questioning. Leah was grateful. There was no way in hell she was telling Ryanne—or Alec—what Death required of her.

Alec returned alone, kneeling beside Leah with that same intense focus as before. "Marcus is taking the body to the lake," he said, inspecting her bandages. "There's a breed of water horse there. Nasty things. They'll take care of what's left."

He leaned in close, so close she could feel the heat of his breath brush her skin. His scent hit her like a drug, sending her pulse into a wild rhythm.

"You've been moving too much," he scolded softly. "Your wound's going to reopen if you don't rest like Ryanne told you."

Leah swallowed hard, then whispered, barely audible: "You didn't say anything about the pregnancy."

He froze. For a long moment, the silence between them stretched taut. Leah exhaled slowly, breaking the tension.

There wasn't another option," she said quietly. "I'm sorry."

Alec shook his head. "Don't apologize—not to me. You did what you had to. Besides…" He hesitated, voice low. "We're friends. I have no right to judge."

His words weren't meant to hurt, but they sliced through her all the same. Friends. Just friends. The reminder settled like a stone in her chest. She lay back, forcing herself to breathe past the ache. She wasn't Lydia. She had to remember that.

When Alec finished changing her bandages and stepped outside, Ryanne fell into step beside him. For a while, they walked in silence toward the fire pit, the bloody rags heavy in his hands. Finally, Ryanne spoke.

"I didn't realize you were as dumb as the rest of them."

Alec stopped, turning to stare at her. "What?"

"You're a fucking idiot if you think she wants to just be friends."

"We are friends."

"You're a liar!" Ryanne shot back without hesitation. "I know you loved Mom, and I know you were faithful to her until the day she died. But don't stand there and tell me there's nothing between you two."

"Even if there is—she's pregnant!" Alec's voice rose. "What the hell am I supposed to do with that?"

Ryanne crossed her arms, unimpressed. "Maybe be supportive, you arrogant prick. She's trying to save our lives the only way she knows how, and the last thing she needs is your pathetic 'we're just friends' speech. The poor girl is about to go through the most traumatic thing a woman can experience, and you just stomped all over her feelings."

Taking her voice up in mockery, she mimicked him: "But I didn't mean to. We are friends!" Then she glared. "News flash: neither of you wants that."

The stunned look on Alec's face was all the confirmation she needed. Snatching the bloody rags from his grip, she stalked off toward the burn pit, calling over her shoulder:

"This is the part where you go tell her you like her, dumbass!"

Alec stood frozen outside the tent, feeling like the world's biggest fool. She was right. He'd made a mess of things. Now he had to figure out how to tell his best friend that he wanted more. What a doofus.

He gripped the tent flap, hesitating for what felt like forever. Then, before he could decide, the flap ripped out of his hand—and Leah barreled right into him.

Her forehead smashed into his nose with brutal force. Alec staggered back, clutching his face as pain exploded between his eyes.

"Fucking hell!" he roared, voice thick with shock and agony.

"Ow!" Leah yelped in surprise, dropping the tent flap shut in Alec's face.

A real pair we'd make, he thought sarcastically, the bitter humor twisting in his gut.

It took Alec two more days before he could bring himself to look Leah in the eye for longer than a fleeting glance. Across the room, when she wasn't looking, he'd steal glances—long, guilty stares—feeling like a complete creep every single time.

This is the part where you tell her you like her, dumbass… His daughter's voice echoed in his head every time he drew near Leah, needling him like a conscience he couldn't silence. Yet no matter how many times he heard that phantom reminder, the words never made it past his lips.

Leah's transformation over the last few days was nothing short of astonishing—and, if Alec admitted it, a little terrifying. She was eating constantly, as if she could never feel full, and her condition was now glaringly obvious to anyone who laid eyes on her.

Once the midwife and surgeon were summoned, the whispers started. The entire village buzzed with talk after the first assessment. Just two days ago, the midwife had declared the pregnancy to be about eight weeks along. Since then, Leah's belly had swelled to three times that size. It was as though time itself had broken its rules for her. By the midwife's latest calculation, Leah had reached twenty-four weeks in only a handful of days. At this pace, they expected the birth to happen within forty-eight hours.

Alec shook his head in disbelief. *She has to do this seven times,* he thought grimly.

The women of the village, however, wasted no time. The moment they heard about the rapid progression, they sprang into action, bustling around Leah like a storm of care and preparation. Once they were convinced she truly was who she claimed to be, they poured their hearts into helping her. Sigils for protection were drawn and placed. Soft furs were laid out for bedding. Cloth for the delivery, gifts for the mother and child, and countless other tokens of love and reverence appeared one by one. These women remembered Leah—remembered her as one of their own. They had loved her, mourned her when they believed she'd died, and now rejoiced at her miraculous return.

And Alec? He couldn't even meet her eyes.

What a worm, the thought coiled in his mind like a snake, striking again and again with its venom.

He spent most of his time sitting on a bench outside the tent, whittling a toy soldier with his dagger. It was the only thing that seemed to keep his hands steady.

A lame gift for a baby, he thought bitterly, blowing wood shavings from his fingers. *Fitting, under the circumstances… but still lame.*

Ryanne's voice shattered his spiral of self-loathing. It wasn't just calling his name—it was panicked, urgent. His heart clenched, and breath lodged in his throat as a familiar terror clawed its way up his spine.

Lydia.

The name came like a dagger through his chest. He hadn't thought about her in years. She had almost died bringing Ryanne into the world. And there had been another—Ryanne's twin brother—who never stood a chance. Lydia had fought like hell to deliver him, nearly losing her life in the process. And when he finally arrived, the boy was too frail, too sickly to last more than a few days.

Just long enough to break Lydia's heart.

She had recovered in time, at least on the outside. But Alec had seen it—the quiet grief that never left her eyes when she looked at Ryanne. The boy's death had carved a hollow in his soul, too, one he never spoke of, fearing to tear open wounds Lydia worked so hard to close.

Now Leah faced that same shadow—but under far worse circumstances.

Alec tore through the tent door like a man possessed, nearly stumbling over his own boots in his haste.

Leah was bent over the wash basin, one hand cradling her swollen belly, the other gripping Ryanne's arm for dear life. Ryanne stood braced at her side, her arm slung across Leah's shoulders, trying to steady her as pain contorted her face.

Leah dragged in a deep breath and blew it out slowly.

"I didn't expect it to hurt so much," she whispered as the contraction ebbed.

"False alarm?" Alec asked, his voice tight, every word measured.

"Maybe… but I doubt it," Ryanne replied, her eyes flicking up to him with quiet dread.

A scream split the air outside—distant but drawing closer. Ryanne's head snapped toward the sound, her face paling. Leah clutched Ryanne's hand tighter, her knuckles whitening as another wave of pain surged through her.

"We need to get to the midwife," she panted, her breath hitching as her stomach clenched again.

Alec stepped forward, ready to help, but Ryanne froze him with a sharp look.

"Something's wrong," she murmured, jerking her chin toward the door.

Alec stilled, listening. The screams were louder now—accompanied by the crackle of fire and the clang of metal.

Something was very wrong.

He ripped back the curtain and peered outside. Chaos. The street was a living nightmare. Villagers lay strewn across the dirt like broken dolls. Flames devoured tents, one after another. And then Alec saw her— the midwife—on her knees in the dust as an army grunt drove a blade through her back.

Detached acceptance settled over him like cold steel.

The curtain dropped from his fingers. He turned on the girls, voice clipped and hard.

"The midwife is dead. We have to go. Now."

"What's happening?" Ryanne's voice tremored with fear as Alec snatched up the sword Leah had kept near her bed. He shoved it into his belt and herded them toward the back exit.

Leah made it as far as the flap before her legs buckled. She stifled a scream, but it came out strangled as she collapsed toward the forest floor. Alec lunged to catch her, wrapping her arm over his shoulder as Ryanne grabbed the other side. Together, they half-dragged, half-carried her toward the cover of the trees.

"Hey, you!"

The shout rang out behind them, sharp and unfamiliar. Alec spun, shoving Leah into Ryanne's arms as instinct took over. His dagger flashed, burying itself in the soldier's throat before the man could raise an alarm.

"Shit—not fast enough," Ryanne hissed as two more soldiers rounded the tent.

Alec didn't hesitate. He rammed the blade into the first one's eye and kicked the corpse hard in the chest, sending it tumbling down the steep incline. Before the second could react, Alec closed the gap and slit his throat in a single, vicious sweep. Hot blood sprayed, metallic and thick on his tongue.

And something inside Alec woke up.

As a dark fae, his bloodline thrived on carnage. Blood was their fire—the source of their strength, their ecstasy. Power surged through him the instant it touched his tongue. His tattoos flared to life, glowing with the same deep magenta as his eyes.

It had been years since he last tasted blood, but the hunger roared back like an old addiction. The chaos, the screams—it made his veins hum with wild energy. He wanted more. Gods help him, he needed more.

That was what had made him so deadly in battle once—the need. The thrill. The kill.

And now it was back.

He took two steps toward the burning camp, toward the screaming… when Ryanne's voice ripped him back from the edge.

"Dad! What do we do?"

Her pleading tone sliced through the haze, snapping his control back into place by sheer force of will. He wrenched himself away from the bloodlust, grabbed Leah, and hauled her into his arms.

"It's okay. It's going to be okay," Leah murmured against his neck like a mantra, whispering comfort even as another contraction ripped through her body.

Here she was, wracked with agony, carrying a supernatural child and bleeding strength with every breath—yet she was trying to soothe *him*.

What a pair we make, Alec thought bitterly.

"We head for the rendezvous—just like we practiced."

Ryanne hovered on the edge of the trees, torn. "I can't leave without Adam."

Alec cursed under his breath. They didn't have time for this.

"Ryanne! I know you love him, but you have to move! Right now Leah needs you if she's going to survive this. Adam knows the drill—he'll meet us there!"

She flinched at his raised voice, but the words struck home. With a shaky nod, she bolted into the woods, clearing the way ahead.

The path was familiar—worn into the earth over years of careful planning. When Ashur betrayed them and the village burned last time, they swore never to be caught unprepared again. This trail was their insurance. Their escape route.

But none of them had planned for this—a woman in full-blown labor in the middle of an evacuation.

Alec leaped a fallen tree just as Leah's strangled cry shattered the forest stillness.

"Stop!" she screamed. "She's coming!"

He skidded to a halt and lowered her to the ground as gently as he could. Her face was flushed, slick with sweat, eyes wide with panic. He touched her cheek, his own breath ragged as he looked deep into her eyes.

"Ryanne's going to take it from here. She's better at this than I am. I'll be right behind you."

He kissed Leah's forehead softly, then pressed his own against Ryanne's in a silent exchange of strength.

"I love you both," he said, leaping back over the fallen log with the grace of a predator returning to the hunt. In one smooth motion, he drew the sword Leah had brought to camp. The cold steel thrummed in his grip, and a familiar darkness bled into his soul like ink spilling across parchment. It welcomed him back, a part of him he had tried to bury for centuries.

The soldiers didn't stand a chance.

Alec lunged forward, a blur of speed and fury, cleaving through the first rank as if they were nothing more than dry twigs. The blade moved with an almost sentient hunger, thrusting, parrying, and slicing as though it could read his thoughts. Every motion felt effortless—natural—like an extension of his very being. It was glorious in its savagery. For the first time in years, Alec felt truly free.

He carved his way through them in mere heartbeats, leaving a trail of blood and broken bodies in his wake. When the last soldier fell, Alec vanished into the shadows of the trees, his breath steady, senses sharpened to a predatory edge. The hunt wasn't over. He could feel them out there—their fear pulsing through the forest like a drumbeat. His dark fae blood burned hot, urging him onward.

The pull guided him deeper, toward a cluster of towering trees where the air was thick with the coppery scent of blood. He flinched at the smell, a part of him recoiling—but the thought of Leah lying helpless in the woods beside his daughter steeled his resolve. If Lydia could see this moment, see what he was doing for them, maybe—just this once—she would approve.

A sudden flash of steel broke his thoughts. A soldier's blade lunged from the grove, aimed straight for his eye. Alec was faster. His hand shot out, seizing the man's wrist in an unyielding grip. With a savage twist, bone snapped like brittle wood. The jagged end of the radius tore through flesh, spraying blood in a crimson arc across Alec's face.

The scent drove him over the edge.

He latched onto the gushing wound, his lips closing over the pulsing artery, drinking greedily as centuries of denial crumbled. Warm life filled his mouth, burning down his throat like fire. Power—pure and intoxicating—surged through him, igniting every nerve with bliss. The sword in his hand vibrated, humming in unison with his hunger. It wanted blood as badly as he did.

A roar ripped from Alec's throat as he tore the man's arm free and cast it aside. Darkness uncoiled inside him, no longer chained but raging, beautiful, alive. He let it guide him, swinging the blade in a wide, merciless arc. The cluster of trees fell like wheat before the scythe, crashing to the earth in a thunder of splintering wood.

Three soldiers stood revealed among the stumps.

One look at Alec was all it took. The first man fainted dead away, crumpling to the ground. The second dropped his sword and bolted like a frightened deer. The third lost control of his bladder, his pants soaking as terror hollowed his face.

***

Leah had never imagined pain like this. The pressure crushing her hips was unbearable, like her bones were being split apart. She screamed, her fingers clawing at the earth beneath her. Ryanne knelt at her side, calm but firm, guiding her through the storm with steady words and gentle hands. The undergarments were long gone—drenched and discarded. Sweat plastered Leah's hair to her face, and tears burned her eyes. Every second stretched into eternity.

Meanwhile, Alec finished the last of the soldiers. When he returned, he was drenched in blood, his eyes still gleaming with that feral light. But his hand was steady as it found hers, grounding her in that moment. She gripped him like a lifeline, summoning every shred of strength to fulfill what felt like the cruelest bargain the gods had ever struck.

And then—relief. The agony shattered, swept away as a sharp cry pierced the air. Persephone entered the world wailing, tiny and fierce, her voice carrying like a battle hymn. Leah sagged back, shaking, as they placed the child against her chest. Warm. Fragile. Alive.

For a few precious minutes, Leah nursed her, whispering nonsense words through cracked lips. Then Alec scooped the newborn into his arms, his expression softening as if all the darkness had never existed. There was no time to linger—they had to move.

Leah was spent, her body limp and trembling, but Alec carried her as though she weighed nothing. She slipped into unconsciousness somewhere along the path, waking only when the rhythmic sway of his stride stopped. Blinking against the fading light, she found herself at the crescent lake, its surface glowing like molten silver beneath the first kiss of dusk.

Alec murmured something about a boat hidden among the trees. At nightfall, they would cross to the far side, scale the sheer rock face, and reach the mountain encampment. From there, they would wait— regroup—until the gods could restore their powers for good. Leah wasn't sure when that would be, or if it would ever happen.

The baby stirred in her arms, pulling her from the thought. An unexpected warmth bloomed inside her, deep and startling. She was no natural mother—at least, she'd never thought so—but there was something undeniable between them. A thread, a tether. Leaning down, she pressed a kiss to the tiny head, inhaling the sweet, new scent of life. The baby cooed softly in response, and despite everything, Leah smiled.

"What have you named her?" Alec's voice was gentle as he lowered himself beside her. His hand brushed the baby's cheek with reverent care, and then he drew them both against his chest, holding them as if nothing else mattered.

"This is Persephone, I believe," Leah whispered, her voice raw but steady. "She's the goddess of spring and new life. She taught me to use my powers—believe it or not." A shaky laugh escaped her. "Not that I've used them lately."

Her laugh turned into a soft sigh. "It sounds crazy, but I swear I aged a thousand years while I was… gone."

Alec studied her face, no judgment in his eyes, only quiet understanding.

"How do you know which one she is?" he asked, his voice low, careful not to wake the child sleeping between them.

"Well… that's the thing. I don't," Leah admitted. "When I left the otherworld, it all happened so fast. There wasn't a plan—no real strategy."

"So…" Alec's gaze flicked to the baby. "She could be one of the others?"

"It's possible, but I find it unlikely. I don't know how to explain it any better than this—she feels like Persephone. Like Hope."

Alec seemed to accept the answer, even if he didn't truly understand it. He exhaled heavily, a long breath that spoke of exhaustion, and slowly pulled away from her embrace. The weight of the day was settling on his shoulders.

"We'll be leaving in a few hours," he said quietly. "You should get some rest."

Leah watched as Alec stepped back, his silhouette outlined by the dim horizon. He had told her he loved her. That simple truth still lingered in her mind like a song she couldn't forget.

"Alec…" Her voice caught slightly as it summoned his piercing gaze. That look—intense, unwavering—always managed to steal her breath.

He was beautiful, and not just in the way most men were. He carried the raw, dangerous allure of a true warrior, a man forged in battle and burdened by scars. Lydia had been a fortunate woman to share a part of her life with him.

Brutal and broken on his best days, downright stubborn on his worst, Alec was still fiercely loyal to those he loved. Family, friends—he would bleed for them without hesitation, giving everything he had, no matter the personal cost. Yet, beneath that strength lived a man haunted by the fear of losing control to his darker nature. She saw it every time he pulled away from her—the silent war in his eyes, the guilt etched deep into every glance he gave her.

"I love you too," Leah whispered, her nerves threatening to undo her. Then, with a shaky breath, she added, "Just so you're aware." The words tumbled out awkwardly, and she instantly regretted how clumsy they sounded.

A slow smile curved across Alec's lips. He rubbed the back of his neck, gave her a funny little nod, and without another word, turned and left.

Several hours later, they set off across the lake, a stretch of black glass under the shroud of night. Silence became their shield. Each of them knew what hunted these waters—what had always hunted these waters.

Crescent Lake was home to countless magical beasts, but the Kelpies were the worst of them. Flesh-eaters, merciless and cunning. They had been hunted nearly to extinction when Leah was still a child—her father had made sure of that.

Those creatures were her mother's creation, born from magic, obedient only to her will. They killed without hesitation, without mercy. Her father had despised them, often calling them her mother's greatest mistake. Their volatile nature made them unpredictable, and soon they became a terror to society—dragging children from the village shores, drowning them as their parents screamed from the banks.

It wasn't until then that her mother finally agreed to their extermination. But even after, whispers of their presence lingered like ghosts in old stories. Rumors of sightings near the beach kept villagers far from these waters.

That was long ago. Leah doubted Ashur cared about anyone's safety now.

Alec muttered a curse under his breath as a heavy fog rolled in, swallowing the boat whole. They were blind. The soft slap of waves against the hull was drowned by the screeching calls of night hawks circling above. The sound set Leah on edge—those birds could betray their position in an instant.

"Daddy, there's a current," Ryanne whispered, clutching the edge as the boat drifted sideways.

Alec gripped the tiller, muscles taut as he tried to correct their course, but the boat kept sliding, carried by an unseen hand toward an unknown destination.

Leah's skin prickled. The night hawks had fallen silent. The sudden absence of their cries was deafening. Then, something bumped the boat.

***

Layla stormed through the village camp, fury burning like wildfire in her veins. If she didn't find the one responsible for Christian's death, she swore the entire settlement would burn.

Most of the villagers had been captured or killed, but that mattered little. Her focus was singular: find Adam.

She had waited a day and a half for Ashur's army to catch up, using that time to observe the village from the shadows. She had listened to whispered conversations through canvas walls, watched them from the darkness, and then—she saw him.

Adam.

His sudden appearance had stunned her. He stood barely three feet away, close enough that she could have reached out and touched him. His mother within arm's reach, and he didn't even know. There had been nothing she could do without exposing herself, so she waited. Watched him like a hawk until the soldiers descended.

When the army swept in, she seized her moment. Her men struck with brutal precision, ambushing the villagers before a warning cry could rise. Survivors were shackled and loaded into wagons, destined for interrogation at the castle.

As Layla crossed the square, a commotion caught her eye—a woman running for her life, three soldiers at her heels. They brought her down hard, pinning her to the dirt. One moved to mount her as she screamed.

Something inside Layla snapped. The memory slammed into her—those endless weeks when she had been nothing more than a gift to the barracks, her body bartered like coin. A violent rage surged.

Her hand brushed the base of her throat where that cursed chain once bound her, and with a flick of her wrist, the soldiers' bodies tore open like paper. They fell lifeless across the shrieking woman.

"Put her in the wagon," Layla said coldly to the stunned commander. "And keep your hands off her."

"How dare you harm my men! Ashur's going to hear about this, you willful bitch!" The commander's voice cracked with outrage, but Layla didn't even glance his way.

"Yes," she replied calmly, "he will."

She knew there would be consequences—some token punishment to appease appearances—but she also knew her value to Ashur. That was a card she would play when the time came.

When the commander grabbed her arm and tried to yank her back, Layla's power erupted like a blade drawn in silence. Her fingers locked around his wrist with crushing force. His scream pierced the night as the bones in his hand shattered, flesh blackening under her grip.

She dragged him closer until her breath brushed his ear.

"You have no power over me," she hissed. "The only reason your men survived my captivity was the chain they bound around my neck. Don't fool yourself into thinking I won't end you—and every man under your command—if you lay another hand on me or any woman here without my permission."

She shoved him back and studied the terror in his eyes.

"Do we have an understanding, Commander?"

He sobbed, unable to speak. Layla seized one of his withered fingers and twisted until he screamed again.

"I said—do you understand me?"

"YES!" The word tore from his throat.

By now, the entire camp was watching.

"Good. Now tell them what I just told you."

When she released him, she let a thread of power spill outward, and the earth answered. Plants withered to dust in a two-mile radius, the air heavy with the stench of death.

"Take the prisoners to the palace," she commanded, her tone like iron.

No one argued. The soldiers obeyed, fear making them swift.

***

Joel had witnessed everything, another fragment of his dreams playing out before his eyes. He didn't understand why this was happening—why visions blurred into reality—but he knew one thing: his strength was tied to her.

Each time Layla opened the siphon, the dreams sharpened, and his power swelled. It had grown steadily over the years since they bound their life forces together. Layla had explained that it would only continue as long as their connection endured.

Joel swung into the saddle, waiting for Layla to finish her display of dominance. When she finally joined him, masked excitement shimmering beneath her composed exterior, he knew what fueled it—Adam. Her son, captured and alive.

Anyone who truly knew her could see it.

What Joel couldn't figure out was how to tell her that Ashur intended to kill him.

Chapter Twelve

Layla rode beside the wagon where Adam was held, separated from the other prisoners. Unsure how to begin a conversation with the son she had lost for so long, she kept her face blank and her eyes fixed on the road. He didn't even know her. The reins bit into her palms and she loosened her grip. Showing agitation during their first conversation would not help her win his trust. My son, the words repeated in a loop in her head. She still could not believe she had found him.

"I understand you're something of a warrior?" she asked, the question lodged in her throat like a stone. Anxiety tightened her stomach until she felt as if it might reject her lunch. How mortifying that would be, she thought, forcing a breath through her teeth.

"What do you care? A lot of good it did me." Adam sat at the front of the wagon, picking mud from his boot with a stub of a stick. Hopefully it was mud, Layla told herself, and not something worse.

"Fucking worthless," Adam muttered, and tossed the stick toward the back of the wagon.

"Don't say that!" Layla had not meant to shout. He looked at her as if she had grown a second head; surprise and a guarded wariness showed in the set of his jaw.

"Don't you realize all of this is happening because of you?" she pressed. Judging from the blankness on his face, she guessed the answer was no.

"Excuse me?" he stammered. Layla noticed, with a small, hopeful shock, that he was actually paying attention. He sat up a fraction straighter.

She chewed her lower lip, uncertain how much to tell him. Wanting to tell him everything, she forced herself to choose her words.

"Your parents have been looking for you. I've been looking for you." Her voice shook; tears pooled hot against her lids.

"What the hell are you talking about? My parents died years ago." His denial cut into her like salt.

"They weren't your parents!" she screamed. Her face went hard, contorting into a mask of rage and grief. The shriek that tore from her startled both of them; Adam clapped his hands over his ears. An unintentional ripple of power surged out from her and slammed him against the opposite side of the cage. He went still, breathless.

Bristling at her loss of control, Layla pulled back and forced herself to calm. She let the mare pick up a longer stride and put some distance between them. She had embarrassed herself—this was not the way she had planned to reach him. She would have to be patient and bring him home. Ashur would be pleased to see him again, she told herself, imagining his weathered face lighting up. A shiver traveled down her spine; she felt equal parts hope and dread.

Return to the palace was slow. The wagons stuck in mud and ruts, requiring frequent stops, but Layla insisted on taking their time. She found it easier to speak with Adam once the day's chores wound down and the camp fires were lit: fewer responsibilities, fewer eyes to worry about. On the third evening they made camp a few miles from the palace. Layla had made very little progress; Adam thought her insane and every argument she made only sounded crazier to him. She drifted back to the fire where she shared a patch of warmth with Joel. He could see she had been crying.

"Are you all right?" he asked, shoulders hunched beneath the weight of the firewood he carried. The arms full of wood kept him from drawing her close—something she would not have welcomed publicly anyway— yet she looked like she needed the comfort.

"He hates me," she managed, before a choked sob seized her and she bolted for their tent. Joel stacked the wood quickly and followed. She folded herself on the bed, her face buried in her knees, the small sounds of her breathing and sniffling filling the narrow space. She looked fragile, and Joel moved cautiously, not to frighten her.

"You know," Joel sat beside her, his voice soft, "I once knew a man who faded with understanding." A long pause stretched out; at last a single, bloodshot eye peered from between her knees.

"So you're saying I have to make him understand?" she asked, muffled.

"I think 'make' is the wrong word," Joel said. "You have to help him see it from his perspective. All he knows is what he's seen and what he's been told. He believes what he's been raised to believe. He's still young in many ways. It will take time to build trust, but I have faith in you." He kissed the crown of her head.

"Thank you," she said, voice small.

On an unrelated note, Joel rose and crossed to the corner where a whiskey bottle lay. Layla sat up, waving away his offer to drink.

"I don't think you should take him back to the palace," Joel said quickly, before he lost his nerve. He put down the glass, poured another, and waited for her. Shock flitted across her face like a moth.

"What? Why?" indignation edged into her voice.

"I don't know how to explain this without sounding crazy, but I think Ashur is going to kill him."

"You're insane!" She laughed, a short, incredulous sound that turned defensive. "What do you mean he's going to kill him? That's his only son out there!"

"I understand that, but I've been having these… strange dreams. I see the three of you—" he faltered, searching for the words. "I'm worried he'll try something."

Layla's laugh turned to fury. "You have a feeling? You want to break up a family because of a feeling?" She rose, fury boiling over.

"That's not—" Joel began, but she cut him off.

"Then explain it to me, Joel." Her tone left no room for equivocation.

Joel could not find a way to make his words hold weight. Layla's frustration mounted until she slapped him hard. "You will not take away my dreams because you're jealous. You have until the end of the night to be gone, or I'll kill you." She spat the words and stormed from the tent.

She wandered the woods through most of the night and finally rested beside a brook that offered a clear, melancholy view of the palace in the distance. It had once been beautiful—the valley full of flowering trees and carefully tended groves—but now brambles and overgrowth claimed what had been tended. Joel had helped her carve a life out of that destruction; she had found a kind of solace in the band of men who followed her. They had all been taken from her in one way or another, and Joel's sudden swell of jealous bitterness felt like another loss. She wept quietly and severed the small, private bond that had held them together. She convinced herself she was better off alone.

When she returned the next morning, Joel was gone. A pang of regret stung, but she stood by her choice—she always stood by her choices, no matter how painful. The company broke camp and began the short ride home. Layla rode at the rear until she spotted the commander at the front, leaning over his mount, his deformed hand wrapped and nursing.

"When we reach the castle walls, I want that man brought to my chambers. Keep your mouth shut about it, or I'll take more than your hand." His eyes were hard as flint; the commander, who had learned caution, bowed and rode on to check the prisoners.

"What would you like me to do with the rest of them?" he asked.

"Torture them until someone tells us what we want to know. Start with the kids—won't take long." Layla's voice held no mercy. She had no intention of letting them slip away again.

"Tell your men to restock supplies and eat quickly. We leave again soon."

Ashur was eating breakfast in the banquet hall when the company entered the palace gates. Layla, flushed with triumph, hurried upstairs to deliver the news herself. At the massive timber doors, she knocked with trembling fingers, her excitement betraying her otherwise composed demeanor.

"Sire!" she said, stepping inside and offering a curtsy.

"Where the fuck have you been?" Ashur roared, hurling his plate across the hall. Layla sidestepped the flying crockery and remained silent.

"Speak, woman!" he thundered, shoving back his chair and rising to his full height behind the banquet table. His shadow stretched across the room like a threat. Layla instantly lowered her gaze, stripping her face of all expression.

"I was searching for the villagers," she answered carefully. "We received a report from a reliable source that they were hiding in the woods, two days' journey from here. The message also said Adam was with them."

Her eyes flicked up, searching for some trace of softness on his face. Instead, Ashur sneered at her, his lip curling with contempt.

"You're still on about that little bastard of yours?"

Layla's mask cracked, her lips parting in shock. She tried to protest. "He's our so—"

The table flipped violently, slamming against the stone floor as Ashur hurled it at her.

"Do you have any idea what's been happening here?" he shouted. "And you dare bring up that worthless personification of jizz to me?"

He seized her by the hair, dragging her to the ground, and kicked her with ruthless precision. Each blow was punctuated with rage.

"If I ever hear his name again, I'll kill you. Do you hear me?"

At last, he straightened his vest, as if violence were nothing more than an inconvenience, and strode to the mirror. He adjusted his hair with meticulous care until every strand was in place.

"Your aunt is missing," he said flatly, his tone shifting to cold calculation. "She apparently leapt from the window. No trace of her power signature remains, and every attempt to locate her has failed. She is assumed dead."

He turned and locked eyes with her as she rose shakily from the ground, forcing herself to stand straight.

"Even without your aunt, the plan is not entirely ruined. Someone was inhabiting her body. Find them—and bring them to me."

"Yes, sire," Layla murmured, managing a curtsy despite the ache in her limbs. She slipped from the chamber before he found another excuse to vent his fury. Once the door closed behind her, she pressed her hand to her ribs and steadied her breath. She made for the dungeons. Someone there would talk.

***

Meanwhile, Leah endured five more births in the span of twenty days. Alec had feared the infants would remain unnaturally small, but to his relief, he was wrong. Persephone, who had already reached womanhood by the time Leah bore the second god, assisted with the deliveries. With her help, the births grew smoother, though no less astonishing.

The second child was named Zeus—a troublesome presence from the start—while the other newborn gods and goddesses ranged from tolerable to intriguing.

The survivors who made it to the rendezvous were far fewer than expected. Alec's heart sank when he saw Adam was not among them. Reports claimed soldiers had been funneling captives into cages. If fortune held, Adam might still be alive among them. Ryanne had been inconsolable since hearing the news. She threw herself into volunteering for messenger parties, determined to bring back aid from neighboring kingdoms.

Once Persephone confirmed the final pregnancy, they would have six days to prepare for their assault on the false King. Alec devoted himself to being useful, though he privately admitted that beyond war, he had little to offer.

When word arrived that their allies would march in support, Alec nearly wept with gratitude. Still, reinforcements would take weeks to arrive, and the risk of discovery before then was real. Vigilance became his mantra. He organized patrols around their temporary encampment, combed through possible ambush sites, and searched tirelessly for the old weapons caches hidden along the mountainside.

Every day felt like an exercise in both strategy and regret. Hunting a rabbit one afternoon, he reflected grimly that he was better at killing than at fatherhood or marriage. He had failed Lydia, failed Leah more times than he could count, and could scarcely believe his daughter still wanted him in her life. War had once thrilled him, but centuries of bloodshed had stripped the joy away. Now it was duty—and perhaps the only way he could still provide for those who depended on him.

He finally caught the rabbit, cleaned it, and set a small fire. As the smell of roasting meat rose, Alec renewed his blood magic, slicing carefully and murmuring old rites. He stared at the black blade Leah had given him. It burned faintly against his hip, almost like a jealous lover.

The absurd thought made him laugh. "I need a new knife," he muttered, though he knew it was a lie. His dwarven throwing knives had served him faithfully for over three thousand years. They had pried boulders, felled beasts, and taken countless lives—yet never once dulled or tarnished.

The sword flared hot in response, rattling faintly in its sheath.

"No… fucking way." Alec drew it slowly, and as he did, waves of warmth and affection coursed through him. He couldn't tell if they belonged to him or the blade.

"King Arthur's sword," he said with a dry chuckle. Trust Leah to stumble across such a relic.

The weapon was plain, the way Alec preferred, though its pommel was uncomfortably large. As soon as he noted the flaw, it reshaped beneath his grip. He tested its balance with a twirl, and with every movement the blade adapted, correcting imperfections until it felt like an extension of his own body.

Excitement stirred in his chest. He launched into a sword dance, slicing and spinning, the steel singing with each stroke. He leapt against a birch tree, using its trunk as a springboard, twisting midair before landing in a sweeping arc. His muscles burned, his lungs heaved, but he was alive again—alive in a way he hadn't felt in centuries.

When the dance ended, he performed the old clan ritual, offering the rabbit's blood to the blade and drinking his share with the weapon raised high. Nostalgia pricked at him, sweet and sharp.

As his vision cleared, the world sharpened. The forest glowed with a vibrancy he had forgotten. Through a break in the canopy, sunlight revealed the distant palace and its sprawling grounds. Drawn forward, Alec stepped to the cliff's edge and looked down.

Below, the King's army gathered in the courtyard. They had less time than he thought. If they waited for reinforcements, it would be too late.

They would need to strike now.

Alec raced back to the rendezvous, already planning the guard schedules in his mind.

Leah felt the moment Hades's soul entered her womb: a hot, nauseous wave that rolled through her and left her hollow with weakness. Her knees folded; she dropped to the floor with a suddenness she had never known. Ryanne and Persephone—who had been chatting over a cup of tea only moments before—scrambled to help her to her feet.

"Maja, Leah! Are you all right?" Ryanne's worry flashed across her face; Persephone's expression was threaded with a quiet, distant sadness.

"Hades is here." Leah kept her voice steady, though Persephone could see tears forming at the corners of her eyes. She managed a reassuring smile for Ryanne.

"I'm all right. I just need to rest a bit." She lied. The air in the tent felt heavy and thick in her lungs; every breath took too much effort. Ryanne's gaze flicked from Leah to Persephone and back, suspicion and concern warring across her features.

Persephone stepped back and, with practiced gentleness, laid Leah down on the bed. Ryanne pulled away, voice trembling as she asked the question Leah had been trying to avoid.

"What did you say his power was again?" The edge in her tone was barely hidden.

Leah sighed and extended a hand. "Life is about balance, little one." Kneeling beside her, Ryanne took Leah's hand as Persephone spoke, nodding toward Leah with grave acceptance.

"In order to bring new life into the world, we must accept the death of the old." Persephone rested a cool palm against Leah's stomach.

Leah's throat tightened. "I don't want your father to know." The words came out small; her chest ached at the thought of Alec and Ryanne being forced to lose her again.

Ryanne shook her head, stubbornness flaring. "No! You can't keep something like this from him. It's — it's too big. You must tell him!" She tried to pull away, to stand, but Leah's hands were firm; Leah's body was too rooted for Ryanne to break free.

"He'll kill the baby." Leah said it with force, shaking her head as if the motion could push the thought away.

Leah's voice cracked. "I've known what kind of man your father is for nearly a millennium. He's not evil, but he loves fiercely. He would kill this child to keep me safe, and our war on Ashur will fail." She studied Ryanne as the younger woman sobbed into Leah's hand.

"But we just got you back." Ryanne's plea was raw. "I can't lose you again."

Leah lifted her chin and fixed Ryanne with an intense, steady look. She needed Ryanne to see the whole picture, not only the immediate danger. She needed her to understand that this decision was agonizing and not made lightly.

A gentle stir in her belly: the baby moved for the first time. Leah heard a whisper in her head—soft, urgent—and images sprang behind her eyes. Hades was sending something through that touch.

"I need to show you something," Leah said.

Ryanne's tears came harder; she rubbed her nose with the back of her hand. Leah closed her eyes, sank inward, and breathed out her intent toward Ryanne. When Ryanne's consciousness followed, she tumbled into Leah's dreamscape and stood in a vision that replayed itself on a loop.

The sky above was black and bruised; storm clouds swirled with an ominous red glow at their center. This was no ordinary storm. Energy crackled in the air so thickly it sounded like distant drums. Down the mountain, Ashur's army marched, ranks moving like a tide. Villagers tried to flee, but the soldiers cut them down where they stood. Even when a villager killed a soldier, lightning arced from nowhere and revived the corpse—only to twist it into something cruel and obedient.

Ryanne had known Ashur was dangerous; she had not imagined this. The vision shifted: a neighboring kingdom's stronghold breached, gates splintered, blood in the courtyard. It changed again and revealed Altrious—Ryanne's grandfather—the gentle old man who had once bounced her on his knee and humored her with dolls. In the vision he charged forward, ax raised, every movement fierce and desperate for someone his age. He fought with unexpected skill but was cut down before he reached Ashur's inner guard. Ryanne watched the life drain from him as if she were watching a memory turned violent.

Every city Ashur took repeated the same horror. No one was left alive. Behind him, an ever-growing horde of monsters trailed; with each conquest, his dragon-priests raised the dead and bound them to Ashur's will. The scenes blurred into one another until the dream snapped back to its beginning — and then, there was a man in khakis and a button-up shirt standing where the mountain path opened.

Ryanne didn't know why she recognized the awkward wardrobe, but she did. Knew them as she knew the man who wore them —Hades— the bringer of death, ender of stars. He looked so normal among the devastation. Simply watching as Ashur's soldiers rushed a stranger; they meant to strike. The man stepped aside as a soldier barreled past and touched the soldier's shoulder. The soldier dropped, struck by lightning that came from nowhere. The man adjusted his glasses, expression bored, as if the carnage barely registered. The soldier didn't move again.

Leah stood beside Ryanne in the dreamscape and squeezed her hand lightly as the scene repeated again and again. Each ne death with the same result. A natural end.

"This is why we need Hades," Leah said. "Even Zeus, the king of the gods, cannot stand against him."

Leah cupped Ryanne's chin, pleading for her to meet her eyes. But Ryanne pulled away, head bowed against the weight of what she had seen.

"You just came home," she whispered. "You're a second mother to me — you always have been — and now you're asking me to do nothing. You're asking me to let you die?" Tears streamed down her face; each word trembled.

Leah wrapped her arms around Ryanne and held her close until the younger woman's sobs quieted.

"I — I'm asking you to trust me," Leah said.

Ryanne hugged her fiercely. "I can't watch. I won't tell him, but I can't watch it happen. My heart won't survive it."

"That's all right." Leah held her a moment longer. "Just know that I love you always." She squeezed Ryanne quickly, then pulled back to arm's length. The tent snapped back into focus.

Leah's voice was a fragile thing when she spoke. "Is there a plan in place already?" she asked Persephone.

"You don't need to worry about that. But since I know you won't listen anyway—yes. It's a pretty good one, in fact."

Picking up a clean dish from the counter, Persephone wiped it nervously. Her anxiety always made her more prone to cleaning. Leah was reminded of the stories her mother used to tell about the forest spirits who crept into homes at night, tidying them not out of obligation but out of care, as though the house itself were alive. She supposed that description fit Persephone's personality perfectly.

Her mother had called them brownies.

Persephone's face had changed, subtly taking on some of Leah's features. Her cheekbones sat a little higher now, her jaw more angular.

With stout hips and a generally larger build, she seemed bigger in every way Leah could think of. Even her hair was different—puffier, with a new auburn hue that caught the sunlight and shimmered like fire.

"Alec is proposing we attack the palace directly," Persephone said to no one in particular.

"I'm concerned," she continued, "with the number of villagers that were captured. We may end up walking into a trap. If Hades were here…" She gestured toward Leah's stomach.

"We wouldn't even need to discuss strategy—just escort him inside and lock the door."

Leah rubbed her belly absentmindedly.

"In any case, we've decided for sure on a Plan B. We'll split into two groups. The first will attack the grounds on foot with Ares, Zeus, and Hera, while the second provides cover fire from a safe distance with Hecate. Phanes and I will be your personal midwives and guards until Hades makes his debut."

"What about Hades?" Leah asked, confused.

"Ah, yes, well…" Persephone slapped the towel over the back of a chair for emphasis. "He doesn't have to be physically present—just alive—for Plan B. Hades can choose a champion. It's one of the perks of being death. He can reach you from anywhere. He'll pick someone, imbue them with his power, and use them as a conduit if necessary. But keep in mind, this is only Plan B. It's not meant to be used at all, so don't start getting crazy ideas."

"Well, what's Plan A then?" Feeling her strength return, Leah sat up straighter in the bed, fully invested now.

"Well…" Persephone and Ryanne exchanged a glance.

"We attack the palace directly," Ryanne said with quiet confidence.

***

As Layla had predicted, it hadn't taken long for one of the villagers to tell them everything they needed to know. One and a half days, to be exact. To her surprise, the defector was a man.

He was stumpy—almost dwarf-like—with broad shoulders and chubby cheeks. A sparse patchwork of dark curls dotted his chin beneath a broad nose, while his eyebrows looked like two fat caterpillars clinging to his brow. Layla hadn't realized until now that ears could define a person's appearance. His stuck out from his head like little wings, as though ready to lift him into the air.

But his teeth unsettled her most. They reminded her of a strange creature she had once encountered, one the locals had called a fairy.

Layla had already ordered the commander to gather his men in the courtyard. They had enough time to replenish their supplies and rest while searching for their new guide, though the search had cost them nearly two days. Stomping into the courtyard, she didn't notice the eyes tracking her from the edge of the keep.

She shoved the rope tied around the villager's neck into the hands of a soldier, sending him to the front of the army. Mounting her horse, she knew it was finally time to end this rebellion.

The sky above the castle darkened, clouds thickening ominously as Ashur's intent coiled inside her chest. His fury slithered through their bond like a snake winding around her arms, raising the hairs on her skin. He would let the world burn before losing his wife again.

And Layla knew this would not end until he discovered where Lux had gone.

For a moment, she thought about Joel. How much steadier she might feel if he were beside her. But Joel had a habit of questioning her choices, and she didn't need that—not today. After today, she would never know unhappiness again. Ashur had promised her that.

***

Joel watched Layla leave, an army of men and dragon priests trailing in her wake.

He had been shadowing her for days, following from a distance, watching helplessly from the shadows as Ashur beat her. The bruises she carried haunted him, but so did her silence.

It had taken him most of the afternoon to search the castle for Adam. The thought that he might never make things right with Layla gnawed at him, but he swore he would not let Ashur kill her son. Joel knew the monster would never allow the boy to live once he found him hidden inside the castle.

At first, Joel had crept through the corridors, cautious and careful to avoid detection. But it hadn't taken long to realize the castle was nearly deserted. Now he walked openly, his boots echoing against the stone.

He stopped outside Leah's chamber door when he heard the crashing inside. Whoever was in there had a vendetta.

Finding the hidden key Layla always kept tucked inside a mirage by the door, Joel unlocked it.

Silence greeted him. The room was dark, the lingering scent of smoke telling him the candles had been blown out.

Joel knew it was a trap, but that knowledge didn't stop him. He was here to save the boy's life.

He threw the door wide open and called into the darkness.

"Adam, I'm here to help."

"Help with what?"

The voice behind him froze Joel's blood. Smooth, rich, and deep, Ashur's words slid across his skin like silk. Joel's legs trembled as he turned, dread seeping into his bones.

Chapter Thirteen

Alec was alerted to the enemy movement almost two days later. He sat hunched over a rough-hewn desk, anxiously scribbling maneuver drills on parchment and scratching them out before the ink had even dried. He had never been good at waiting, and the endless anticipation gnawed at him. When the messenger finally brought word that the enemy was advancing, he felt a wave of relief before fear had the chance to take hold.

He gathered his sword and daggers from the chest beside the bed, fastening them to his belt with steady but impatient hands, then stepped out into the early evening air. The fading light painted the camp in tones of fire and shadow.

Leah, Ryanne, and Persephone were already waiting for him. Behind them, Alec noticed Phanes, his sharp gaze fixed almost unblinking on Leah. Another god of life, Alec had been told. Leah's pregnancy was maturing with alarming speed—faster than the others before it—and yet something about this time unsettled him. Persephone and Ryanne rarely left her side, but Phanes never left her at all. Alec doubted the man had closed his eyes in days.

He had tried to broach the subject with Leah, voicing his unease, but she brushed it off, claiming his hyperawareness was getting the better of him again. Still, the way Phanes's presence clung to her felt purposeful, even necessary, though no one—including Ryanne—would acknowledge it. That silence only fed Alec's growing conviction that something was very wrong. Perhaps, he thought grimly, he was simply growing paranoid with age. His Uncle Farron had gone the same way—

sharp and sound until the month before his death, then suddenly raving, muttering to walls no one else could see.

Alec pushed the thought aside and took Leah's hand, pressing it to his lips.

"Are you ready?" he asked, forcing a smile. He was terrified for her, but there was nothing more he could do than fight—to hold off Ashur's army until the last god had entered the world. If the timing was true, Leah would be in labor within hours. The enemy would need most of the day to crest the ridge, which meant her pain and his battle would arrive almost together.

Leah smiled back, calm despite the strain in her eyes.

"I'll be with the mages until it's time for Hades to make his debut. The least I can do with these primordial powers is put them to use while we have the chance."

"Just be careful," Alec said softly. "I want to see both of you home after this."

He pinched her chin affectionately, kissed her, then kissed Ryanne goodbye before turning to join Ares at the front of the rebellion.

Ryanne waited until Alec was out of earshot before speaking. "He's never going to forgive us for this," she murmured, then walked away without another word.

Phanes and Persephone steadied Leah as they guided her to the western cliff face. From there, the world unfolded beneath her. The mages stood two hundred feet below, their positions marked by faint glimmers of power. Through the breaks in the trees, she caught flashes of metal—Ashur's soldiers pushing forward beneath the bleeding colors of sunset.

The gods eased Leah onto a rocky ledge. She sat, clutching her stomach, and stared across the Moro. Her homeland—beautiful, fractured, forever changed. Yet she still had the chance to save it. She had to, for Alec and for Ryanne.

Without Alec's watchful eyes upon her, she no longer bothered to hide the pain. All morning it had been building, clawing at her insides as Hades turned restlessly within her. A brutal kick sent her reeling off her mat. She fell to her knees, retching violently onto the stone.

Phanes and Persephone rushed to help her, steadying her shoulders as her body shuddered. Leah lifted her gaze to Phanes and noticed sweat streaking his brow, his focus honed solely on channeling life into her. Her pain dulled, though the relief was fragile.

"Thank you," she whispered through heavy breaths. He only nodded, his jaw tight, as she turned back toward the horizon.

The sun was sinking low. This would be her last sunset, she knew. She clung to it for just a moment longer.

Hecate's traps lay in place, stones charged with the unstable magic she had siphoned from Leah in the spirit world. They lined the perimeter of the mages' range, sensitive enough that the vibrations of marching feet would trigger catastrophic blasts.

The army was nearly upon them. Soon, the stones would detonate, and the mages would unleash their fire, sowing confusion for Alec's ambush.

Leah inhaled deeply, reached into the growing darkness, and pulled it into herself. Above, clouds thickened into a roiling black mass streaked with veins of violet. Lightning licked across the sky as Zeus fueled her gathering storm. Thunder rolled over the cliffs, the wind slicing cold across the rocks.

Her powers swelled, amplified by the night itself—and by the presence of her unborn son. For now, Hades's magic was still hers to command, but it came at a cost. Her body strained under the pressure. Bones shifted. Organs compressed. Sweat poured down her face as she fought to contain the torrent.

Phanes clutched her shoulder, his own breath ragged as he forced more life into her failing body. Persephone steadied her from the other side. Leah must have been a terrifying sight—an omen of death tethered to the world by the hands of gods.

Her hair lifted in the wind, raven strands bleaching into white. Her eyes widened until the pupils swallowed her irises, the whites bleeding red. Thin rivulets of blood trickled from her nose, ears, and eyes as the strain shattered her vessels. Her skin shriveled, her flesh greying as though already claimed by the grave.

Leah screamed, a sound that split the air like steel tearing, and then she released it all. Power ripped free in a cataclysm, carrying her life with it.

***

Layla had not expected to contend with lightning as she led Ashur's forces up the mountain. Drawing on his power, she countered as best she could, whipping walls of air to deflect the strikes. It was exhausting. She was the only one strong enough to hold back the storm, while the dragon priests at her side proved utterly useless. Once again, the burden of the army's survival rested on her shoulders.

She felt a bitter satisfaction when one bolt collapsed a trail ahead, taking an entire platoon down with it. But irritation soured it quickly. She wanted this over—wanted to return to her son. Her thoughts strayed to Adam, and a pang hit her chest. She had wanted him to meet Joel.

That single thought was her undoing.

The stones behind her detonated in a chain of explosions. Her horse reared, throwing her violently into a tree. Pain exploded across her skull, and the world tilted.

The daisy chain of blasts tore through Ashur's ranks. Soldiers who should have revived under his power lay still, unmoving, corpses sprawled in grotesque shapes. Confusion gnawed at her. Why weren't they rising?

Shadows surged. Rebels charged, screaming as they fell upon the survivors. Layla drew her sword, cutting one man down and driving her blade through his neck before he could rise again. Blood smeared her hand as she pressed it to her head, trying to steady the spinning world.

She fought her way forward, but the press of attackers and the absence of her own soldiers forced her into retreat. Smoke and darkness thickened the sky, forcing her to siphon more of Ashur's strength just to see.

She caught sight of her men through the chaos—running. Running for the castle, abandoning her.

"Fucking cowards!" she screamed, slashing one villager's throat and hurling his body into another. But she could not hold her ground.

She turned and fled after them, fury burning in her chest.

A sudden sonic boom split the air. Layla froze, eyes snapping to the sky. A black sphere of roiling smoke crashed into the mountainside, spilling outward like a tide of death.

The mist devoured everything. Soldiers choked, their flesh dissolving in their own hands. Others seized and collapsed, writhing as the poison took them.

"What the actual fuck is happening?" she whispered, scrambling onto a boulder to escape the creeping death.

Through the haze, she saw him. A lone figure standing unyielding in the mist. Tall, lean, auburn-haired, with spectacles glinting over sharp features. An odd garb draped his frame.

Then the lightning revealed the truth.

The illusion burned away, and his flesh vanished. A skeletal face stared back at her, empty sockets burning with venomous yellow light. His grin—slow, deliberate, predatory—made her heart pound with terror.

He moved toward her with dreadful purpose.

Panic took her. Layla teleported back to the palace, trembling, her body still shaking from the horror.

Alec and his men waited for the advancing army to reach the trap laid out by Hecate. She hadn't explained much about how the devices functioned; however, Alec had seen a similar technique during the war. The mages would gather excess energy, pressurize it into containers, and once those were placed, a magical tripwire would be attached to the trigger, activating the device.

Like with any other ambush, Alec and his men simply had to wait for the opportune moment. When the devices finally went off, they worked even better than anticipated. The enemy army was effectively divided in two, and the rebels wasted no time exploiting the chaos.

Alec flew out of the trees like a madman. The enemy had been utterly unprepared for the ambush, and Alec's men struck with a ferocity that sent soldiers crumbling in their wake. They carved their way through the ranks with such relentless force that Alec almost felt guilty when the enemy broke formation and fled. Almost.

A flurry of fire magic rained down from above, scorching the air and striking the fleeing soldiers as the mages provided cover fire. The sword in Alec's hand seemed to sing in ecstasy. Every clash of steel against steel brought him a surge of exhilaration. Raising the blade high, he gave the order.

"After them!" he bellowed.

The answering war cries erupted from his men, savage and triumphant, bringing a grim smile to his face as they charged down the mountain. Off to his left, a female voice screamed, "Fucking cowards!"

Alec turned toward the sound and spotted a woman gripping a sword slick with blood from the slain villager at her feet. Rage burned in her eyes as she seethed at the sight of the broken and retreating army. For an instant, Alec thought it was Leah. But no—this was Layla.

It had been centuries since he had seen her in person, back then she had been in her *own* body. The one that was now safely away from the war front, giving birth to a god. The wildness of her hair, the fire in her gaze—it pulled him back to memories of the war. Chuckling at the recollection, he twirled Arthur's sword in his hand and began stalking in her direction. He would savor dismantling her one piece at a time. There was no rush. He was a gentleman, after all.

His savage fantasy was cut short when Layla suddenly took off after her retreating men, her rage propelling her forward. Alec snarled at himself for missing the moment and followed at an easy run.

Just as she was catching up to her soldiers, a thunderous sonic boom cracked across the blackened sky. The vibration shook the earth beneath

Alec's feet, and instinct hurled him into the nearest tree. Persephone had warned him that when death arrived, the ground would be swallowed in toxic smoke. Ares had advised the rebels: if the fallout came, their best chance was to escape through the tree branches.

The warning proved true. A massive sphere of black smoke ripped through the forest, swallowing a large portion of the fleeing army. Layla quickly covered her mouth, while the men caught within the rolling fog screamed and choked on their own blood. Their bodies broke down in grotesque spasms, limbs disintegrating into pools of flesh that splattered with a wet slap as they collapsed one after another.

Alec couldn't help but marvel at the brutality. On a nearby boulder, Layla scrambled up to avoid the deadly fog, her chest heaving. An involuntary growl rumbled in Alec's throat. *Calm down. There's plenty of time,* he reminded himself.

Layla let out a startled cry, staring not just at the remains of her men but at something else beyond them. Alec followed her gaze. Through the haze, a male figure emerged, his approach slow and deliberate, heavy with menace. Layla vanished from the rock in a blink.

"No!" Alec roared, furious. He had lost his chance again. Self-disgust burned in him. He clenched his teeth, cursed his arrogance, and berated himself for letting the opportunity slip away.

In his fury, he failed to notice the danger his outburst invited. When he opened his eyes again, a man crouched mere inches from him. Instinct jerked Alec's sword up as a barrier. The stranger's unassuming clothing could not disguise the chilling gleam in his yellow eyes.

Lightning split the sky, illuminating the grotesque face before him. Alec was no stranger to violence, but this figure—this *thing*—was something else entirely. It had but one purpose: to kill. Its eyes left no doubt of that.

Hades' hands twitched ever so slightly in Alec's direction, and the sword in Alec's grip thrummed with anticipation. For a fleeting, horrifying moment, Alec wondered if he might be the first victim of death insanity.

Yet Hades did not strike. The terrible viper's gaze softened; the yellow receded, replaced by warm golden irises. His body sagged, and with a sudden clumsy motion, he toppled from the tree.

Alec exhaled in relief as a groan echoed from the forest floor.

"You okay?" he called down, grateful to the stars.

Flat on his back, Hades gave a sarcastic thumbs-up.

"Good. Get up. We have a witch to catch."

***

Meanwhile, in the castle, Joel stood frozen in the doorway to Layla's chamber, gripped by anxious confusion. Several things were wrong with this picture. First, he had already searched the castle—it was supposed to be empty. Second, he had not expected to be caught so easily. And third, Ashur wasn't even supposed to know his name.

Joel took a steadying breath and turned to face the intruder. Confidently, he proclaimed, "Help with your escape, Adam."

But the murderous rage on Ashur's face told Joel he had made a grave mistake.

Ashur's fist drove into his gut with such force that Joel was hurled across the chamber, crashing to the floor in a heap. The pain was immediate, but worse was the humiliating realization—he was fairly certain he had just shit himself.

Striding forward, Ashur slammed the doors shut behind him, sealing Joel inside. From the shadows came a skittering sound, and a small round pot rolled gently across the floor. A short fuse jutted from a wax seal at the top, holding the contents tight within.

The only question—what was inside?

A spark flickered in the darkness. Then another. Joel realized Adam was trying to send him a message.

Grunting theatrically, Joel forced himself to his feet, stumbling backward in a calculated show. Keeping Adam out of Ashur's line of sight, Joel summoned the pot into his hand and hurled it at the god.

The container shattered against Ashur's head, releasing a cloud of white powder that filled the air and coated his body.

"Flour? Really?" He looked at Joel as if the man had lost his mind.

Ashur shook his head, sending another puff of white dust into the air. Joel wasn't entirely sure what Ashur expected him to do either, but with a shrug, he flung a pitiful little ball of fire into the suspended particles. His mana had been badly drained since leaving Layla in the woods, and it showed. Yet the reaction was nothing short of obscene.

The flour ignited with a thunderous explosion that ripped through the chamber. Ashur was swallowed in a wall of flame, and Joel stumbled back in shock, only to collide with something fast and solid. The impact shoved him forward before a rough grip caught him by the collar, yanking him off balance. He realized, in a dizzy second, that it was Adam dragging him toward the exit.

Adam had anticipated the chaos and wasted no time seizing the chance to escape—dragging Joel with him whether Joel agreed or not.

Ashur, however, recovered quicker than either of them expected. With a snap of his will, a gust of wind tore their feet out from under them. Joel and Adam crashed in a tangled heap of limbs, groaning against the marble floor.

"You didn't actually think it'd be that easy, did you?" Ashur's voice dripped with contempt.

With a flick of his hand, he levitated them both until they dangled upside down at head height. Joel and Adam twisted helplessly in the air, struggling to break free. Adam spat curses at Ashur, defiant even while bound, when Layla appeared in the doorway.

She was a ruin of herself—covered in blood, streaked with dirt, panic flashing across her wild eyes. Her chest heaved as though she could barely draw breath, and the sword trembling in her hand betrayed both exhaustion and fury. She froze for half a second, taking in the sight of Adam and Joel suspended helplessly before her. Then rage surged through her, sharpening her fear into something deadly.

"What the fuck is happening here?" she screamed, her voice cracking.

Ashur raised his hand, sending Joel and Adam higher toward the ceiling. He turned to face her fully, dismissing them as if they were mere nuisances. A twitch of his fingers sealed Adam's mouth shut, muffling his continued curses.

"It seems," Ashur said dryly, "we have rats."

His lips twisted into a cruel smile. "You've been keeping animals in the castle again, Layla."

The mocking tone dropped from his face in an instant, replaced by something darker. A malignant shadow flickered over his features as his eyes glowed with a piercing, terrifying blue light.

"Why. Are you. Here?" Each word came like a hammer strike, slow and deliberate.

Layla stiffened. She should have been with his army, far from the castle. He knew where she had been sent and what her mission was supposed to be. Her sudden return made no sense—and Ashur's suspicion clawed at her throat.

Panic gnawed at her, but she forced her trembling lips to move. She stammered at first, earning the arch of his brow. Then, with a stomp of her foot and a desperate attempt at pride, she spat the words.

"Your army ran like cowards. We were ambushed by rebels before reaching the village, and those fucking idiots fled like dogs."

Her voice cracked but held its defiance. The silence that followed only deepened the weight of her words.

Ashur tilted his head. "But why, are you here?" he pressed again, his tone colder.

"I—I came to warn you," she blurted, grasping at the first excuse that might hold water.

But Ashur was no fool.

"You're lying," he sang almost gleefully. Then, without warning, he slammed Joel and Adam into the ground. The marble split beneath them with a bone-jarring crack. Joel's scream pierced the chamber, raw with pain, as the sound of snapping bone echoed against the walls.

"No!" Layla shrieked.

She hurled herself at Ashur with every ounce of fury she possessed. Wrapping her legs around his waist, she rained her fists against his head and neck. The centuries of torment, betrayal, and pain she had endured burst forth in a violent storm.

"I hate you! I hate you! I hate you!"

Her voice rose to a frenzied pitch, each repetition more savage than the last.

"Keep your hands off my son!" she roared. Her face flushed hot, blood vessels bursting in her eyes until they ran crimson. Black smoke erupted from her body, swirling above like a predator circling prey. She pulled raw power from the siphon Ashur himself had bound her with, funneling his gift against him.

Ashur staggered under the onslaught, tucking his face into her shoulder to shield his vulnerable throat. But his irritation boiled swiftly into rage.

A pulse of energy blasted from his body, hurling Layla across the room. She struck a bookcase with devastating force, splintering shelves as her spine cracked audibly. The impact left her vision swimming, ears ringing until the world dulled to a muffled haze.

Still, she clawed at the siphon, dragging power into her battered body. Ashur loomed, seizing her by the throat and hauling her up. Blood trickled from her ears and mouth as her face darkened from red to purple, air cut off entirely.

She smiled.

Even as he cursed at her, even as her strength bled away, she smiled. She didn't care about his words anymore.

Ashur shook her violently as she slipped toward unconsciousness. Her eyes darted past him, landing on the empty indentation where Joel and Adam had once been. Relief flickered across her face.

Then her neck snapped in his hands.

For the briefest moment, perhaps for the first time in her long life, Layla felt free.

***

Adam staggered down the corridor, half-dragging Joel who winced with every step on his ruined leg. He didn't understand what had just happened in that chamber, but he clung to the distraction Layla had bought them. Every instinct screamed at him to abandon Joel, to save himself while he still could. But his conscience wouldn't allow it.

"Left," Joel rasped, grimacing as they reached an intersection. Adam pulled him down the corridor as quickly as Joel's twisted leg would allow.

A thunderous boom rolled through the halls behind them, rattling the walls. Joel glanced back, pale.

"We have to go!" Adam snapped, dragging him onward.

"Leave me," Joel panted through clenched teeth.

"What?"

"Leave me. It doesn't matter what happens to me, as long as you get out. I can die knowing it wasn't in vain."

Adam faltered, staring at him. Why would this man—who had once hunted him so relentlessly—be willing to sacrifice himself now?

"Why did you do all of this?" Adam demanded, anger and confusion twisting his expression. "What purpose did my capture serve you?"

Joel's face fell with shame. "Your mother wanted to know you," he said softly.

Adam froze. Layla. His mind replayed every strange, fleeting exchange he'd had with her. The missing piece finally clicked into place. She was his mother.

"Dammit," Adam whispered, closing his eyes. The word escaped with raw frustration as his head sagged in defeat. He hated the decision even as he made it. He was going back.

"I hate you people," he muttered, stepping away from Joel and turning back toward the chamber.

Joel panicked. "Where are you going?"

Adam didn't look back. "I'm going to get my mother."

He jogged down the corridor, the sound of his footsteps swallowed by the silence that grew heavier the closer he came.

The chamber door was cracked open, and through it, an unnatural stillness pressed against his chest. He pushed the door wider.

Layla's body lay at Ashur's feet, her head twisted at an impossible angle.

"She just couldn't let you go," Ashur muttered, almost disapprovingly.

Adam's blood turned to ice.

"I suppose it's my own fault," Ashur added, voice sharp with bitterness. "I hadn't intended to get her pregnant in the first place."

The weight of those words sank into Adam like a blade.

Ashur turned toward him. His movements were jerky now, faltering—whatever Layla had done had drained him, and Adam knew it. She might not have been there for him in life, but she had died to protect him. That was enough reason to fight.

"To be clear," Adam said, his voice measured and dangerous as he stepped forward, "that would make you my father, correct?"

Ashur gave a small nod, even humming as though testing the word on his own tongue. His expression carried disbelief, as though he too struggled to accept it.

"Not that it matters," Adam continued coldly. "I have no intention of letting you leave here alive."

Ashur smiled grimly. "Good. Because neither do I."

The two men collided on the stairs with such force that the castle walls shook. Ashur was weaker than Adam had expected. Whatever Layla had done to him just may have evened the odds, though he was still formidable.

They grappled at close range, Ashur's face just inches from Adam's. For a brief moment, Adam found himself staring into blue eyes—his own reflected back at him. The distraction cost him dearly. Ashur seized the opportunity, slamming Adam against the wall with such violence that the stone cracked open, throwing him into the adjoining bathroom.

Adam groaned, pushed himself upright, and brushed the dust from his clothes. Without hesitation, he teleported. The sudden move caught Ashur off guard, giving Adam the opening he needed to drive a crushing blow into his jaw. Ashur staggered, dazed. Adam grabbed his collar and struck again, sending him sprawling to the floor.

But Ashur wasn't finished. He thrust both hands forward, and a blast of wind slammed into Adam's stomach, hurling him across the room like a rag doll. As Adam arched through the air, he vanished, reappearing mid-motion and kicking Ashur full in the face.

Ashur spit blood and disappeared just as Adam's boot came down where his head had been, the floor cracking beneath the force. From his left, Adam caught the flicker of movement and narrowly dodged as a razor-edged slice of air tore past him, grazing his ear and shearing its tip clean off. The attack was blisteringly fast, but Adam was faster.

With every strike he evaded, his confidence grew while Ashur's faltered. Adam dropped low, sweeping his leg to knock Ashur off balance, but the man vanished before hitting the ground. Twenty feet away, a shimmer in the air betrayed his reappearance. Adam recognized the ripple just before Ashur could fully solidify.

He had him.

Adam charged, feinting an attack. Ashur took the bait and vanished again. But Adam had already tracked the telltale ripple to his right. He teleported, materializing directly behind Ashur, and unleashed every ounce of strength in a single blow.

Had Adam attacked from the front, he would have seen the flicker of surprise on Ashur's face transform into terror. For the first time in his life, Ashur tasted fear—sharp, undeniable—just as Adam's hands crushed his skull. The sound of bone collapsing echoed in Adam's ears, followed by the wet crunch as Ashur's head burst apart.

Panting, Adam collapsed, relief flooding through him. He lay on the stone floor, every nerve in his body aching as the adrenaline drained away. The pain of battle revealed itself in full, searing through his ribs and limbs. For several long minutes, he lay there, forcing air into his lungs, before pushing himself upright with a groan.

He had to get back to Joel. He had to get home.

***

Gathering Joel, Adam headed for the nearest exit. Joel, still pale from his wounds, pointed toward the back courtyard. The front echoed with the clash of steel and dying screams.

They hurried through the garden, but Joel stumbled over a loose stone and fell. Adam rushed to help, but Joel pushed him away, sweat running down his pain-stricken face.

"Go," Joel gasped. "I have an idea."

In the far corner of the courtyard lay the massive corpse of a giant, its flesh being torn apart by dragons feasting like carrion birds on a carcass. The sight was grotesque, yet strangely mesmerizing.

"What can I do?" Adam asked, his voice firm.

"I need you out of the way. Run into the forest and don't stop."

"I can't just leave you here."

"Yes, you can. And you're going to." Joel's tone sharpened. "You don't owe me anything. Besides, your mother would never forgive me if I let you die here."

Adam hesitated, torn between loyalty and reason.

"Go, damn it!" Joel shouted, his voice breaking. "You're putting your people at risk. Just go!"

Adam looked toward the dark line of trees, the cries of dying soldiers echoing through the forest. At last, he relented.

"Thank you," he whispered, then sprinted toward the woods.

He didn't see Joel draw the dagger from his robes or hear the first words of the incantation. But he felt it—the tremor underfoot, the sudden splitting of stone as the ground shook. A low rumble grew behind him, and against his better judgment, Adam glanced back.

Horror froze him mid-step. Joel had raised the giant. The grotesque body, stitched together by necromancy, stirred with dreadful life.

***

Hades, Ares, and Alec tracked the enemy back to the castle. The gods had proven invaluable in keeping the undying army truly dead. Hades' very presence prevented their regeneration, while Ares filled the soldiers with unbreakable resolve. The air around the god of war carried a weight that pressed on every heart, hardening their will. Alec himself felt a fire in his chest, his doubts silenced.

His men sensed it too. Many had instinctively rallied around the two gods, their spirits lifted in ways words could not explain. Together, they had pursued the rebels to the castle gates, where the cowards had locked themselves inside.

The mages were still more than an hour behind, clearing the forest of lingering monsters on their descent. Until they arrived, there was no breaching the walls. Alec and his soldiers would have to wait among the ruins.

But waiting brought its own peril. Blood scented the air, drawing predators. Alec turned from the gate, his eyes sweeping across the skeletal remains of his former home. The ruins were unnervingly still.

The silence unsettled him. His grip on his sword tightened, the blade humming faintly in response to his anticipation. Above him, soldiers manned the walls, their eyes searching the distance. Alec ignored them, his focus locked on the shadowed forest beyond.

Then it came—a guttural roar that reverberated through the trees. The sound froze every man in place.

His sword quivered in his hand, eager for battle. One by one, the men turned their heads toward the dark tree line. Shadows shifted, and the valley fell deathly silent.

"The sun is setting! Get ready!" came the order from the wall behind Alec.

Ready for what?! he thought in mild panic. Taking a defensive stance, he gripped his sword tightly and glanced at his men.

"You heard him, get ready!" he commanded.

They were trapped with nowhere to run. Alec knew with certainty that his men would be fired upon from behind. His only hope was that whatever was approaching from the tree line would be dreadful enough to distract the archers and delay their fire until the confrontation was over.

The ground trembled. A second roar split the air, and the trees parted to reveal a giant. Normally, giants towered above the world, their heads grazing the clouds, their colossal feet flattening cities in a single step. But this one was different.

It was corrupted—something beyond the touch of ordinary dark magic. The creature crept forward on its stomach, its head grotesquely twisted upside down. A wide, deranged grin split its face, hungry and manic. Parts of its body were missing, as though it had been gnawed alive. Its legs were gone from the knees down.

Scanning the area, Alec noticed patches of forest scoured clean, trees flattened, and mounds of dirt heaped in jagged ruts. This abomination had been here before.

Hades began to laugh and stepped forward to stand beside Alec, casually resting his hand on Alec's sword. Turning to Ares, he shouted,

"This thing is dead!"

Ares threw back his head and started laughing as well. He dropped his sword and wandered away, still chuckling to himself. His strange reaction sent a ripple of uneasy laughter through the rebel ranks. Up until now, Ares had been instrumental in the slaughter of their enemies.

With him suddenly abandoning the fight, Alec wasn't sure how it would affect the battle's outcome.

Hades shook his head.

"Take your men and go," he said firmly. "This pathetic creature is under my command now."

Alec stared at him in disbelief.

"What?" he sputtered.

"It's dead. I am Death. It belongs to me."

As if to prove his claim, Hades raised his arm. The giant mirrored the motion. When Hades swung downward, the monstrosity brought its arm crashing down, smashing a section of the wall and killing three soldiers instantly.

"Take your men and go," Hades repeated.

"Yeah, no problem. Get out of the way!" Alec barked. He rallied his men and led them after Ares. It was time to rest.

The rebel army looked on as Death himself unleashed ruin upon the castle and those trapped within. Alec kept expecting Ashur and his dark queen to appear, but neither came.

When reinforcements arrived two days later, only a handful of men remained alive, most of them mages. Among the ruins of the palace, they uncovered Layla's body buried in the rubble. But Ashur's remains were never found.

Adam was intercepted by the mages as they descended the mountain. He was alone, battered, and half-dead. Though questioned incessantly, it would be years before he could confide in Ryanne about what had happened that night. He knew that the death of his birth mother, and the truth of his fathers nature would plague his dreams for decades to come.

Meanwhile, Alec returned to camp only to discover Leah's death—and Ryanne's role in it. His heart hardened, and forgiveness never came. Not for her, and not for the gods around her. Grief consumed him, driving him into self-imposed exile. He made his home deep in the forest, far from the reach of kingdoms, men, or gods.

Only Hades was permitted entry into that solitude. Over the years, the two spoke often within the quiet of Alec's sparsely furnished hut. Most often of the women who somehow made them feel whole. Through this uneasy companionship, Alec eventually heard of his daughter's engagement. That autumn, Ryanne invited him to attend her wedding in the spring.

The most Alec could do was watch from afar. On the day of the ceremony, sunlight bathed the glen where Ryanne and Adam exchanged vows. He prayed silently for their endless happiness and for the safe birth of their children. Yet he dared not draw closer, fearing his presence would shadow their joy with his unshakable sorrow.

After the vows, Hera stood among the guests at the altar. Across the ravine, she caught Alec's gaze. They exchanged only a solemn nod before he turned back into the forest. He knew that because of Leah's sacrifice, Hera would grant his unspoken request.

When Alec entered the clearing where he had built his home, dew-bright flowers opened beneath the morning sun, light cascading gently through the willow trees. The sight reminded him of Leah. He had chosen this place for that reason alone.

Behind the house, he had cultivated a small garden of flowers and vegetables—the same ones Leah and Lydia had once tended together with joy. The memory cut deep, and sorrow overwhelmed him. He was so lost in it that he failed to notice the open windows, the fresh smoke curling from the chimney, or the spring air drifting out from within.

He stood in the clearing, eyes closed, listening to the brook's gentle murmur. The sun warmed his face as he prayed quietly for death in the serenity of the forest.

Then came the sound of squeaking hinges. His front door swung open.

"Do you want to come inside, or just stand there all day?"

Leah's voice.

Hades and Persephone stood behind her, grinning like fools.

Alec surged forward, scooping Leah into his arms. He kissed her fiercely, pouring into it every ounce of longing that had consumed him for years. Holding her close, he vowed never to let her go again.

"How?" he breathed clutching her to him.

"Turns out I'm pretty hard to kill." She sniffed, tears of joy cracking her voice.

Alec pulled back, a prick of apprehension climbing up his spine.

"We never found Ashur's body."

Leah gave him a grim smile, touching the stubble covering his chin with a soft scratch.

"That's a problem for another day."

www.ingramcontent.com/pod-product-compliance
Lightning Source LLC
Chambersburg PA
CBHW061119100726
47911CB00013B/612